The Man in the Dark

John Ferguson

Originally published 1928
London, U.K.

This edition published 2023 by

OREON

an imprint of

The Oleander Press
16 Orchard Street
Cambridge
CB1 1JT

www.oleanderpress.com

ISBN: 9781915475220

Sign up to our infrequent newsletter
to receive a free ePub of
Fatality in Fleet Street
by Christopher St John Sprigg and get
news of new titles, discounts and give-aways!

www.oleanderpress.com/golden-age-crime

A CIP catalogue record for the book
is available from the British Library.

Cover design, typesetting & ebook: neorelix
Base image: Wallace Chuck

Contents

*'What song the Syrens sang,
or what name Achilles assumed when he
hid among women, are questions not
beyond all conjecture.'*

BOOK ONE

The Murder in the House at Ealing

I

Along the Embankment the fog was even worse than it had been in the Strand. Kinloch thought it queer that in so short a distance there should be so much difference. But worse it was. The sulphurous taste became intensified, while in addition a new and acrid flavour, probably the river's contribution to the mixture, made its presence felt on the roof of his mouth.

But progress was far easier on the Embankment. Up in the street he barged into and cannoned off some other pedestrian at every step. The handling he suffered! Hands some of them, it is true, gently warding off the impact of body on body; but others there were who thrust one impatiently aside, digging hard with elbows, so that, for a fellow in Kinloch's condition, the street quickly became something like a nightmare. But down on the Embankment, though his advance was still slow and uncertain, he had more room to feel his way, and to breathe freely, for that road was as silent and deserted as a Scottish village street on a Sunday afternoon.

With such sounds as did come the fog he found played strange tricks. Some it magnified and others it muffled up. The cough and sneeze of an occasional pedestrian would come quite audibly across the wide road; and while the rumble of a train crossing the bridge sounded like thunder, the chimes of Big Ben striking seven came through the sheeted air refined, as if by increased altitude, into a faint and silvery whispering.

At the foot of Villiers Street, however, he once more stumbled into the stream of hurrying people. Now, at least, there was no risk of missing the Underground. He was jostled inside the vestibule by a quick-footed crowd all going one way, and all equally eager on such a night to reach the shelter of their suburban homes.

As he moved on in the queue towards the ticket grille the sharp tones of the clerk, the smash of coins on the counter and then the scurry of feet running for the stairs made him contrast his own case with that of all these bustling, purposeful people. He had nothing to hurry for.

Nobody listened for his latchkey. Time was nothing to him. The fog? He counted on being back in the thick of it within a couple of hours. It was curious how much alone he felt. He went down the stairs, clinging to the hand rail, while numberless people flitted past him, not one of them more to him than a tattoo of rapid feet, swarming for the trains. Yet had he been sensitive enough that feeling of being so alone in the crowd might well have served as a premonition. It was perhaps Fate singling him out, and separating him off from his fellow men for the strange sequence of events destined to begin that night. Fate seems to work like that, using a man for a purpose he cannot see at the time. He goes down one street rather than another, for no apparent reason, and something happens in that street which alters the whole of his life.

When Kinloch left the train at Ealing Broadway the fog was still there, coming cold and dank to the face, though some of its more virulent ingredients had gone. After getting the direction from a forlorn but kindly taxi man who must certainly have seen from his clothes that he was not a possible fare, Kinloch set out to grope his way to Albany Road. It was in Albany Road Peter Dunn lived; and on Peter Dunn his hopes were centred. A man who lived in the same doss had looked him up in the medical directory at the municipal library; and it was this same man – a begging letter writer by profession – who advanced the amount of the fare to Ealing. A sporting fellow he was in his way, for their combined resources did not run to more than the ticket from Charing Cross to Ealing, and even at that it meant the pair must go supperless to bed if Kinloch failed.

It was the first begging call of his life and, though he never doubted about success, the fact that it was an old friend to whom he was applying made the journey very distasteful. This surprised him in a mild way, for he counted himself pretty tough at that time. And so while he stumbled on in the dark, and as if to fortify his resolution, he fell to thinking over Peter Dunn, mentally recounting all the incidents in which, in happier days, he and Dunn had been associated. It was the worst thing he could have done, to think of the old days. It forced up the contrast between what life had been and what it had become; between the lad he looked at in the early days and the man he was at the moment, hardened, bitter, and almost unscrupulous. In a word, while he looked at himself as he once had been he saw himself as he was.

Hugh Abercromby had brought them together, the unforgotten, the unforgettable Hugh, beloved of both. A fine, fresh day in spring it was when he first met Dunn on the links at St Andrews – all three were third-year students. At first Peter and he had eyed each other askance, like two young dogs each jealous of the place the other might have in Hugh's affections. But Dunn proved to have a taste for literature, and though he kept this taste under control, so that it never, as in his own case, interfered with his professional studies, yet it served to draw both together. Many times they fell out, for Dunn was of a queer, dour temper, and his mental processes, if sure, were annoyingly slow in working. Then Kinloch's mind turned to their last meeting. To him, then, that also seemed long ago. It had taken place in the General Hospital outside Boulogne to which he had been brought with his first wound. Coming into the ward Peter must have recognised him as he lay tossing uneasily, that hole in the shoulder making itself a centre of pain that gathered almost all thought to itself, so that he could give heed to little beyond its small circumference. Unperceived by him, Dunn in his white overalls had seated himself beside the bed in which he lay, feverish and stifled by the hot motionless air and the fire of his wound. Then bending forward Dunn began slowly, and almost in a whisper, to recite certain lines, the first words of which made him jump:

> *St Andrews by the Northern Sea*
> *A haunted town it is to me.*
> A little city, worn and grey,
> The grey North Ocean girds it round,
> And o'er the rocks, and up the bay
> The long sea rollers surge and sound.

Startled by the familiar words, Kinloch had twisted round to look at this man who from what he said might at that moment have been eavesdropping at the door of his heart. 'Peter!' he had cried, recognising the broad face, so rugged, and the grey eyes bent over him. But Dunn put him down again by laying a hand on his chest.

> O broken minster looking forth
> Beyond the bay, above the town,
> O winter of the kindly north,
> O college of the scarlet gown!
> And shining sands beside the sea,
> And stretch of links beyond the sand,
> Once more I watch you, and to me

It is as if I touched his hand...
St Andrews by the Northern Sea
A haunted town it is to me.

Well, as has been said, all this, and much more, came back as Kinloch was fumbling his way along those desolate Ealing roads and avenues. One may wonder why these memories gave him no confidence. It is, perhaps, the measure of the abyss into which the man had fallen to say now that such memories daunted rather than encouraged him. The more he remembered and the nearer he got to Dunn's door, the more clearly he saw what he had become. A false pride was in it too. The hash he had made of life, while Dunn had prospered. And – another thing – for the past six years he had heard nothing of Peter Dunn.

How much may happen in six years! The truth is he feared to find his old-time friend with a wife and perhaps a family; a settled and sedate medical general practitioner. For, as he used to argue in the old days, in no calling is the change from roystering youth to smug and portly respectability so rapid and complete as in the medical. There lurks something of a poet in the wildness of the medical student; but once that student becomes a G.P. he treats his poetic soul as a disease; and invariably it yields to treatment. Invariably! The thought made Kinloch pull up short. Peter's wife instantly grew terribly real to him. He visualised Dunn as ill at ease about having to introduce an out-at-elbows friend to her; and he saw the lady herself regarding him with a fixed smile, and hostile eyes, while she wondered whatever the parlourmaid would think.

Then as he stood hesitating in that deserted road, a prey to sickening indecision, struggling between a sense of shame and a knowledge of his pressing needs, the heavy tread of a policeman sounded at his back.

Fate had stepped in and again decided for him. He was, little as he knew it, being pushed on to his destiny, and the choice as to whether he would go on or turn back was now less than ever in his own hands. For as he automatically resumed his walk the following footsteps quickened and a heavy hand descended on his shoulder.

'What are you loitering here for?'

'I have lost my way.'

He spoke like a child, confusedly, as one coming back too suddenly from a dream. He was a little frightened. Lost his way! So indeed he had. But long before that night. Some vague perception of this may have added to the bewilderment with which he spoke. This the policeman took for guilt. The walking stick was dexterously twisted out of Kinloch's nervous hand.

'Gammon! A clearer case of loitering with intent I never saw. Had my eye on you for the last half hour. You come along.'

His grip shifted to the coat collar.

'I am looking for 28 Albany Road,' Kinloch protested, now fully awake.

The policeman gave a grunt of scorn.

'Dining there, I suppose.'

'No – er – consulting Dr Dunn.'

'Don't try that gaff on me. Dr Dunn has no patients of your class – except when he acts as our casualty surgeon. Now then!'

He gave Kinloch's arm a twist, and at the same time trod heavily on his left foot. The old Sandy Kinloch fired up momentarily.

'Are you trying to make me a casualty?' he asked, shoving him off.

The man was on him with a bound, in joyful brutality. Kinloch had heard tales of his sort from other unfortunates. The wantonly inflicted pain was probably intended to provoke resistance, which of course would serve as corroboration of any serious charge. Why should a guiltless man resist? Kinloch knew from experience that here and there a type of officer still remains who believes he must produce cases to justify his own existence.

His foot throbbed with pain, but he restrained the natural temptation to prolong the struggle.

'All right,' he said. 'So long as I see Dr Dunn it's all one whether you take me to him or bring him to me.'

Have you ever tried to make a policeman change his mind? A forlorn hope it usually is. It puzzled Kinloch as to how he succeeded with that animal. Possibly the careless indifference of his last words had an effect; but more probably it was due to the memory of some recent reprimand for an equally wanton arrest. Anyhow the thick fingers gripping his garments at the back of the neck again shifted to his arm. The officer said:

'Albany Road is on our way. We can call in as we pass.'

But his grasp was less assured than before.

Albany Road indeed proved to be round the next corner, and the man had just pushed open a gate a little way along it when Kinloch heard a door bang. He could not tell whether it meant someone entering or leaving. Hastily he felt at his torn collar and tried to get it down to meet the tie, also damaged by his recent rough handling. Then a voice boomed out from the doorway:

'What is it, officer?'

The policeman pulled his captive forward, half uneasily.

'This man, sir, I got him loitering. Says he knows you, and was coming here.'

'Says he knows me, does he? Put your lantern on his face.'

The next moment a cry came.

'Sandy – Sandy Kinloch by all the –' Dunn broke off short. He must with his quick, professional eye at once have observed the other's affliction. The policeman dropped the arm he held as if it had burned his fingers.

'Oh, Sandy, my poor lad, Sandy!' Dunn said in a low voice.

The policeman here returned the walking stick, and stepped out nimbly for the gate. A mighty relief it was to hear him go. Dunn slipped a hand under his old friend's arm.

'Och, och, come away in,' he said.

'But, Peter, you – your wife,' the other stammered.

'My what?' he cried, pulling up.

'I'm in rather a disreputable condition. Will she mind?'

'You mean about her chintz chairs and so on, I suppose. Who told you I was married?'

'Nobody; I guessed it.'

'A bad guess, Sandy: there's no minx here to mess up my place with china ornaments and female fallals. So wipe your feet on the bass, lad, and step inside.'

Dunn has said that he saw at the first glance just what Kinloch's condition was. No doubt this is correct; his professional eye would give him information not so apparent to others. He says, however, that he made no comment at the time on his old-time friend's affliction, though he admits making a joking remark on the length of Kinloch's hair to put him at his case. This remark the other turned aside, probably because Dunn would not have understood that where Kinloch had lived for the past year there was a prejudice against the owners of close-cropped heads. Most close-cropped heads in Rowston Street were cropped, without their owner's consent, at their country's expense.

In Dunn's cosy study that night, after such a meal as had become no more than a dim memory to him, Kinloch told his story. Much more of it was told than need be set down here. Not so much because of its dull and sordid details, but because it has no direct bearing on what was to follow. The real story in fact only began that night – little as either of the men dreamed so then.

Dunn heard it out in silence, except for an occasional grunt or sign of indignation. When he had finished the doctor hit the coal a resounding blow with the poker, as if he wished it had been Maxtone's head. For Kinloch had rounded off his story by telling him of his experiences with Maxtone. Maxtone was the editor who had turned him down. At the end of a long silence Dunn's voice broke in plaintively:

'I never could understand why you did it, Sandy.'

'Did what?' the other asked, coming back startled from his memories of Maxtone.

'Took up this silly writing business, and wrecked such brilliant prospects.'

'Because I couldn't help it, Peter.'

Dunn gave a grunt of incredulity.

'I had leanings to poetry myself, once,' he said, 'but it was one of the few temptations I've found it easy to resist.'

Kinloch laughed the first mirthful laugh for many a day.

'Yes, you old pill-pusher, and proud you are of it. But then you will never know the joy of creation – to take up an idea and give it flesh and blood, to see the germ of excellence spring out of nothing.'

'Ay – and lead to nothing.'

The sharp disgust in this muttered rejoinder was probably due to what seemed the extravagant enthusiasm of the other's previous words. But at that moment, when Kinloch was over-sensitive, and in great need, it came to him suddenly that Dunn was now anticipating an appeal for help, and was half-resentful over it. It was like a cold douche after his mirth. His long lost pride came back, as other things came back that night. He would show Dunn he would ask for nothing. So taking this reproach as a warning, he got to his feet. But Dunn took no notice.

'Well, I must he going,' Kinloch said with a flourish.

'Going,' he repeated; 'going where?'

'To the place this scribbling has led to – a cubicle in a doss in Rowston Street,' Kinloch replied bitterly.

Dunn shoved him back in the chair with some violence.

'You needn't be so touchy. If I am angry it is solely for you, Sandy, knowing what your capacities once were. Man, man, but you were aye an unco thin-skinned lad.'

Dunn, like many of his race, was accustomed to use the broad dialect of his country whenever he was under the stress of some strong emotion of which he was half ashamed. But well as the other knew this national trait he was too fantastically sensitive by this time to be influenced by that knowledge.

'What is the good of reproaches now?' he said wearily. 'After all, as things have turned out, what else could I do but write? What sort of a doctor could I make now, after the war has done with me?'

It was here that Dunn blundered.

'No; but if you had qualified in medicine you would never have been in the fighting line, and so have escaped your present calamity,' he persisted.

Kinloch fired up at once.

'Been safe at a *base* hospital, you mean,' he retorted hotly.

After that things somehow went from bad to worse. There is no doubt Dunn had intended to stand by his friend. When the other had leisure, with a cooler head, to think over what happened, he saw that, for he knew that Dunn was not of the sort who give good advice when they mean to give nothing else. Dunn no doubt meant to do probably a good deal more than his friend had hoped for, but on that very account he claimed the right, like the dour Scot he was, to improve the occasion.

The rupture came suddenly, before either was aware.

Dunn, hot-headed, began to preach at him, and Kinloch, sore and sick with the picture of himself as drawn by his candid friend, stung him with a gibe that smacked of the den from which he had emerged.

Dunn rose in wrath.

'You spoke of a *base* hospital just now,' he cried. 'It might have been better for you had you died in that same base hospital; it might have saved you from a base existence.'

Both were now on their feet; and this time Dunn made no effort to detain the other. He was breathing heavily, and his keys jingled in a hand trembling with anger as he opened a drawer. But Kinloch rejected the money when he offered it: it was not possible for him to do otherwise after the particular gibe he had used, and the retort Dunn had made to it.

'As you please,' he said.

'Fortunately I'm not quite penniless,' Kinloch proclaimed with ludicrous dignity and entire untruth. 'It would be painful to have to pocket your insult with your money.'

'Oh, I did not mean to insult you,' the other man said, almost humbly.

Kinloch said nothing.

When they reached the door Dunn gave a sudden exclamation.

'Lord, I had forgotten that!' he cried.

'What?' Kinloch asked, surprised at his sharp exclamation.

'The fog. I can't let you go, Kinloch. It's thicker than ever. Even a beggar's dog would lose his way tonight.'

It may have been his unaccustomed use of the surname – never had he been other than Sandy to him – or perhaps his reference to a beggar that touched Kinloch on the raw once more. Without a word he stumbled quickly to the gate.

'Come back, Sandy,' Dunn called, following. 'On a night like this –'

'Fog makes no difference to me, Dunn,' Kinloch cried, as with an affected laugh he slammed the gate.

Touched with remorse the other started after him, but Kinloch hurried away; and it needed but a few steps in that fog to be beyond finding.

Kinloch, indeed, had not gone far in the fog before the awkwardness of the situation pulled him up. It was somewhere after eleven, he was many miles from Rowston Street, and with not a penny in his pocket to get there. Cool enough he was now as he stood against a wall and under a dripping, overhanging tree in that sodden, deserted road.

For half an hour he must have leant against that wall dully considering the plight in which his foolish quarrel with Dunn had placed him. His clothes, too, had suffered much in his brief interview with the policeman. Though worn threadbare, his suit had been of good quality originally, and he had always taken care of it. It is extraordinary how important the condition of a last suit becomes to a man who has reached the end of his resources. At an interview with a possible employer boots can be more or less hidden, and a shabby hat can be held negligently behind one's back, but one's suit takes the eye, and supplies the first impression by which most men judge. But these were not thoughts that occupied him for long. His one thought soon turned to how he could get back to Rowston Street. For the Underground barriers cannot be passed without a ticket. Then he remembered the Ealing Great Western Station, close to the District. If he could slip into a carriage there he should reach Paddington, where, in such a large station, it would be easier to evade the collectors at the exit. If not – well, arrest at least would provide a shelter for the night.

He had gone some distance towards the station when a new thought came, one which would probably never have occurred to him but for the recently recovered memories of better days. It was this: if he had to risk arrest he must see to it that his name did not come out. It is almost comical that he should have been so sensitive about this all at once.

Anyhow the fact remains that he went methodically through every pocket, and tore into scraps every paper that could serve as a clue by which his identity could be traced. Dunn must not know – this was his motive, probably. So all along those suburban roads and avenues he laid down something like a paperchase trail, and only when the job was finished and he had left himself with nothing in his pockets did he begin to heed where he was going.

The fog seemed to be as thick as ever. Behind its almost impenetrable wall he knew there lay on each side of him rows and rows of houses, each separated by no more than a yard or two of turf from the road, but for all that showed of the life within them he might as well have been limping through a dead city.

A little later, finding himself alongside a great line of massive iron railings, so stout that he knew they must have been built with public money, he felt that he was passing beyond the sub-urban villa region, and became doubtful of his direction. When the road began to make a great sweeping uphill curve, doubt became certainty: he knew he had not come that way.

Something like a tremor of anxiety passed through him, while he stood, doubtful as to what course to pursue. It was very cold, in a raw, penetrating fashion; for by this time his clothes were fairly sodden from exposure to the fog. Eagerly as he bent for any sound, his ear caught nothing but the eerie drip, drip, drip of the condensing moisture falling from some trees inside the railings.

Using the stick on these same railings he worked along them, trusting to come on the gate of some house at which he might obtain guidance. Failing in this he crossed the road in the hope of finding houses on the other side, and eventually after fum-bling along a high blank wall he came on a little iron gate that certainly belonged to a villa. Without one thought as to the late hour, Kinloch mounted the steps and pulled the bell. By this time he was so eager for the sound of a human voice that if any inmate were only to lift a window to curse at him he would have welcomed the voice. But that did not happen. No one responded. Peal on peal he sent through that house before realising from the hollow, ghostly re-echoing of the bell that the house was empty.

Up and down how many roads he went after that in search of something human he never knew. What, however, he could never forget is that in rounding a new corner in a dull despair he walked suddenly into something soft and human – a stout man of middle height in a thick overcoat with fur collar and cuffs. The man gripped at Kinloch to save himself from a tumble.

'Damn you,' the stranger cried, irascibly shaking him.

'Are you quite blind?'

The unexpectedness of the meeting more than the violence of the collision left Kinloch for a moment speechless.

'Sorry, sir, but you were certainly going the faster,' he said.

The stranger was passing on, but stopped at the other's words.

'H'm, a man of some politeness. You recognised who I am, no doubt.'

When Kinloch haltingly explained his plight, he emitted a quiet whistle; but not, as it turned out, from any sympathy.

'Not acquainted with this neighbourhood?' he queried, coming nearer again.

Wondering who this man could be who expected to be recognised by any chance passerby the young man explained that, so far from being familiar with the locality, he had not the least notion of where he then was. If, he went on, he could be put on the way to a railway station he would be very thankful. For a moment the stout gentleman said nothing, but seemed to stand there in the fog debating something with himself.

'I can put you on the way to something much better,' he said at length. 'You are just the man I want. There's something providential in our meeting. Yes, sir, I seem to detect a Higher Hand in this, though I am not a superstitious man.'

When he took him by the arm, his hand trembling with eagerness, it struck Kinloch that the man was in a state of agitation or anxiety. He freed himself half uneasily.

'Look here, come to business. What do you want?' he asked.

'A small service, for which I will pay much.'

'How much?'

The man in the fur coat hesitated. It is significant of Kinloch's desperate condition rather than of his nationality that he inquired as to the amount of the reward before asking the nature of the service.

'Five pounds for half an hour or so seems ample.'

Kinloch laughed, exhilarated by the prospect held out to him. The stout man evidently took the laugh for one of derision.

'Five pounds. It's surely enough,' he said.

'That depends. I've gone through half hours I wouldn't repeat for five hundred.'

'But this is merely to sit still in a chair, in a quiet room, and rustle some papers.'

Kinloch's heart sank as he realised the man must be a lunatic, a harmless wandering lunatic. Of course he was! Who else would be abroad on such a night – owning a furlined coat? When he recalled, too, that the man had expected to be recognised, no doubt from supposed portraits in the papers, suspicion of his insanity turned to certainty. Kinloch's hopes sank to zero.

'If you tell me where you live,' he said soothingly, 'I'll take you home. Your people must be getting anxious.'

'You think it too little?' the stranger said sharply, and the tone was not that of a man with wandering wits.

Kinloch shook his head.

'No; too much, unless something shady lies behind it.'

'Nothing lies behind it that need concern you. I offer you so much because, to be quite frank, I admit that if I had searched all London I might not have found a man better suited for my purpose. Come; time presses. Is it a bargain?'

But his ill-concealed eagerness roused a new suspicion.

'You must be more explicit,' he said, wondering to find himself so curiously unwilling to go with the man.

An impatient exclamation came. A masterful, domineering man Kinloch now judged him to be, certainly no lunatic in the ordinary sense. It was evident that he could barely restrain his temper while the young man dallied with his proposal. With quite apparent effort he now spoke calmly:

'An important interview lies before me at my own house. A man is coming to confer with me, and it is essential that a third party should be present. Not to see, still less to overhear what is said, but simply to make it evident to my visitor that I am not alone. Now I am the last man in England to be caught in a corner, as you would know if I were to reveal my name. So, needless to say, the witness had been arranged for; but he has failed me. This cursed fog,' he burst out uncontrollably, breathing heavily. 'Chance has got lost in it, no doubt.'

'Chance?' Kinloch repeated, bewildered.

'Did I say Chance? Well,' he laughed, 'chance has put five pounds at your disposal, my needy friend. You agree?'

'Sir,' was the reply, 'I am one who has had to part with most of his scruples, and to earn five pounds at this moment I would do much.'

From the other came a grunt of coarse satisfaction.

'So I judged,' he remarked. 'A gentleman on his uppers! Just the man for my money; I cannot understand why you hesitated.'

But the coarse joviality of his new tones had an effect opposite to that he probably intended.

'I said most of my scruples. Unfortunately I have still one or two left.'

'Set your mind at rest, then. Had you retained as many as your maiden aunt, you might still come with me. You are not engaged for housebreaking or deeds of violence. You will expose yourself to no danger of arrest, for I am asking you to my own house solely for my own business. Is that enough assurance?'

'Quite,' Kinloch agreed with great relief. 'So long as the police are not in it, five pounds will do.'

And, as the stranger slipping an arm through Kinloch's began to lead him eagerly down the road, the younger man puzzled over the way in which the other had used the word 'chance'. In his own mind no doubt existed that, despite his clumsy attempt to use the word in another sense, Chance was the surname of the man whose job he was now undertaking. The name had slipped out in the stress of the other's anxiety and excitement. Chance: it was a name too uncommon to be readily forgotten.

But, however that might be, the man in the fur coat meant to let nothing else slip out; for, as if annoyed with himself, he remained silent till they reached his house.

Having opened a door with a latchkey – a door which was certainly not the main entrance to a house of the size this proved to be – he led the way through a corridor into his study. The room was very long, and rather narrow. A big, crackling fire diffused a warm glow as they passed it to reach the niche at the far end which it appeared had been prepared for Mr. Chance to occupy. This niche seemed like a semicircular bow window opening possibly on to a lawn, and into this apse he was placed after stumbling against the screen drawn across its entrance to prevent Mr. Chance from seeing – or being seen. Only when he had Kinloch seated at a table behind the screen did he speak again.

'Your part in this comedy is not a speaking one,' he said. 'All you have to do is to prove your presence when I give you the signal. Then you may make a rustling noise as if busy with papers. But on no account are you to speak or show yourself. And remember this' – his stumpy forefinger tapped Kinloch's ribs – 'the signal may not be given at all.'

'What is the signal to be?'

'Three taps with the poker,' he replied promptly. 'We'll rehearse it now.'

It was at once evident that all had been carefully arranged – even to keeping control of the poker, Kinloch said to himself, while feeling about on the table for the paper with which he was to operate. When his host returned after making three audible taps and the alert young man remarked that he appeared to have forgotten the paper, the man threw something on the other's hands.

'There, try that; it will sound like music in your ears.'

Kinloch tried it, and it made an admirable sound, the crackling sound that a new crisp Bank of England fiver always makes. Still, as Kinloch remarked, it wouldn't be so audible at a distance, and in the midst of talk might be unheard.

'Then you are to cough. Yes, as the night is raw you may cough. Indeed, it may be well to do so from time to time - of course after I have given the signal – as a reminder to my caller of your presence.'

He left his guest alone after that. What he did, or where he went, Kinloch did not know. And at the moment he did not care. For at once he fell to spinning glorious dreams as to the spending of the fiver. He held it between his fingers, making it talk to him with its cheery, crackling whispers.

Untold wealth that crinkly note seemed to him then. To the passage of time he gave no heed. But to judge by the number of things he decided to do with the money it was certainly an underestimate on his host's part to say that the business would only take half an hour.

Then with a start he heard the murmur of voices at the far end of the room. A door shut. Kinloch came out of his dreaming and sat up attentive. Chairs were moved about, as if for more comfort before settling down to business. But when he heard the clink of glasses that spoke of friendly intercourse, it struck him that his host had been unduly timorous in engaging anyone for protection.

Very little of the talk come to Kinloch's ears for some time. Both men were speaking in an even murmurous undertone which might have been chosen either to be persuasive or to prevent him from hearing. Not that he had any other thought than to be alert for the signal and honourably earn the reward he had already received. He was happy in a quiet way, feeling assured that his luck had turned, that his dark hour had passed, and he sat behind the screen with his hand motionless on the fiver which he dare not play with any more for fear of prematurely indicating his presence. In his damp clothes he was hard put to restrain from the coughing which was not yet required.

Then quite abruptly, heat and excitement broke out between the two men. One voice rose in pitch as if to warn Kinloch the crisis approached.

'So you think you have me cornered!'

In a flash Kinloch thought he understood – a blackmailing visitor.

'That depends entirely on yourself.'

'How?'

'Tut, tut. For a man of the world like you, that is surely a needless question to put.'

'Ah, needless, is it? Yes, I suppose so – to put to a devil like you.'

'No devil at all,' said the other, neither devil nor angel, but just a plain businessman ready for a deal. Do not pretend that anything in this takes you by surprise.'

'It does not. I am prepared for it.'

There was something in the way the man snapped out these words that Kinloch at least found ominous. A quiet laugh came.

'In that case we had better get down to business at once.'

The last three words were accompanied by three distinct taps as if to emphasise the statement. So anyhow Kinloch took them, for he promptly made the prearranged reply.

'What was that?'

To leave the man in no doubt he followed up his signal by a cough, and a very genuine cough it was.

'We are not alone,' he heard his employer say in a bantering tone. 'I, too, prepared for our meeting here tonight.'

Again there was a pause. The stranger seemed to be read-justing himself to the new situation created by the revelation of Kinloch's presence. He did not take long.

'By God, so that is your game, is it? This time you've mistaken your man!'

There came a sudden quick scramble of feet: a crash of glass followed as a table overturned with a dull thud.

'Keep off, keep off!'

The sudden, wild scream sent Kinloch's nerves leaping. He rose amid the struggle and the thud of chairs overturning on the thick carpet. He knew the man who had hired him was stumbling towards him, calling for help. But almost before he could move there came a sound he recognised – a sound more horrible to the ear than the startling cry of pain or terror – a tired kind of sigh followed by the noise of a heavy body collapsing in a heap on the floor. Starting up in the dark Kinloch blundered into the screen, plunged forward in an effort to retain his balance, tripped over a chair and shot headlong to the floor. Groping about quickly with both hands to recover his stick as a weapon, his hands went slithering into something warm; and wet.

'Ah, the rat leaves his hole!' a voice cried viciously.

He knew the man was coming for him. He came slowly, though, walking as if he himself had been hurt, or was impeded by the scattered furniture.

Kinloch worked rapidly along the wall with some dim idea of finding a window or a door. He heard the man close behind, but by an instinctive swerve he evaded the clutching hands and went on. The room was silent now, so silent that in the darkness Kinloch could hear the man's quick breathing, and the smothered oath that followed his own momentary escape. Yes, the man appeared to have been hurt himself in the struggle, for his soft padding steps sounded uneven.

Then abruptly the stillness was rent by a piercing cry:

'Don't. Oh, don't!'

It was a woman's voice, and at the shrill and imploring cry, which revealed to Kinloch the unguessed presence of a woman, he stopped dead. In a moment the man was on him. One hand clutching his hair, pulled the head backward. The strength of madness was in that man.

'Safe bind, safe find,' he shouted fiercely, as if it were some sort of slogan.

In the horror of that paralysing moment Kinloch's nerve snapped, and he began to plead, weakly re-echoing the woman's entreaty.

'Don't, oh, don't! Look at me, I –'

But something struck him heavily. A brilliant light flashed through his brain, and he went in a heap to the floor.

II

Consciousness came back to Kinloch at no definite moment. It was like rising slowly to the surface through deep waters. What he first recalled was a sound, a low murmuring that somehow had determination in it, and never ceased. For a time he thought the sound was in his head, and with that the remembrance returned that someone had just knocked him on the head. He felt horribly sick and shaken, and the instinctive attempt he made to move showed him he was lying full length on his back, helpless.

So he lay still, nerving himself at first for the second blow he expected to fall, and was unable to avert. Then as the blow did not come at once he remained motionless in the hope of escaping another by pretending it was needless.

For a time he lay like that, still as death, but thinking brokenly about the nasty, violent business into which he had walked. He knew the man meant murder, knew that the flutter of an eyelid now would be enough to make him finish the job. So, shamming death, he listened hard, seeking to catch a hint of the other's movements in the room.

It was very difficult to hear anything because of that dull, continuous drumming in his head. He tried to ignore it, to listen, as it were, through the throbbing sound. But nothing else could he hear. In a dazed way he then began to be surprised that so soon he should feel so cold and stiff. It was exactly like what he had experienced when he lay for hours against a shattered wall at La Boiselle with his first wound.

But there was a difference. Then he had felt no resentment towards the hand that had struck him down. Then it had been a fight for life on equal terms. This time he had been helpless, defenceless in the hands of a man who had shown no mercy. And as he remembered how his broken spirit had forced from his lips the cry for mercy his shame gave birth to a hatred of the man, all the more intense and enduring because he must lie there incapable of fight. To have to die like a dog cowering on the floor in a corner.

Was that to be his end? How much better to have died at La Boiselle then than in this sordid way, in some quarrel between two blackguards whose names he did not even know! He felt so sick and cold and stiff. Then with a start the question burst on him: had he been lying where he now found himself for a long time – a longer time, at all events, than the man was likely to stand over him to see if he were dead? A gleam of hope came. Remembering he had been struck down close to the wall on his right along which he had been feeling his way, he cautiously stretched out a hand with the notion of verifying that wall.

But it was not a wall he felt: it was something that recoiled from his touch with a smothered exclamation. The cry was instantly followed by a metallic click exactly like the sound made in releasing the safety catch in an automatic pistol.

'Oh, damn!' he cried, thinking that he had after all betrayed himself.

A hand was laid on him gently but firmly.

'No need to be afraid. You are safe now.'

The voice was a woman's, and, remembering, he did not doubt it was she who had tried to stop the man's murderous attack.

'Has he gone?' he asked in a whisper.

Again there came that ominous, metallic click.

'You have a pistol,' he said. Lifting his hand, he found his head and half his face swathed in bandages.

'No, no, that was the switch for the light under the dash you heard. I turned it on to see if you were all right. Try to sleep again. I must watch the road.'

But he did not go to sleep. He lay awhile trying to piece together what she could mean, wondering most as to why she must watch the road. The noise in his head made thinking very difficult. It was like the word 'thud' repeated unendingly, in a low, murmuring tone, yet infinitely more rapidly than mortal lips could articulate the word.

All at once he understood. That dull pain was indeed inside his head, but the drumming sound was an external sound. It was the beat of a motor engine. Instantly the woman's words about the light under the dash, and about having to watch the road became intelligible. She was carrying him off. She was taking him out of danger. They were out and away on the open road!

How that perception changed his feelings about that drumming engine! So long as he thought the noise was in his own head, it wearied him. Now it seemed unutterably friendly, and he lay prone, rejoicing in the sound, feeling from the engine's eager strokes that it was whole-heartedly on his side. He gave little or no thought to the woman, or where she was taking him; he did not then even wonder who she could be. His whole thought went to the purring engine that whispered continuous comfort to his ear. To him that engine was, even more than the silent woman, a living thing, making heroic efforts to carry him into safety. Lying prone he thrilled to think he was safe so that, sooner or later, he would get even with the man who had struck him down...

The next thing Kinloch remembered was the sound of a great bell, sonorous and so exalted that it might be the bell on some lofty cathedral tower. It struck six times, with a magnificent slow dignity between each stroke, and he began to wonder in a half dazed fashion what little town owned so great a clock. That it was a little town he knew because presently he felt from the ceasing of all echoes that the car had left the narrow streets and was speeding upwards on a straight, smooth road.

Afterwards, however, he was glad at having heard that bell, glad that its tone stuck in the memory. But just then such thought as he was capable of filled him with shame. The woman had heard him plead for his life, bleating like a sheep, he put it to himself. The remembrance made him shiver with mortification.

Her pity flayed him like a whip, for he fancied there was in it a tinge of contempt. Later he heard the click of that switch again.

'You are putting on the light,' he cried, almost involuntarily; for he did not wish to be seen by her at that moment.

'No, turning out the headlights. It will soon be day.'

They must then have been running along a wood-lined road, for now he could hear the twitter of birds, that preliminary twittering and trial of their notes they all seem to make in the early dawn. He lay awhile listening. The air was cold but dry. Presently the chatter of the birds faded and died out behind.

Almost at once the woman spoke:

'Why do you come to be associated with evil men? Your face is not – not altogether an evil face.'

After his kindly thoughts of the woman and the car the question surprised and wounded him.

'Is it light enough to see that?' he asked in sarcasm.

She hesitated a moment as if not quite understanding.

'If you will sit up and look you will see the daybreak,' she said, 'and the light creeping through the trees, and – and' – a catch came in her words – 'and the birds.' The horn sounded for something on the road. 'But,' she added in a changed voice, 'I suppose a person like you cares for none of these things.'

'No – not – not now,' Kinloch said.

'Used you to? I would like to think you not a bad man at heart.'

There was an almost eager note in her voice that irritated him again.

'Look here,' he said shortly, 'don't you start worrying yourself about my heart. My heart is no better than my face.'

Now, at all events, he began to wonder who this woman could be. Evidently she had mistaken his previous hesitation, and imagined her description of the morning had touched his better nature. She was so sure of his badness too!

No doubt, he admitted to himself; he must look, that morning, with his bandaged head, torn clothes, frowzy, unshaved and unwashed as he was, an offence to the pure dawn. He could imagine the contrast present itself to her. But, after all, he was no criminal. His mild feeling of irritation deepened.

No more was said then. But she had started him off thinking things out, and presently, when the car turned a corner, and was clearly taking a side road at a reduced pace, it occurred to him that he had a right to put a few questions on his own account.

'Where are you taking me?' he demanded.

'Not much farther; I am going to drop you on the road.'

'Drop me by the road! What for?'

'To get rid of you – a better fate than you deserve,' she said.

On that he awakened to realities.

'Is that man dead?' he asked in a whisper.

'Oh, yes. There are worse things than death, you know.'

Kinloch shuddered violently. He thought she was referring to his own pitiful pleading for mercy, and tried to be cynical.

'Are there? I wonder if – if he thinks so?' He paused, breathing heavily. 'This is a hanging business, then.'

'Well, you will be out of it – unless the police take you,' she said.

'I see, it is for the murderer's safety, all this. You thought I saw the man who did the deed, and on his account it was judged better that I should not fall into the hands of the police. An awkward witness I might have been against that man! So you propose to drop me by the roadside.'

She heard him out in silence. Then after a pause she coolly said:

'Yes; you so far profit by my interest in his safety.'

It was her calm assumption of his badness that he found exasperating. She took his evil character for granted, and seemed to regard it as an accident that he himself had not committed the murder. He struggled to a sitting posture, cold with anger.

'Your interest in the murderer must be very deep,' he retorted. 'How is it you come to be associated with such an evil man –

you who seem to have such high standards of morality, and care so much for the clean sunrise and the guileless birds?'

That touched her up. He heard her sharp indrawn breath. Presently, with the car slowing down to a creep, she said:

'After all, I've had some trouble to save you from arrest, and may have saved your life. Why shouldn't I be glad to know that life is not so worthless as it looks?'

'Drop me here,' Kinloch said shortly. 'Your preaching makes me sick.'

Promptly the brakes were applied.

While he was fumbling with the catch of the door she bent forward and undid it herself, flinging the door wide open. Kinloch stumbled on to the road.

'By Heaven, you are a cool creature,' he remarked. 'How old are you?'

'Not so old as I look this morning.'

Standing there on the road he laughed derisively, and then got his parting-shot ready. For he had a parting-shot, and a nasty one, he considered it.

'If you only knew it, you might have gone to bed, and left your car in the garage: there was no need to carry me so far.'

'Oh, Jane doesn't mind,' she said.

'Jane?' he repeated, mystified.

'That is what I call my little car. Plain Jane, for she has no frills.'

The flippant tone of the remark, and the fact that it delayed the retort with which he meant to crush her, irritated him again.

'And you are plain too?' he said.

There was no response to this impertinence, except that the engine began to throb more quickly, as if in indignation. Then the brake was taken off with a sharp clatter of metal over the stops.

'If you will kindly remove your hand from the door –' she said icily.

But he held on, grimly nodding up at her, taking the opening at last given him.

'I'd like you to know this first,' he said. 'I never saw the man who was murdered nor the man who – who did the deed, so I could never have been a damaging witness against him.'

'That is incredible,' she said coolly. 'Impossible unless you were quite blind.'

'Quite impossible,' he agreed, 'unless I were quite blind.'

It took her a moment or two before she understood. Then the engine ceased racing as if her foot had slipped from the accelerator. He knew she was staring hard at him now.

'Blind,' she whispered. 'Oh – it – it – can't be – it can't be! I'd need to be blind myself not to have seen that.'

The man laughed harshly.

'Sharper sight than yours missed seeing that last night, in that fog, which makes you all grope about like the blind,' he said.

But she did not seem to be listening.

'Oh, dear God, what am I to do now? What am I to do?' she said, her own eyes riveted on the careworn face and the unseeing eyes of the man on the road.

Kinloch was taken aback by the blank horror in her voice. What difference could this make to the plans she had formed for his disposal? She ought to feel safer. He recalled the man in the fur coat. It had made him laugh aloud with relief. So ought she to be glad – at least after, as was natural, a little irritation over her needless journey. Why didn't she say something? Why didn't she clear out? The news of his blindness should be good news to her and to – Then his ear caught an unexpected sound; it was like someone quietly weeping.

III

The breakdown was at once so utter and so unexpected that it amazed Kinloch. He could not understand it. It was the last thing he expected from her. Up to this point she had shown such cool, masterful self-assurance, and, as he judged, such calculating selfishness, that he had been sure she was either a tough, middle-aged, hard-bitten woman of the world, or one of those modern young women who are without the least grain of tenderness, even for themselves.

Hard she might be, but evidently she had her breaking point. As the man stood silent, feeling helpless in the face of this distress, the tinkle of a bicycle bell recalled him to action.

'Someone is coming,' he said quickly. 'Pull yourself together.'

Then going down on his knees beside a wheel, with his back to the road, he affected to be looking at some damage to the tyre; for it were well, he thought, if she could not control herself, to make it appear as if she had some cause for distress. While so engaged he heard the soft whirr of wheels flitting past on the gritty lane. Only when he heard the bell again as the cyclist dropped down to the main road did he stand up.

'He stared at you,' she whispered over the side.

'Who was it?'

'A policeman, a country policeman, on his round.'

It startled the man queerly to find himself so soon after the incidents of the previous night in contact with the police. But the ruse he had adopted to divert attention from himself to what he was doing pleased him.

'I pretended you had a puncture.'

'Oh, dear,' she cried, no wonder he turned round to look at you. 'Didn't you notice the tyres are solid?'

His hand went out to be assured she spoke the truth. He had never heard of a solid-tyred car till that moment.

'We had better push on,' she said, throwing open the door. 'This is a bad beginning.'

'They can't possibly have heard yet,' he argued.

'No, but when the news comes out that policeman will remember us.'

Her voice was so full of foreboding that Kinloch was surprised.

'Oh,' he said, with an attempt at reassuring her, 'the thing may make a noise in Ealing, but after all –'

A strange sound cut him short. He could hardly believe his ears. She was laughing. Not that it had any mirth in it. He noted that. And it ended as abruptly as it began.

'What did you laugh at?' he asked sharply. 'Seems to me you've not much to laugh at.'

'No. But that wasn't laughing.'

He became suspicious.

'It really happened at Ealing, didn't it?'

'Oh, yes.'

'Well?'

'If – if – it would make a noise only in Ealing,' she said with a sigh, as if to herself.

But he overheard.

'You go on' – he spoke almost gently – 'I dare say you're not a bad sort, and I'm too dangerous for you to have on your hands.'

'No. I can't leave you here.'

There was a world of quiet decision in that utterance. But the man thought she spoke from mere impulsive sympathy, and had not calculated the dangers.

'My dear lady, look at me, and then look at yourself. What sort of a pair do we make – to sit together in a car? The difference must be a difference that would excite notice wherever we went.'

'Then we must in some way reduce the difference, that is all. Leave you here to be caught by the police I dare not.'

Kinloch stood awhile, his head still throbbing with pain, so that clear thought was impossible, trying to envisage the situation. As he hesitated a cry came from her.

'O God, there is the policeman coming back. I thought he would. Oh, be quick,' she pleaded in an agony of dread.

Kinloch got somehow into the car, and she raced it up and shot away.

For about half an hour they ran on without further speech. He was afraid some word of his might unnerve her again. But from the turns and twists he knew they were among lanes with the main road far behind. After that she began, as it were, to breathe more freely. He sat wondering how it would all end, and was rather bewildered by the quick march of events.

'Where are you taking me now?' he asked at length.

There was no tremor in the voice that now replied:

'Where I had meant to go myself for a time – a queer lonely village on the top of this ridge. It's shut in with gates at either end, and has a village green – well, I suppose it's more of a common than a village green, for it's a mile long and has clumps of trees on it, and furze.'

She appeared in fact to be talking to put him at his ease.

'And when we get there – what then?'

'There's a house – someone I know has a little bungalow which he uses only in summer. An old woman, a neighbour, has the key. It will be all right; she knows me. You can stay there for a few days to get well and to see what has happened – whether anything has been discovered. Not one soul need know you are there.'

'What is this place called?' he asked.

She hesitated over her answer.

'Ah, you don't want me to know?'

She did not reply, so he added: 'Never mind, I know it isn't many miles from Chichester.'

She seemed to give a start of surprise at his shot, and after a moment said:

'Why do you think so?'

'From the bell striking six, and the time we took to reach the small town in which there was such a bell. Besides that, the way we've been going up and down among hills would tell me these hills can only be the Sussex downs.'

After a moment she said:

'If you are wise you won't try to find out where you are.'

The reply let him see exactly where he stood with her. Evidently he was to be told as little as possible. He nodded his understanding of that fact to himself. So, in spite of her earlier breakdown and her tears, she was now on her guard, with all her wits about her, and knew how to take full advantage of his want of sight.

Later, when they approached the village, she left him in a thicket a little way off the lane, and went on to interview the old woman who had charge of the house. It needed considerable trouble to fix things up, evidently, for she was away about two hours. The old woman was then getting the place ready. She had shown no surprise over the unexpected arrival. The doings of the town people – foreigners as they were called – were always odd, even when they were not altogether mad. Much more, while he ate, she told Kinloch sitting beside him on the rug. Although she seemed to be talking for talking's sake, he noted that she did so warily all the time, for nothing to give him a clue as to where he was slipped out.

'What is this village called?' he asked, as if forgetting for the moment her previous reluctance to tell him.

'I call it Minnis,' she said.

And he gathered from her tone that it was so called by no one else.

Another thing he noted: for all her volubility there were occasionally sudden, oddly abrupt silences. He could feel she was thinking hard. He thought she was troubled, nervous, strained. And in those uneasy silences from among the wood below there came the clear strokes of a woodman's axe.

It was, of course, impossible for him to enter the bungalow before darkness came. He must stay where he was till nightfall. So after she had slipped away again he had nothing to do to keep him from thinking. His thoughts went straight back to that room in Ealing. What had that man in the fur coat been up to to get himself blackmailed? Beaumont – it was unlikely that was his real name – the begging-letter writer in Rowston Street, had told him tales of that fashionable crime. Not that blackmail was Beaumont's own game; he hadn't got the nerve for it, he had admitted. Nothing paid better; but, unfortunately, it was dangerous, he said. Then another thing Beaumont said came back to Kinloch – that in almost all cases of blackmail there was sure to be a woman somewhere. A lady of high position, he had said, smacking his lips, whose reputation afforded the leverage necessary to extract substantial amounts. It was only in such cases, he asserted, that sufficient pressure could be applied. And as Kinloch filled a second pipe his mind turned to the woman in this case. Was this the woman? Something of what was afoot between the two men she must have known. But she came into the room just too late. That fog again, he thought. The man must have envisaged murder from the start, for he had carried a knife, and no man carries a knife capable of inflicting death at one stroke – Kinloch had heard the heavy sigh that follows the use of steel too often not to draw that inference – except with murder in his mind. Besides, his hand had gone into that pool of warm fluid in about a minute after the blow.

At this last remembrance he sat up in sudden apprehension, the match burning itself out over the unlit pipe. Had he left any traces of his presence there? The man who came prepared to do murder, thoughtfully choosing a noiseless knife rather than a revolver, he was unlikely to scatter proofs of his own presence, or of his identity, around. But he himself could have had no such forethought; and it gave him a sudden qualm to remember he had left his stick in that fateful room.

No, decidedly, it would be safer to lie low for a time. Remote as the place was, newspapers would no doubt penetrate even there, and with safety he could hear what they contained from her. Meanwhile no one had seen them come there, and no one need see him enter the bungalow. So she had said. He was rather content to take the course she proposed, for he did want to know more about the case, and about this girl's part in it. His first dislike of her had passed away. She was not quite what he had first thought; and, anyway, he determined to see the thing through.

It was very cold lying among the damp trees on the northern slope of that ridge; but he had lain in worse places. And it consoled him to remember that if the January day is raw it is also short.

IV

He started up at the sound of a snapping twig, aware that he had been nodding with fatigue and sleep. The next instant a hand was laid on his shoulder.

'Come,' she murmured, 'it's safe now.'

'Is it dark?' he asked with surprise.

'Quite – a black night.'

Walking was difficult at first, for he was stiff and numb with inaction and cold, and as if from the long exposure the wound in his head began to ache and throb worse than ever. But taking his arm she guided him through the undergrowth, and out on to the road. Close as she was to him he could hear her draw a sharp breath now and then, though whether from some fancied alarm or painful memory he could not say.

After a time they passed through a heavy gate across the road.

'Now,' she breathed, 'quick as we can go; we are on the open common beside the first house.'

For a village, that Minnis was a queer place. Once inside the gate his feet were on a road as smooth and even as is the drive to some great house. And when they left the road for the turf, which they did very soon, he found the turf as springy and level as any lawn. But there was gorse on it, and bracken too, in patches, for once catching sight of some object looming up a short way ahead she made him lie down in a clump of bracken while she herself went forward to reconnoitre.

Kinloch could tell when they were nearing the house from the way in which her hand tightened on his arm, and her breathing quickened. From her movements, so close was she to him, he knew her to be glancing this way and that, peering into the darkness. All around them the night was as still as the grave, and on that turf feet made no sound. What with all this dread of being seen, and the convulsive grip on his arm, an uneasy feeling came to him, a vague sense of disquiet as to what he might encounter in that house. But before this feeling had time to grow very strong he found himself at the door.

The sharp, deep sigh of relief too, with which she shut and bolted that door, gave him the measure of her previous anxiety. He knew terror had gripped her lest they should be seen. She must have sunk down into some chair as soon as they stumbled into the room. Kinloch, left to himself, after standing at a loss for a little, groped about to discover another chair. There seemed to be very few in the room, but coming on one he drew it towards the glow of warmth that told him where a good fire was burning. For the slow, cautious crawl they had made from his hiding place among the trees had done little to restore his circulation, cold and numb as he was with so many hours of inaction and exposure.

But the first thought she showed afterwards was one to take note of. For her first act as soon as she recovered breath was to attend to his damaged head. She undid the bandages, and having deftly snipped the hair from around the wound, and washed it carefully, she readjusted the bandages in a way that revealed experience. From this he concluded that his mystery woman had probably done nursing at a war hospital. Then from her movements he knew she had set about preparing a meal.

After a little, as he sat holding out both hands to the blaze, she came over beside him to kneel before the fire.

'How do you feel?' she asked.

'Like a piece of frozen mutton.'

By the simile he meant to convey no more than that he felt very cold indeed; but she appeared to imagine he had laid emphasis on the last word.

'You cannot blame yourself for what has happened,' she said. He noticed now that her voice seemed almost youthful, clear in tone, yet low in pitch. But blame himself! He was far from doing that! He wished the man who knocked him out had been there. He'd have done more than blame him. He had a score to settle with him – one day sooner or later. But he kept quiet about that intention then. He said:

'Well, as to that, I've been in the control of others in this affair all along – at their disposal, I mean, driven like a sheep – an ignoble part.'

She began to stir up the fire. From the abstracted, mechanical way in which she used the poker, he gathered she was deep in thought. In the end she left him without saying more.

Kinloch listened hard to see if he could detect the presence of anyone else in that house. As the numbness melted out of him before the log fire, and his faculties began to thaw, the first human quality that seemed to come back was a quickly growing curiosity about that woman. That she was deeply involved in the affair was plain enough; that she had carried him off to save the other man he felt certain. Yet it was not upon such facts that his thoughts now mainly turned, not even on what the graver issues of the tragedy might be, but merely on who she was, and what she was like. And here, once for all, certain facts set forth afterwards by Dr Dunn, need to be understood by all who possess their eyesight. They are these: the mind of a blind person tends to be more active and alert than that of a sighted person. He lives in his mind more exclusively, for he is thrown in upon himself in a variety of ways, and is almost certain to make up for lost physical activity by an increased mental life. In consequence, and as if in compensation for the lost sight, certain other senses become more acute – touch and hearing immensely more, and his memory and imagination – are more developed. The point in asking that these facts should be remembered lies in this: many people regard a blind man as a more or less helpless creature. He is so only in regard to one of his five senses; in the

other four he is not unlikely to be more efficient than the person
who pities him.

Thus, for the answers to the questions as to who this woman
was and what she was like, it might be thought that Kinloch was
helpless except in so far as she chose to enlighten him. But that
was not his view; and he made up his mind, sitting there that
night, to get an answer to them, and to others. For he did not feel
under any weight of obligation to her. It was clear enough that,
though she had carried him away from what might have proved
more than an awkward situation, she had done so only because
his story of what had happened might, if it were believed, make
things much more awkward for the other man, and perhaps
herself also.

The woman too, he thought, must have begun to do a lot
of thinking just then. Whether it was that the house in Minnis
had associations connected with happier days, or whether she
had little chance and less liking for thought up to the time they
reached the shelter of the house Kinloch didn't know; but she
had precious little to say to him that night. Still, she must have
had her eyes on him, for after the meal, when he returned to the
fire, she at once perceived the drowsiness that stole over him,
and packed him off to his room. It would be time enough, she
said, to talk plans over in the morning.

The next morning, however, Kinloch was made aware that
even in that lonely house their situation was not without its
dangers. Very early he was awakened by a peremptory tapping at
his door, followed by a summons to breakfast. The decision in
the knocking caught his attention: it was that of one who had
taken command. He was unwilling to stir at once, wishing to
luxuriate awhile in such a smooth, warm bed as he had not lain
in for ages. And when he sat up and felt his stubbly chin it did
not add alacrity to his movements. But he scrambled out, feeling
almost glad he could not himself see what he looked like.

Over breakfast the delicacy of the situation was made known
to him. The old woman, Mrs. Spedding, was coming to do the

housework, and he would have to be concealed for the two hours she would be moving about the house. But this seemed easy. He had only to stay in his room, a room which, since it was supposed to be unoccupied, the old dame would have no occasion to enter. As it chanced, they were almost caught straight away; for he had not finished eating before the old woman was at the door. In her eagerness to please, she had come before the time appointed. Kinloch was breathlessly smuggled into a sort of cloakroom cupboard in a corner of the little lounge hall in which they were breakfasting. But she got the door shut just as the old woman opened the other. He heard all that passed.

'Mornin', ma'am. Thought I'd best be a bit early this first morning in case anything 'ad 'appened.'

'That was good of you, Mrs. Spedding. Did you think I'd burn the bacon or spill the milk?'

Mrs. Spedding chuckled.

'No, miss, not zackly, though I might 'ave, you not being used a-doin' for yourself. What was in me mind was that you might be scared outen your wits your first night alone, what with all them there cat burglars we reads on nowadays.'

When the girl laughed, or rather tried to, Kinloch knew she was standing with her back close against the cupboard door, more afraid of Mrs. Spedding than Mrs. Spedding would have believed. Afraid, too, she must have been of what the old woman might let out in his hearing.

'Well, you see I'm not a bit scared.'

From her shaky tone Kinloch would have said she was in mortal terror; but the old woman cackled wheezily.

'No, miss – ma'am, I mean – but all the same if you'll 'scuse me, you've lost your roses. Quite pale you be. Last night I was putting it down to your travels, but now I sees 'tain't.'

The voice stopped abruptly and then there came rather tremulously the question:

'What is it, Mrs. Spedding?'

'I thought you was alone here.'

What the old woman had seen Kinloch could not guess, but he felt as if their game was up already.

'What makes you think I'm not?' came faintly from the other side of the door.

'The table's a-laid for two, and two's been using the things!'

Then in the horrible pause that followed the old woman laughed.

'Ah, I see how 'tis – seein' them two cups give me quite a turn; but that on t'other side be the one you used last night, I reckon.'

'I was so tired last night, Mrs. Spedding.'

There came a quick clatter as the old dame began to collect the dishes. Kinloch waited for another exclamation. Fortunately, however, her eagerness to gossip kept her from discovering what he expected her to discover, what his own touch would have instantly told him – that both the cups were warm.

'Ah, reckon the air of the Downs will put ee to rights. You used to thrive on it when ee was a little un.' She sighed reminiscently. 'Folks ain't forgotten you 'ere, Miss Stella. And that reminds me, we all saw your fortygraft in the papers the time you was wedded. Tolputt – you remember Mr. Tolputt at the post office – ee twisted it round a pot o' treacle for Mrs. Prebble, and never noticed it were you. But there, men don't never notice nothin', except it hits them somewheres. But Mrs. Prebble saw who 'twere – trust her! – and she cut the fortygraft out, and showed it all round. It was that picture of your stepping out o' church under a harchway of swords, and you holding a nosegay. 'Appy you looked! I'd have knowed your smile anywheres. Yes, I reckon it were that smile first showed us who 'twas.'

The door behind which Kinloch stood creaked as if someone had leant heavily against it, and after the cheerful Mrs. Spedding had stumped off with her loaded tray he heard in the empty room something between a sigh and a sob. And this at least was more than he wanted to hear.

Mrs. Spedding came bustling back in a moment, however, brushing the cloth as she resumed her talk.

'Jane Prebble, she put the fortygraft in her Prayer Book next Sunday to show the folks coming outer church. It was wonderful to see how it waked them all up. Crowdin' round her they all came. Farmer Noakes first 'ad it in his hand, and what with all the rest a-craning of their necks over his shoulders to see what 'twas, while he was getting out his glasses – well, if he didn't have to set down on the late Mrs. Uden's tomb to keep 'em off his back. But all the same some on them cried out your name afore ee got the glasses to his nose. "So 'tis," ee says, holding it out and a-cockin' his head, "so 'tis. Townified of course, but Miss Stella it be." Then ee hold it outen to show 'em. "Folks," ee says, "who'd a-thought of that grand lady once a-riding my old Buller bareback and a-straddle, as bold as brass?" Old Jacob Wytch caught up the talk then. "A taking young 'ussy she always were. Whoi, masters, afore I knowed who she was didn't I catch her in the orchard among my cherries one marnin', and dang me if I didn't find myself afore I knew a-showing 'er where t' best ones was." Young Bob Ames, ee cut in then: "'Twasn't perticklar like you, Jacob Wytch, that wasn't," he says. But Mr. Noakes nodded as he tooken off his glasses. "No," he says, "it wasn't like Wytch to act so, but it were main like she to get un." And all the folks laughed so hearty at Jacob. "So t' little maid's married?" Mr. Noakes says. Then young Bob, he says, "Let's look at the fellow she's a-wed to," taking over the picture. But Jane Prebble snatched it away, proper angry, and Jacob Wytch cuffed young Bob's ear. "Be that a way to speak of the high nobility? Fellow indeed," he says.'

Mrs.. Spedding might apparently have rattled on, but a sudden pause almost coincided with a sort of moan that came from the other side of the door.

'Bain't you feeling well, ma'am – m'lady I mean?'

From her tone Mrs. Spedding was aghast.

'Oh yes – quite – well. Just a little – faint after – after yesterday. A glass of water, please.'

'There, drat me if I haven't wearied you out with my gabble!'

The old woman hobbled off to the kitchen. In a moment the other, as if recovered from her faintness, had Kinloch out of his cupboard and along the passage, pushing him into his own room. The rapidity of the change left him breathless. For the clever fashion in which he had been manoeuvred out of earshot by a woman who had seemed to be on the point of collapse gave him food for thought. His sympathy, he now felt, had been wasted. He was almost certain that that sudden faintness, with the demand for water, if real at all, was due less to the dread of detection by Mrs. Spedding than to the fact that the old woman was on the verge of saying more than the lady would wish him to hear. Of course she did not trust him. Her refusal to tell him so much as the name of the village proved that, and now he felt sore over that distrust – and the sympathy he had wasted. In consequence, at lunch, after the old woman left, he said:

'So your name is Stella?'

'Yes.'

'Stella means a star.'

'Yes.'

'I've been wondering how to address you; it's awkward to be with a person who is – well, anonymous as well as invisible.'

'You may call me Stella.'

'But I don't want to. A star means nothing to a blind man – doesn't exist for him.'

She said nothing at all to this.

'She called you "m'lady" once,' he reminded her.

'That might be better.'

'That means nothing either – just a poor old woman's courtesy.'

'So as I don't know your surname I shall have to call you Stella?'

'Circumstances give you that privilege,' she said coldly.

'Well, it does seem a little over-intimate after one day's acquaintance.'

He waited in vain for any response.

'So I am going to be told nothing?' he said at length.

'The less you know the better.'

'Better for whom?' he asked.

'Yourself.'

'Is that a threat, then?'

He heard the door shut as she left the room.

V

From that day a silent fight began between them. Piqued by her distrust of him, and heedless of her warning, Kinloch appears to have become determined to find out all he could about the affair at Ealing and the people concerned in it. And the lady seems to have been quite confident that he could only know what she liked to tell him.

He did not use her permission to call her Stella. When he called her anything it was 'm'lady'; and just because he did not think she had any right to that form of address, the title came easy to him in the half serious fashion in which he used it.

But he was certainly wholly serious in his determination to dig out the facts. With her he had no quarrel. Indeed he thought he rather liked her. The fingers that dressed his wounded head were very gentle. And he had learned to judge people's souls by their touch. But whether she were innocently or guiltily involved in the Ealing affair he was quite sure that for his own sake, and probably for hers in the long run, he must get at the facts.

He began by cross-examining himself on what he already knew or could safely infer. Why had he not been left lying in that room with the other victim? Why take him away at all? To have left him there to be found with the murdered man – wasn't that the real game to play? For what could he say, when he came round, to explain his presence in that house? Anything he said would count as nothing in the face of what the eye could see: the man lying there murdered, and himself a wandering vagabond of disreputable appearance. His tale of being invited to the house by the dead man – how ridiculous and fantastic it would sound! Indeed, the case against him was blacker than the real criminal knew. For a blind man's weapon naturally would be a knife and not a revolver. And the murderer, leaving him where he fell, could have placed the knife in his hand and so put the halter round his neck as surely as – Kinloch pulled up suddenly. A strong motive for his own removal became apparent to him. He himself had been knocked unconscious; there was the wound in his head to witness to that fact. Therefore when he was found in the room the question would arise as to who had inflicted that wound. Obviously the dead man couldn't have struck him down after he was dead! And if this blow that knocked him out had been struck before the other was dead, the man who received it would never have been able to strike back. Therefore that wound in his head would testify to the presence of a third person in that room, and so far support the otherwise incredible story he would have to tell of that night's happenings. Have to tell?

Kinloch's thoughts fastened on the words. Yes, have to tell if he had been found lying unconscious in that room. But, he asked himself, would he volunteer the story now? Could he come forward with the tale now? And in the answer he gave to the question he found a sufficient answer to the questions as to why he had been carried away from the Ealing house. It would never have suited the criminal that an unconscious man should be found in that room – a man who, when he came round, could, for all that was known to the murderer, fully and accurately describe the man who struck the blow. But it would not suit himself now, with the wound in the head almost healed, to fall into the hands of the police. A cock and bull story it would all sound at this date, especially if he had to end it up by admitting that he did not even know the name of the village to which he said he had been taken!

Then, sitting on his bed, thoughtfully nursing his knee, he saw with sudden, startling clarity the problem he had to solve. He must find out the name of that village. He had to know where it was, as safeguard against future chances. He sat a long time racking his brains over this. For the first time he became fully aware of the woman's quiet determination to keep him ignorant of where he was, and of the terrible danger this ignorance might yet be to him. He didn't feel hopeless, though, about beating her. There was that great bell he remembered, and the little town through which they had passed. Was this queer scattered village somewhere in Sussex as he had guessed? He went over Mrs. Spedding's gossip. How easily the name of the place might have slipped out! But it hadn't. Still, there were all those names the old woman had mentioned. Many names had, he knew, a place connection.

From a surname you could often tell from what part of England a man came. Tyldesley, for instance, meant Lancashire; Fosters were common in Worcestershire. Were Prebble, Ames, Tolputt, Uden, common names in Sussex? He did not know; but he knew there were men who were authorities in such matters. And these names, taken together, had the air of belonging to some particular locality. And yet this was not much to go on. Rather like clutching at straws, he felt. He must somehow find out the name of the village she called Minnis. The problem, he saw, was a double one: to find out where he was, and to find it out without letting her know that he knew. For he had a suspicion now that this knowledge would be a very hazardous possession to him if it were known he had it.

Yet for all his brooding on the subject, on that day and on others following, he was quite unable to see how he could come by the information.

Once, a few days later, he almost got what he wanted by accident. And again it was through Mrs. Spedding. Of course after that first mischance the lady had taken care there should

be no more surprises of the sort. But this once she was caught
napping.

One of her precautions was to keep out of Mrs. Spedding's
way whenever the old lady was at work anywhere in the house
within earshot of his room. In consequence he never heard them
talking together except at a safe distance, the lady never entering
her room, the door of which was almost opposite his own, till
Mrs. Spedding had left the house. On this particular morning,
however, Kinloch heard Mrs. Spedding come stumping along
the passage and, the door evidently having been left open, he
heard her voice at once.

'The list of things you want, Miss Stella, it can't be right.'

'Let me see.'

He heard the flutter of paper.

'Sakes alive, you can't 'ave used all them things already. Unless
it be as Ben Horrockes is a-givin' short weight.'

Kinloch, suddenly aware of a new and unforeseen danger,
bent forward to listen. The lady seemed to become aware of the
danger too.

'I – I – like to – don't like to run short,' she said.

'Lor', Miss Stella, but ye do eat 'arty, nowadays, though
you've little enough to show for it,' the old woman grumbled,
'you not bein' nigh so plump as a young girl oughter be.'

He heard the lady attempt a laugh.

'You don't think I – I look right, Mrs. Spedding?'

The uneasiness was obviously misinterpreted by the old
woman.

'Oh, m'lady, don't you worry about your looks. You've no
call. Folks here think you better looking than ever you was,'
she said reassuringly. 'Why, even that old nabbler, Jacob Wytch,
must a got 'is head turned when he saw you yesterday; turned
'im into as big a nissy as young Bob Ames, the sight of you did.
Didn't I 'ear him myself telling old Uden as hadn't seen y' yet,
that you was lovelier than the Queen of Sheba in a chariot what

they'd got painted on the walls of Brooky church where he was a lad nigh sixty years agone. But I wasn't meaning them sort of–'

The voice diminished as the old woman was led or hustled out of earshot, and he heard no more.

Kinloch, however, sat very still for a long time thinking over what he had just heard. And at first his thoughts had nothing to do with the discovery he was so keen to make.

Up till then he had scarcely ever wondered what the lady looked like. To a blind man people's looks didn't matter much. The voice counts for more, and from her voice, deepened perhaps by her own recent experiences, he had vaguely judged her to be older than it now appeared she was. But what a light this revelation threw on the whole of the tragedy at Ealing! He recalled Beaumont's words, that behind most crimes, if you could only find her, there was a woman. And this one must be beautiful indeed. There was the impression she had made on Jacob Wytch to prove that. Kinloch was deeply impressed by the effect she had made on old Wytch. The sight of her had reawakened in this old man, after an interval of sixty years, the memory of what, in his youth, had no doubt stood to him for a vision of all that was beautiful in woman. It almost awed Kinloch to see the significance of that. And his mind went back to recall the names of the fair women, good and bad, women like Helen of Troy, Deirdre, Cleopatra, Queen of Egypt, and Mary, Queen of Scotland, whose beauty had brought men to ruin and death.

He was startled by this revelation. More lay behind the affair at Ealing than he had supposed; the waters were deeper than he had guessed. But startled as he was, he soon perceived that in more senses than one now he must know where he was.

So he was thrown back on his original line of action. He began to ponder over Mrs. Spedding's words, from a new angle. But what he knew seemed precious little. The old woman had mentioned Brooky Church. Yet though that was definite, it might well be a long way off; and in any case it seemed to be a diminutive of some fuller name. Still, he stored the name of the place in his memory, for possible future use. He had, on the whole, more hope from the peculiar dialect words Mrs. Spedding had used. She called Wytch an old nabbler who had been turned into as big a nissy as young Ames by the sight of the girl. The two words, nabbler and nissy, he had never before heard, but the very sound told him their meaning. They were dialect words, certainly not in common use, yet, like all dialect, familiar in a more or less restricted area. The scent was strengthening. Kinloch, pleased with his astuteness, was quite sure that a professional detective would have let these two words pass unheeded. They were not the sort of clues he would understand. For himself, he was resolved to let nothing pass.

But his self-satisfaction proved to be short-lived. Days went by and brought nothing to him – nothing but a growing conviction that the girl was going to be too much for him. She countered his every move. One day she said suddenly:

'You haven't found out very much, have you?'

It was the first time she had openly referred to the struggle between them. And from this open reference he saw she considered him beaten. There was even a touch of pity in her voice as if she took him for a rather naughty child.

'Not much,' he admitted.

'Nothing,' she said, in the tone of one who had the situation well in hand.

'Only that you are younger than I thought, and something of a beauty, it appears.'

'And that is hardly what you hoped to find out.' She almost laughed.

Kinloch fired up, responding with grim humour.

'Well, you'll find I'm impervious to beauty's eyes, anyhow. Here's one man, at least, whose head isn't to be turned by any woman's looks.'

But this was said merely to cover his sense of defeat. She had no need, he knew, to turn his head with her beauty, for he had not discovered anything likely to make him dangerous. He went straight off to his room. And there, sitting on his bed, kicking his heels, he started to think the thing out afresh. She had almost laughed at him. How sure she must be that she had him in her pocket! And he must stay there, it seemed, till – Kinloch sat up suddenly, under the shock, as an idea struck into his mind, an idea that had about it the brilliancy of an inspiration!

That same night he was sitting with her before the fire behind the closely curtained windows. The strong southwester that had sprung up with the fall of night made it safe for them to talk above the usual subdued monotone.

No one approaching the house unseen could hear voices above that wind. He said to her:

'I can guess what a derelict I look.'

'There's no one to see you but me,' she said.

'It's not a matter of vanity. If anyone else chanced to see me, wouldn't it be dangerous?'

'Dangerous?' she echoed sharply.

'A man like me seen in the house.'

'But you're not going to be seen.'

'It might happen by some accident. You can never tell. Anyway it's a needless risk to run when you could so easily get me some new clothes.'

She seemed doubtful, and he felt her eyes on him when he produced the crisp, clean fiver he had received from the man in the fur coat.

'The nearest biggish town,' he said. 'You'll find some outfitter with a selection of ready mades. How far will you have to go?'

'Oh, not very far,' she said evasively. 'I can go in the car tomorrow afternoon after Mrs. Spedding has left.'

She seemed pleased to find him so thoughtful of a danger that had not occurred to herself. He showed her how to take his measurements with a piece of string.

But the next afternoon a disappointment came. She returned without the clothes. It was early closing day in the unknown town, and the shops were shut.

'Didn't you know?' he asked disappointedly.

'No. Most towns close on Wednesday,' she replied innocently.

Kinloch instantly forgot his disappointment. Another clue had been presented to him. Putting things together he now knew that the house in which they were hiding was one in a village of widely scattered houses which stood on a ridge of downs not more than – to judge by the time taken in going and coming – ten or twelve miles from a town whose early closing day was Thursday.

'And tomorrow will be market day,' he said, fishing.

'What do you mean?'

She seemed a trifle startled, for the words came quickly.

'It will be very busy,' he prevaricated, 'if it's market day.'

'Oh, I'll get the things tomorrow,' she said, leaving him no wiser as to whether Friday was or was not market day. So he failed to get that further clue as to the identity of the town.

But had she seen him open the parcel next day she would have been still more startled. He, however, did not open it before her. When he got to his room with the new clothes the first thing he did after locking the door was to feel the inside of the coat just below the collar. A thrill came as he found what he sought. Yes, it was there, the small square of silk that bore the name of the outfitter from whom the suit had been bought – the name and, his fingers told him, the address. He could not read the lettering; and there was, as yet, no one whom he could ask to read it for him. But, he said to himself, while shaving with the new razor, it was a satisfaction to know that he now carried the information about with him!

And he fell to thinking of how easy it would be to ascertain the identity not only of the village but of the woman herself. For, the name of the town once known, it would be simple to identify the village about ten miles distant which among its inhabitants had people of the names of Prebble, Ames, Tolputt, and the rest, not to mention a farmer called Noakes; a village which had in the churchyard a tomb to a lady evidently of some position, named Uden. As for the house, he could describe every corner of it. But that wouldn't be necessary. For Mrs. Spedding once found, the lady's identity could no longer be concealed. Kinloch was so full of all this that, his toilet completed, he returned to the sitting room without thinking of the very different appearance he now presented to the eye. A smothered cry followed his entrance.

'What is it? Anything wrong?' he said. And then he recalled his altered appearance. 'Is it as bad as all that?' he asked.

'I – I – didn't know you at first,' she stammered. 'I thought someone had come to –' She broke off and added tamely, 'I didn't know clothes could make so much difference in a man.'

He brushed this aside.

'You were frightened, not surprised,' he said.

'No.'

'You thought it was –'

'No, I didn't. Come, here is your chair.'

Kinloch put out his hand. She took it in her own to lead him, and he found that the hand in his shook like a frightened bird. Beyond doubt she had taken him for a police officer. But her eyes must have been on his face.

'What has happened?' she asked as soon as he was seated.

'Happened?' he repeated, taken aback in his turn.

'You look so different tonight – happier.'

Inwardly Kinloch cursed his tell-tale face.

'Of course I do. Who wouldn't after getting rid of those rags?'

'Sorry I didn't think of it before,' she said humbly.

'So am I. Feel ever so much better now.'

He certainly did. He was tremendously conscious of that little square of silk at the back of his neck, just on the spot at the nape of his neck where the knot of the hangman's halter might have come one day, he reflected.

VI

With the last days of January a week of wild rough weather set in, the wind, accompanied with alternating showers of sleet and drenching rain, blowing in great gusts over the exposed uplands. The storm kept people to their houses, and the few outdoor winter occupations in that remote agricultural region were at a standstill. There were days when even Mrs. Spedding did not come to the house. Now and then a lonely horse and cart, with the driver huddled up, and heading into the blast, might be seen crossing the common among a sea of tossing gorse bushes. But scarcely another sign of life showed for several days.

Inside the house the storm, and the increased sense of isolation it brought, had the effect of making the man and woman draw somehow nearer to each other. Thrown together they had been by a strange stroke of Fate, but with fear overshadowing them and mutual distrust between them, there had been so far little scope for understanding. Now, however, when Kinloch felt he had the secret sewn on to his coat, his half-felt antagonism died away, and the girl, no doubt feeling the change, without knowing its real cause, responded to that change in him. Kinloch, in fact, had come to regard her as much more the victim of the man whose identity she was struggling to hide than he was himself.

One night while brushing out her hair – she had probably come to see there was nothing in letting down her hair before a blind man – she said to him suddenly:

'Didn't they give you a disability pension?'

Kinloch, who had been listening to the long soft swish of the brush and trying to judge of the length of her hair from the length of the stroke, was taken aback.

'Oh, yes,' he said, 'but I commuted for a lump sum.'

Her insistence amused him. But the brushing stopped even before, his own short laugh.

'You squandered it, I suppose. Is that why you laugh?'

'No; it was your inquisitive questions. So like a careful, old-fashioned wife, before the days of shingling, cross-examining a husband.'

He heard the brush get to work again, but more slowly, as if she were looking at him thoughtfully through the strands of her hair.

'Look here,' he said defensively, 'I didn't "blow" the money – not in the usual sense anyway. It went into tea shares, Kalindar, a company a friend told me of. Ninepence each they were then, and I believe there are thousands registered in my name, all quite unsaleable. They mostly belonged to the friend who advised me to buy and who swore they were bound to rise.'

After this outburst he was surprised to find himself so anxious she should not think ill of him.

But although she was always ready and even eager to talk about his past and his future, he did notice that the moment he turned the talk to her own past and her own future she became dumb at once. He could see she dreaded all questions. He was certain, too, it was to head him off herself and keep his mind occupied that she not only read aloud, to him but set him on to study the Braille system of reading for the blind. But he had quite enough of the embossed letters, sitting on his bed fingering away at them in silence during the three hours Mrs. Spedding was at work about the house. Then the Braille book saved him from infinite boredom; so that, presently becoming keen about it, he made rapid progress. In the evenings she would listen to his stumbling efforts to read her some passage. It was exactly like some child learning to read. The same halts, hesitations, long pauses, and false starts. But having at last attained the end he would seem still more like the small boy in his deep sigh of satisfaction, and his face lit up by sense of triumph. Then she in her turn would pat him on the back and he would glow with pride. Thus insensibly, but very effectively, her mental ascendancy over him grew. She was the schoolmistress, he the scholar.

But the man in him reawakened sharply one night. They were seated before the fire, the lamp unlit, the big book with its embossed characters on a small table between them. He had, with the usual stammering and straining, and puckering of the facial muscles, just got through his day's task, and was about to sit back when he felt her hand take hold of his. That had happened before when she wished to test his progress by putting his hand on some unfamiliar new page in the Braille book. But this time he felt the touch had in it a different quality, and as he heard her turn the pages he found himself detaining her hand, and somehow thrilling and responding to her touch. For a second this lasted. He felt the soft warmth of the hand. Then hastily she put his own fingers in contact with the page.

'Read me that,' she ordered.

But her voice had a break in it and was not at all like that of a governess. And as he bent to read he felt her breath like a caress on his cheek, while a strand of her loosened hair touched his face.

He jumped up. Was she trying to dominate him, to capture and subdue him? To put him in her pocket and make him safe? A suspicion of this flashed to his mind.

'What is it?' she asked, with an appearance of astonishment.

'Not any more tonight. You're – you're pushing me too hard, you know.'

'Sorry. Shall I read to you, then?'

'Yes, it's your turn.'

She got up, and while lighting the lamp asked:

'What shall I read tonight?'

'*Travels with a Donkey*,' he said promptly, now conscious of the ascendancy she had won, and of how near he had come to making a fool of himself.

'But we have no Stevensons,' she said.

'Then for a change let's have the newspaper.'

Not for an instant did he believe she would read him anything of the sort. She had never even admitted that she saw a newspaper. So he was correspondingly surprised to hear her presently unfold a paper. But he was amazed when he heard the first words. He had supposed she would choose some innocent political leading article, or something about the present condition of the Iron Industry, or the prospects of the Boot and Shoe Trade. A leader it was, but not one on politics, and she began in a voice not quite in perfect control:

'*THE EALING MYSTERY. That section of the public which has begun to fear that the present day police methods in the detection of crime are too stereotyped will have had their fears confirmed by almost everything that has happened in connection with this case. While ourselves not entirely in sympathy with the blame now being so freely showered on New Scotland Yard, we are bound to admit frankly that it is very disquieting to remember that already two weeks have elapsed since the date of the tragedy without an arrest having been effected. We stress this fact not to disparage the Yard, whose methods are admirable in some respects, but as palpable evidence of the fact that the new type of criminal who has arisen in our midst calls not only for new methods but for a new type of officer. Unfortunately there seems little chance that we shall see this new type yet. The authorities still adhere to the rule that all detective officers must first serve as ordinary police constables. The absurdity of this rule is manifest when we remember that the ordinary policeman is selected more for his muscular than for his intellectual endowments.*'

This was the first time he had heard a word from the outside world about the crime. And it made him realise the thing in a new way. He felt somehow solemnised. When the reading stopped he said nothing for a moment.

'Why did you read me that?' he asked quietly.

'Because you wanted me to.'

'No! You knew I've wanted news all along, and you wouldn't say a word. Why do you read this to me now?'

He heard her folding up the paper before she replied.

'To reassure you,' she said. 'Nothing is known. You'll soon be able to go your way and I mine, safe.'

Safe! The word took his ear.

'So,' he said, 'up till now you have hidden what you read because the news was not good?'

'Partly,' she admitted.

'You read things in the paper that made you feel we were not safe?'

'Oh, yes.'

Again he felt awed. He could now visualise the forces of the law and all the wide-flung resources of the Press combining to hunt them down.

'Well, m'lady,' he said finally, 'if you keep the newspapers from me after this I'll know what to think.'

She came over and sat down. He heard her take up the paper and stir the fire in an abstracted way, as if thinking of something else.

Perhaps they might have parted and gone their different ways after that night but for the gale that began in the early hours of the morning. Probably she had to wait for instructions from the man for whom she was presumably acting. Kinloch certainly meant to go. But the wild weather came and it lasted eight days. Eight days and never an hour in all their number in which Kinloch did not remember the small hand he had held for a moment, nor feel the place where her hair had touched his face burn like fire. But he was on his guard once more against her. Knowing from that newspaper how soon they could now part, she had attempted those blandishments to capture him, to make him safe, to ensure his silence, if any doubt about that remained. Perhaps she had even been acting on instructions in what she did – caressing him by order! Under his breath Kinloch swore.

On the fourth day of the storm he said to her:

'You have read me nothing more from the newspaper.'

'I haven't seen it. I've to go to' she checked herself – 'a long way to get it.' Then she added, 'tomorrow I must see one, whatever the weather.'

Next day he was waiting for her when she returned.

'Well?' he said.

'There's nothing, not a word of any kind in it.'

His ear detected uneasiness in her voice that made him sure she was lying.

'No news is good news. Why are you frightened?' he asked contemptuously.

He expected a denial to his question.

'You – you still feel sure you can't be traced?' she said hesitatingly.

'Quite,' he replied, wondering what this meant.

'You think you can't be connected with – with what happened?'

'Don't see how. I left only a walking stick in that room.'

'A walking stick can be traced to its owner.'

'Not this one,' Kinloch asserted. 'Men who live where I lived don't have their names and addresses engraved on their walking sticks.'

'But the policeman who stopped you that night, he would know you again?'

'Perhaps. But I'm not going to let him see me.'

'He couldn't fail to see you were blind.'

'It's what he did fail to see. Otherwise he would hardly arrest a blind man for loitering with intent. And you must remember that for the short distance we had to walk he held my arm, leading me. I didn't tell him I was blind; I kept that fact in reserve till we should reach the police station. I owed him one, you see, for he was rather a nasty brute.'

'But surely there's someone who will miss you?' she persisted.

Kinloch laughed grimly.

'Not a soul. Not one will have raised a clamour, unless it's Beaumont, the begging letter chap who lent me the fare to Ealing that night, but he'll say nothing about my disappearance.'

'Why not?'

'Why, don't you see, he'll take it that I didn't return so as to escape repaying him. I'm sorry for that: his estimate of human nature is low enough already. Now,' he added, 'will you tell me the meaning of all this. You have read something in the paper, haven't you?'

'No, there's nothing in the paper about the case; but there's something in it about you.'

'About me?' he cried incredulously.

'Listen. It's from the "Agony" column:

'Alexander David Kinloch, last seen at Ealing on the night of Monday, 15 January. Will any person in a position to supply information as to his present whereabouts kindly communicate with Messrs Selwyn & Smith, Devon Chambers, Chancery Lane. Liberal reward.'

He was utterly amazed and bewildered.

'Somebody seems to want you for something,' she said doubtfully.

The remark brought a smile in the midst of his perplexity.

'It isn't Beaumont anyhow – he'd have cut his losses long ago.'

'The police?' She breathed the question.

'Might be. Read it again.'

While she read he noted the peculiar form in which the notice was put. It did not, as was usual in such advertisements, invite Alexander David Kinloch himself to reply. Why not? They either knew that he could not or would not. Then another peculiarity caught his attention: '*Last seen in Ealing.*' Last seen by whom? He asked himself. The more he thought of it the less he liked it. Even if the thing did not come from the police it would certainly attract their attention. For the night of Monday, 15 January, on which Alexander David Kinloch was last seen in Ealing, was also the night of the Ealing murder. And that coincidence was certainly one into which they would inquire.

'It looks,' he said to her finally, 'as if they were after me.'

There was no fear in his words. He was simply surprised. He could not imagine how it had been done: how they had managed to connect him with the case.

They were both silent for a time.

'We must stay on,' she said. 'No one can know where you are.'

He then remembered a saying of Beaumont's. There had been a discussion in their doss on the best way to avoid the police. The subject always led to lively and animated arguments there. It was Beaumont's contention, he remembered, that the police owe more to the stupidity of the men wanted than to their own cleverness. 'Lie low!' That was Beaumont's advice. 'It may take some nerve but it's the correct game. Once they get you on the run that's telling who done it, and then you're as good as lost.'

'Yes,' he said to her, 'it seems best to lie low here for a bit.' He listened to the wind raging outside. 'If this isn't a safe place there isn't any.'

And up to the last day of the storm they lived in peace, seeing no more newspapers. Then the thunderclap fell. And from a quarter both had overlooked. Mrs. Spedding had just left, and the girl was in her room getting ready to dash away for the latest newspaper. Kinloch was about to emerge from his own room when he heard quick, determined steps coming down the passage. A peremptory knock sounded on the door opposite. Then he heard Mrs. Spedding's voice.

'Miss Stella!'

'Yes?'

'I got a question to ask you. This can't go on no longer. I can't keep it back no more, I can't, I can't!'

The old woman's voice was charged with high excitement, and this time the reply, if there was any, he did not overhear.

But he heard the question easily. It came with a rush, loudly, uncontrollably:

'Be there a man in this house?'

VII

He expected some such question after he had noted the excitement under which the old woman was labouring. But the lady appeared speechless with surprise, for it was a moment or two before he heard her stammer a reply:

'A – a man in this house?'

'Yes, a man you're a-hiding.'

'Are you crazy? The question is an insult. What gave you such a ridiculous suspicion, Mrs. Spedding?'

'Several things, m'lady. Perhaps I am crazy.' She sighed heavily. 'It is a crazy question, come to think of it.' She paused doubtfully.

'Then don't think of it any more, Betsy. The weather must have got on your nerves.'

'Maybe 'tis so. That wind a-whistling all day and a-howling all through the night gives you the idea there's voices all round ye. Last night while I lay wakeful in bed I could have took my oath I 'eard Joe Spedding a-callin' to me from the garden, though ee's lain up in the churchyard nigh thirty years.'

The old woman seemed shaken. Kinloch heard the low murmur of sympathy with which she was led away down the passage.

Later they talked over the incident. Kinloch thought she should have found out what had raised the old woman's suspicion of his presence. But it appeared she had been too frightened to ask, and had preferred to leave well alone. Mrs. Spedding had gone away reassured, and would probably be thoroughly ashamed of herself next day. But all the same he noted that she had now put off her intention of going for the newspaper as soon as the old woman left. He himself shared in the feeling of vague insecurity he divined in her. Discovery by Mrs. Spedding neither of them had ever thought likely. Yet something had quite evidently awakened the suspicions of that unsuspicious creature. What was it? Neither of them could guess. But they would have to find out if the same danger was to be avoided in the future. For the old woman's suspicions once awakened would be more easily reawakened, but not be so easily dispelled a second time.

Kinloch brooded long over the situation, when after dusk fell he was left alone in the house. His thoughts were not about himself. He had no apprehension for his own safety. Once he might not have minded much had Mrs. Spedding seen him and been able to identify him afterwards and so far corroborate his story. But now that he had all that was necessary sewn inside the collar of his coat, identification by her, if arrest came, was unnecessary. By a hundred details of the life in that house he could prove his presence there, and secure Mrs. Spedding's support in what he said. But he was conscious now that he was unwilling to see the girl come to grief. She carried some dark secret, and was fighting well. He tried to analyse his feelings about her. What if the man for whom she fought was a criminal? Many a good soldier has fought in a bad cause. Like himself she was the victim of that man. And he saw now, it was because he did not mean her to be left in that man's hands that he had been content to remain with her in that house.

A long time he sat absorbed in the thoughts that followed. But a moment came when he sat up with a start, all at once alert and fully conscious of his surroundings. Something had happened to disturb him. He saw that. But it puzzled him to think what it could be. A noise in the house? He listened hard, and heard nothing beyond the wind whistling on the roof. Then a door banged. The wind, he told himself, only half believing. But if so the noise had been caused by a sudden inrush of air as some other door or window was opened... He waited, rigid with attention. Then he heard a board creak. There was a loose one

– he knew it well – at the threshold of the sitting room. *That*, at least, was not the wind. His mouth went suddenly dry, and he sat petrified. He could hear the wind moaning above the interior stillness. Then the distant door banged again.

After a long time he ceased to listen and began to urge himself into a belief that it was nothing, that no one had stared at him from the open door. Doors do sometimes bang mysteriously, and even a mouse can make a board creak. Anyway nothing had happened. He was getting as nervous as Mrs. Spedding herself, and far more fanciful. They had nothing to be afraid of. It was impossible that the police could trace them to that lonely house. Any clue they might have held would have been used long ago. And since none had been used it was now obvious they had none to use. He ought therefore with every day that passed to be getting less and less, instead of more and more, jumpy and uneasy.

And yet some unknown sense seemed to be telling him as he sat on that danger was drawing nearer. The storm seemed to have spent itself, for the wind had dropped quite suddenly, half an hour ago. And now there had come what seemed after those days of unending tumult a great calm in which nothing moved. He was almost sorry the storm had passed. That gale was like a wall that shut off the rest of the world from them. But in this sudden hush and stillness there was somehow not peace but expectancy. The world seemed stilled with the sense of something terrible about to happen.

Yet it was a good hour before he heard the sound for which he had sat listening, the quick, sharp click of a key in the lock of the front door. He stood up to meet her, noting the hurry of her approach.

'You have news,' he said to her.

'You know?'

'Felt it in my bones. What is it?'

She did not reply, but when he heard the glass shade tinkle as with a trembling hand, when she removed it to light the lamp, he knew both that the news was bad and that it was something she must read to him. He heard her spread out a newspaper on the table.

'*THE EALING MYSTERY – ARREST IMPENDING. Events continue to move rapidly in connection with this crime, and the general public will learn with relief that it is not one destined to be added to the long list of unsolved mysteries which have of late so frequently baffled the police. The strictures this paper was impelled to make on the out-of-date methods of the police will yet be fresh in the memory of our readers. In consequence of the strong exception taken in certain quarters to what we then said, we may now reveal the fact that to justify our contention this paper set a specially selected crime expert to work upon the case. And the peculiar qualifications possessed by our agent have yielded the most gratifying results. Working along lines quite different from those being followed by the many police engaged on the case, he is now so close on his quarry that an arrest may be looked for within the next twenty-four hours.*

In the interests of justice we must of course still write in the most guarded terms. But in amplification of what we have said in previous issues we may assert that the public interest will not cease with the arrest of the man and woman concerned in this remarkable case.'

Kinloch heard her put down the paper. He was silent too. It was not the confident tone of the paragraph that shook him, but the reference to the man and woman implicated. The precision of that reference impressed him; and from its correctness he did not doubt that much was known which was left unsaid.

He heard her get up and begin to walk about the room. There might be a doubt as to whether the wanted man were the other man or himself; but there could be no doubt that this was the woman wanted. And now Kinloch found that he wished to save the woman. That was the discovery he made as he sat there. He wished to save her. Men, he told himself, are what they make themselves, and women are what men make them. His hands clenched in hate of that man. Her voice came in a hoarse whisper:

'How long do you think we've got?'

'Is that today's paper?'

'Yes. Oh, I shouldn't have minded the weather. The weather! And there were things in the paper that would have shown me sooner what was coming. But for five days I haven't seen a paper, on account of the bad weather. Oh, but I felt so safe – safe with you here.'

He was not listening to her. If this was that day's paper then they might expect to hear that peremptory knock on the door at any moment now. Half hypnotised by the expectation he lifted his head to listen. And it was so quiet after the storm that he could hear the girl's steps, and even her breathing, as she passed restlessly up and down the room.

'Is it worthwhile trying to get away – is there time?' she asked, stopping in front of him.

He shook his head doubtfully.

'Don't know.'

Then just as he spoke his ear, tuned to listening, caught a sound somewhere in the house. The remembrance of his earlier suspicion of someone in the house returned. He knew it now! Of course that had been no fancy: they had merely waited till she came back to take them both together.

He held up his hand.

'Listen,' he whispered sharply. 'Listen!... There is the answer to your question.'

And the quick indraw of breath told him she too had heard. But the next moment she had him on his feet, and half leading, half pushing, scrambled him into the embrasure of the nearest window. Kinloch yielded himself, aware of the uselessness of the attempt at concealment. Not till the house was surrounded would they be offered a chance of escape by a window. But, making no attempt to open the window, she stood him behind the curtains and herself stepped back into the room. Though

he believed this to be equally futile he played up to her, leaning
back against the glass to avoid contact with the curtains. There
followed the briefest interval in which nothing happened. Then
a sharp exclamation came from the girl. This Kinloch read as
meaning that the intruder was not the person she had expected
to see.

'Oho,' the voice came, 'popped out o' sight again, 'as ee, that
Jack-in-the-box o' yourn?'

'Mrs. Spedding, what on earth –'

The girl's indignant expostulation was cut short.

'Oh, I seen 'im, not 'alf an hour agone, and not for the first
time neither, and seein's believing, they say. Locked 'im in, did
ye, while you was away? Yes, but I unlatched the kitchen window this morning. So I crept in and had a good look at 'im
settin' before the fire. Leastways I saw enough of him to know
from the picture in the paper that *he* wasn't the man what went
to church with you.'

The old woman was almost shrill with reproach and anger.

'The innocent I was! I believed you about them two cups on
the table the first mornin'. But I didn't know I'd been doing
only half the washin' up ever since. Nor the lot you eat didn't
start me suspecting. Nor even the smell o' baccy. Nor nothing
else, till I saw you was buying things elsewheres. I knowed it
from the printed names on the bags as ye sometimes forgot to
burn. See? "Something queer, 'ere," I says to myself.'

'And you came to spy?'

'That's just what I done,' the old woman cried defiantly. 'But
with no bad in my mind. You wouldn't 'ave me to sleep 'ere as I
wanted to do, and the thought of you all alone wouldn't let me
rest o'nights. So I began to come round 'ere in the dark to see if
you was all right. Yes, but I soon found out you wasn't so lonely
as I thought for.'

'But he's only a friend, you silly old thing.'

This assurance seemed to exasperate rather than to mollify
Mrs. Spedding.

'Only a friend, is he? Didn't I see ye setting with him last night? Didn't I see ye through the window whenever the draught swayed the curtains, and you a-brushing your hair wi' your arms and shoulders white in shameless nakedness afore his very eyes? "That ought by rights to be 'er 'usband," I says, "but if so," I says to myself, "if so, why be she a-hiding of un?" So I made up my mind as I'd have a closer look. See?'

'But there's nothing wrong.'

'Nothing wrong? Then what's he a-hiding for? Having a game of peek-a-boo with old Spedding, I s'pose, like what you played in the old days? I reckon not! Townified ways this – us country folk don't hold wi' them. It ain't proper for him to be livin' 'ere, not you and him alone.' The voice began to quiver and break. 'Us – us country folk knows the same conduc' as we 'olds to isn't to be expected from gentlefolk, but –' Mrs. Spedding broke down.

Behind the curtain the man stifled the curse that rose to his lips, and listened to hear the girl defend herself. Not a word came from her. And so still was it in that room that he could hear the old woman's heavy, agitated breathing.

'You're – you're in love with him, that's how 'tis.'

'Y–es. Of course I – I love him. Why else should he be here?' The words came quickly.

So that was the line she was taking! Well, it did explain his presence.

'Oh, it ain't right, it ain't right.'

'One can't help one's feelings. They get too – too strong before you know.'

'Oh, but we can all help what we do. And oh, Miss Stella, even if you can't, why didn't ee go somewheres else? Why didn't ee take him where ye wasn't known, and leave us free to think on ee as us used to think?'

Mrs. Spedding seemed to go closer, raising her voice in a quick passionate appeal.

'Give him up,' she cried. 'No good can come of it – nothing but scandal. And that mayn't be so far off, neither.'

She drew near to whisper loudly. 'Look, m'lady, when I was a-coming across the common I came on a stranger man.'

'A stranger?'

'Yes, a man I didn't know, and who didn't know the common from the way he was movin' among the gorse bushes. Didn't 'ear my feet on the grass, and he seemed to be looking for something. Then the thought came to me. "What if it should be her husband?" I says to myself.'

'What was he like, this man?'

'Couldn't tell. It were too dark. Turned away soon as he saw me, but he was a big man, and nobody belonging to these parts. Oh, I don't go for to say as 'twas your husband, but it's a warning, it might as well have been. So give him up, m'lady, give this other up.'

There was no reply at first. But presently the words came in a rush:

'Yes, I'm taking him away tonight – tonight. You'll never see or hear of him again. But you'll tell no one, will you? If – if anyone came asking about him, you won't tell, Betsy?'

'Tell? Tell a thing like that? Wild 'orses couldn't drag it from my mouth.'

Half an hour later Kinloch was sheltering in the lee of a haystack in the corner of a field. He had been hurried out of the house by the back door; and they had scaled a fence and wormed a way through several hedges to reach this shelter. Then before either had recovered breath she had gone back to get the car, bring it round as quietly as possible and pick him up.

Left to himself Kinloch made some of the hay into a little heap and sat down against the rick to think things out. She had warned him that she might not be able to come back for a long time. Who was this man who had been seen nosing about on the common? Mrs. Spedding, to frighten her, had suggested it might be the girl's husband. Well, it might be. But on the whole the man was more likely to belong to the police. Anyhow she might have to face this man, and even outwit him, before she could get away with the car. Kinloch here considered a notion that came suddenly to him. Why not go away alone? Walk clean out of the business – and leave all trouble behind. His presence in that house had put the girl into a horrible position with Mrs. Spedding, forcing her to lie brazenly, and in the end forcing her to pretend to be in love with him. With him! She said that unwillingly – he recalled her low, halting murmur – and only when hard pressed by the necessities of the situation. There simply was nothing else left for her to say. That, and that alone, certainly was the only convincing reason, short of the truth, which she could give for keeping a man hidden in that house.

Yet the curious thing was that, lie though he felt her pretence of love to be, ever since he had heard her faltering admission to Mrs. Spedding, he wanted to help her. Up till then he had fought her to find out what he could – fought her not unfairly considering his handicap. It had been a struggle between them, each wary of the other, fencing, feinting, each alert, he for what he needed to know, and she determined to conceal it. But now, as he sat there with his head leaning back against the pungent hay, he was conscious of a complete change in his attitude towards her. In the presence of this new danger he felt wholly on her side. And the question arose in his mind as to whether the best help he could give her would be to go away, to disappear before she returned. Was not that, he asked himself, the decent thing to do? But no sooner had he reached this conclusion than a doubt arose in his mind. Would it be fair to go off and leave her uncertain as to why he had gone and what he meant to do? He tried to imagine what her feelings would be when she came back and found him gone. Would she feel relief or fear? He could not decide. He did not know enough. Perhaps, if he fell into the hands of the police, they could infer from whatever he told them more than he meant them to know. He might blunder out some damaging fact which he himself took to be quite innocent. He could not tell. It depended on how much the police already knew. That advertisement asking for information about Alexander David Kinloch's whereabouts seemed to show they knew something about himself. At least they seemed to know he could not read. And if it were known he was blind, how quickly they would get their hands on a blind stranger found wandering about a neighbourhood which they were evidently then searching. No; he must stay there till she came back. And having reached this conclusion he was surprised to find himself rather glad.

Then in this moment of danger Kinloch's thoughts ran back once more to the thing's beginning, and the tragic night when he had become involved in the crime. The murdered man himself had no desire to be known, he remembered. There was his delight, his unconcealed delight, on learning that he had found a blind man who did not know who he was. Kinloch smiled grimly. Too clever by half that man had been. The carefully staged trap, and all his neat pre-arrangements to frighten his visitor, had only served to make the assassin's job easier. Probably the deed would not be discovered for hours afterwards. For the victim who, like the murderer, had laid his plans so carefully, would have seen to it that there was no likelihood of any intrusion into that room by any member of his own household.

But someone must open that door sooner or later. The speculation as to who it would be somehow fascinated Kinloch. In the end he decided it would be a housemaid, a sleepy housemaid, early next morning. He pictured her opening the door, pulling up the blinds with a yawn, and turning broom in hand to begin her work. And then he could see the wild-eyed horror come suddenly to her face, and the stupid stare, before she began to scream, when she saw what lay there on the floor.

BOOK TWO

Narrative of Godfrey Chance, Journalist

VIII

AT the time he was murdered Ponsonby Paget was one of the most popular men in England. It is true he was eyed askance by some of his colleagues in Fleet Street; but that was on personal grounds, and none of them ever denied his journalistic genius. There were those indeed who said he could interest anyone in anything he chose to write about.

On matters affecting public morals he put into words what the plain man felt but could not express, and he was a master of that piquant and witty paragraph of society scandal which all women love. Where he got his information none of us knew; but he was certainly familiar with the private, and even secret, lives of the most distinguished people in England.

With the masses he enjoyed a reputation second to none for blunt, outspoken honesty. He never claimed to be spotless, but he never ceased to proclaim that he was British; and the public, taking this to be much the same thing, took Ponsonby Paget to its heart. On the platform after he entered Parliament he was immense. His squat, full-bodied, bull-necked figure topped by the blunt, rugged face made him so like an incarnation of John

Bull himself that his audience believed what he had to say before he had time to say it. But, trenchant orator as he was, his real forte was journalism. He wrote prose as brilliant as Macaulay's. And it was in the *Eye Opener*, the weekly paper he owned and edited, that his genius found its full vent.

The *Eye Opener* has now passed into other hands, and like some of those who were pilloried and exposed in its columns has changed its name. Statesmen are no longer apprehensive, nor do, I imagine, society ladies tremble or gloat, as the case may be, while they turn its pages. It is not what it was in the days of the Ponsonby Paget *régime*, when I, an apprentice in journalism, carried it in my overcoat pocket against my heart. In those days genius was stamped all over that paper – even on the buff-coloured cover. On the upper half of the cover appeared the head and nude shoulders of a massive woman with a very long neck and features of classic beauty. Her head was thrown proudly back, the lips apart, and each eye was shut by a penny piece, twopence being the price of the paper. I remember pointing out the symbolism of these two pennies to Matheson, my chief on the *Record*, when, in my early days on that journal, he caught me with the *Eye Opener* on my desk.

'For twopence she opens the eyes of the British public,' I said.

I was a callow youth then, having lately left a country town for Fleet Street, or I would have known better than to try to teach him anything. Matheson sniggered as he eyed the female bust.

'It doesn't say how much it costs to shut her mouth. Probably that price varies,' he sneered.

I knew what he meant: that rich rogues who liked to pay the price could escape exposure.

'Nothing can shut that mouth,' I asserted hotly.

And now – the thought comes with sudden solemnity – something *has* shut it – Death! The great Ponsonby Paget is dead. White as alabaster and incredibly still I saw him lying, murdered, in the police mortuary at Ealing, with two penny pieces on his own eyes.

*

As we viewed the body in the presence of the police that day, my thoughts returned to the day on which I had first seen the man on whom my eyes now rested for the last time.

My acquaintance with the late Mr. Ponsonby Paget had begun with a contribution I sent to his paper. The subject matter of that article was derived not from any gossip in the sub-editors' room, but through my association with Francis McNab, the private inquiry agent, a man of whom I shall have to speak presently. The *Eye Opener* returned my article; but instead of the usual rejection slip there came back with it a personal note from the editor asking me to call and see him.

How vivid is my first personal impression of the man! After a few inquiries into the sources of the information my article had contained, and also as to my position on the *Record*, he talked on nothing but literary style. He held out hopes of employing me provided I could liven up my style.

How I hung on his words! Hung on them like a new gospel, as he paced that room, a stout, short-legged figure, more like an English farmer talking on turnips than a master discoursing on English prose.

'Above all,' he said, 'shun parenthetical clauses. The English don't like them. The English are a blunt, straightforward people, and they like language like themselves. There's always something Frenchified about a parenthetical clause; it sounds as if you weren't quite sure; and it seems to shilly-shally with the subject. And don't be afraid of repeating yourself. It is necessary to repeat yourself. You can no more get a point home to the British public by saying a thing once than you can get a nail home by hitting it once. Besides, the English like repetitions. They like repetitions for the same reason that they like the big drum. The big drum is the only instrument in the band they understand; it is the only instrument that keeps on saying the same thing over and over again, and therefore it sounds in earnest.'

And yet, looking back, I now recognise that with all his surface simplicity and directness there was in Ponsonby Paget a subtlety and adroitness equally exceptional, though less evident to a raw recruit in journalism, as I then was. In the column of his paper headed *P. P. Peeps*, which he himself wrote, things were said about distinguished people, public men, and society ladies, which no other paper would have dared to print. Not because the things were false, but rather because they were true. For these things he was never prosecuted. Partly, no doubt, he owed this liberty of speech to the place he occupied in the nation's heart, and partly to his known skill with juries; but most of all probably he owed his immunity from actions for slander to the fact that no man in England could suggest so much in words so apparently innocent.

Such was the man I found lying dead, that black January night, on the study floor of his Ealing residence. Matheson had never viewed my acquaintance with him with favour, had in fact warned me against him; but Matheson owed it to me that his paper appeared with an exclusive report of the tragic discovery. And it was one of the biggest sensations the *Record* ever created. How well I remember lingering in the street to witness the sensation our news of his awful death would create when the newsboys appeared with their papers and placards. Weary, hungry, heavy with sleep after that terrible night's experiences, I yet lingered on to hear the cry that would startle London. My eager ear caught the yell they made afar off. Like a flood they burst along the Strand, every one with a big armful of papers, and this bill dangling against their legs:

DAILY RECORD
MURDER!
PONSONBY PAGET
MURDER!

As I turned away to seek my long overdue sleep I felt sure Mr. Ponsonby Paget would have approved of that bill – had he himself, that is, not been the subject of it. For there was in it not only the repetition that he favoured but also that irresistible appeal to curiosity in which he delighted.

One, that is, had to buy the paper to know whether Ponsonby Paget was criminal or victim, or even to be sure that the bill was not an incitement to murder by our own paper. No doubt that bill was the grim Matheson's own idea; but anyhow the matter behind it had been provided by me. And it proved to be one of the finest selling bills that has ever appeared on the streets of London.

*

This is the story of how I came to be the discoverer of the crime.

About one o'clock on the day of his death, which was Monday, 15 January, Mr. Ponsonby Paget rang me up as I was going out for lunch: could I, he inquired, dine with him at his house in Ealing that night? The invitation sent a pleasant glow coursing through me; it marked such a definite step forward in one's career to be taken up by a man of his standing in the world of journalism. But my heart fell as I recalled that I was booked for duty at the big political meeting in the Albert Hall that night. When I explained this regretfully there was what sounded like a muttered oath at the other end of the phone. This startled me, for he was not given to swearing. Then his cheery laugh came through.

'You're my second disappointment,' he said.

'Sorry to be that,' I rejoined, 'but Matheson wouldn't let me off; so it's useless asking him.'

'Look here,' he said briskly, 'what time will you be free – by ten?'

I considered a moment. To come back to the office and turn in my copy would not take half an hour. Before I could reply his voice came again, rather eagerly:

'What I want to know is: can I rely on your being here by eleven?'

'Oh, certainly.'

'You are absolutely sure?'

The emphasis he put into that question was startling and I replied with becoming gravity.

'I'll let nothing stand in the way, Mr. Paget, you can depend on that.'

'Good!' Then his cheery laugh came again. 'Take the sack rather than disappoint me. It is a big thing for you. Afraid you'll get no dinner, though.'

'Perhaps I may hope for a little supper,' I suggested jocularly, meaning to respond to his change of tone.

'Eh?'

I repeated the remark.

'Oh, well, a man on whom I can rely may hope for more than that – before long,' he added significantly. And when the jar of his receiver came through as he rang off, I felt like a man whose future is assured.

*

It was the fog that led to his death. But for the fog Ponsonby Paget would be alive today, for I should have reached Ealing in time to save him. The fog came on about four o'clock, as night began to fall. Matheson had sent me round to see Francis McNab about a promising crime story I had reported from Bow Street in the forenoon. From the little window in McNab's office, which was in the Adelphi, right on the top of a lofty edifice overlooking the river, I watched the Surrey side gradually being washed out as the fog crept up, like waves of smoke rising out of the river. I watched it idly while waiting for McNab, attaching no sinister importance to its coming, my thoughts for the moment turning on the little man for whom I waited.

For some considerable time the *Record* had specialised in the treatment of crime; not, of course, pandering to depraved tastes for the grotesque or the morbid, but, all the same, supplying matter unobtainable through the ordinary channels. The paper had come into touch with McNab rather curiously. At the time when the mysterious Acton Green affair was creating such a splash in the press, McNab sent us a letter propounding a theory on the crime so startling and apparently far-fetched and incriminating that Matheson, as I have heard, not trusting the wastepaper basket, himself put the communication, spitted on the end of the poker, into the fire. When, however, subsequent events proved McNab right in regard to the highly-placed criminal, Matheson grabbed the private detective as a special contributor. He it was who over the *nom de plume* of 'The Lamplighter' contributed those illuminating articles on current crime which were so long a special feature in the *Record*.

Well, just as I was giving him up McNab came into the office. He was, with his thin, clean-shaven face and thoughtful eyes, more like a youngish doctor than a detective – except that there was nothing affable about him.

'Hullo, Chance – business or pleasure?' he asked with a nod.

'Matheson's business: my pleasure,' I returned. 'Come over to the Blue Bird and have tea.'

'And pay half a crown for threepence worth of tea? No, no, laddie.'

Then he struck a match and lit the gas ring upon which a kettle stood ready prepared. This done he sat down astride a chair to read Matheson's letter.

McNab was painfully Scotch. Matheson was Scotch too, but it flattered him to be taken for an Englishman, which was the one thing I liked about Matheson. McNab, however, was of the brand of Scotch labelled extra special. His accent made his English sound like a foreign tongue. Yet he was the only Scotchman I ever really liked, and the only acquaintance I had who never made puns on my name. At first this fact led me to infer he had no sense of humour. How well my mind goes back to that afternoon in McNab's office: it was the calm before the unsuspected storm.

'Business slack?' I inquired as he poured out the tea.

He sighed, nodding at Matheson's letter.

'So-so. A sort of haberdasher's time I'm having, big turnover but small profit.'

'Matheson says he's found out you had a university training and took high distinction in logic at Aberdeen,' I blurted out like an interviewer.

He threw up his hands in protest.

'Heaven forbid – not Aberdeen! I resent the accusation.'

Then I broached a matter that had puzzled me for some time.

'An English university man would never think of taking up your kind of work, you know.'

'Wouldn't he? Why not?'

'He'd have more – well, ambition.'

'Ambition!' he cried. 'Man, man, do ye not see the World is full of men just *not* good enough for their jobs? And what is responsible for that? Ambition. Ambition pushed them on to take jobs just beyond their powers. Whereas, if they'd been content with a job well inside their capacity, they would be successful men. But no! Ambition is the itch that spurs them on to make a hash of it.'

Then, Mac,' I protested, 'if these are your opinions why in the name of Samuel Johnson didn't you stay on in Scotland?'

His dark eyes twinkled at me.

'Laddie, now you are making yoursel' more stupid than Nature intended ye to be. Why didn't I stay in Scotland, ye ask? Well, in the first place Scotland is an honest, law-abiding country; in the next place, in England intelligent competition is less severe.'

He handed me over the biscuit tin, leaving me doubtful as to how much of all this was seriously meant.

When we had finished tea, and cigarettes were produced, I sprang the surprise on him which I had kept to the last.

'Mac, I mentioned your name in a letter to my people the other day, and I hear my maternal grandmother was Scotch.'

'Not so bad. But it's highly diluted.'

'What?'

'The Scots blood that's in you; it will be swamped, I doubt, or will only show in exceptional moments.'

'I'm told she had red hair, and came from Aberdeen.'

'From Aberdeen? That alters the case. They're all made of granite up there, like their city. So I'll not deny that the Aberdeen fluid isn't the better of a strong dilution. It needs a large infusion of the soft English blood to give it a touch of humanity.'

That is the kind of man he was. One could rarely be sure whether he was serious, although he always looked so. But as I took leave of him later, thinking on this, I little thought of the seriousness of what then lay so close ahead.

*

After my duty in connection with the Foreign Secretary's speech at the Albert Hall was over I found myself with an ample margin of time to reach Ealing before eleven. But I had no sooner put my nose outside the door than I determined not to surrender control of my progress to the District Railway. The risk on such a night of a probable hold-up in some tunnel was too great. I therefore took a taxi – they were having a pretty thin time of it that night. A taxi if slower and more expensive was surer. Besides, I reckoned on getting clear of the fog belt somewhere beyond Kensington.

At first our pace was no more than a crawl; but this I had expected, and it caused me no uneasiness since my driver asserted he was so familiar with the route that he could travel to Ealing blindfold.

There is this to be said for the man; he ran into nothing, nor did he once touch either kerb or refuge. Indeed, to me it seemed miraculous how he divined his track to an inch merely by the dim glow overhead that marked the position of the invisible lampposts. When, however, my watch showed 10.15 uneasiness began, for we had not yet passed beyond the fog radius. In a few minutes more the brakes jarred, and as the cab came to a halt the figure of a policeman loomed up alongside. My heart sank as

I saw his uselessly extended arm giving directions to my driver. Hastily lowering the window I heard him speak of taking the third on the right and the second on the left: we had crossed the direct road a couple of miles back!

I am not going to give the history of our further wanderings that night. Heaven knows where we went; but at no time did we get free of the fog. In the end we found ourselves in Ealing before knowing we were near it; and I left the cab and, on the plea that it was a matter of life and death, got a policeman to take me up to Mr. Ponsonby Paget's house in Tookworth Avenue.

When he left me to return to another section of his beat I stole a look at my watch. For a long time, sitting in that wandering vehicle, I had not dared to look at it. It was almost one o'clock. I pulled up in the drive to consider what to do. The large house I dimly discerned ahead stood eerie and ghost-like in that, veil of mist, without a lighted window.

Was it worthwhile, I asked myself, to go on? To decide the question I determined to walk round the house and see if any window behind showed a light. It would be something, at least, to prove to Mr. Ponsonby Paget that I had done my best to keep my word to him. Scouting about, I came on a bricked path, circling in among shrubbery, and taking this, found that it led me on to the lawn fronting the house. Crossing the lawn I turned the corner at the far end, and at once saw light streaming out from the windows of what appeared to be a one-storey addition to the main building. There was no door that I could see, but the brick pathway took me right up to the single step that gave entrance to the room by means of a French window. This window was slightly ajar.

After waiting a moment I tapped on the glass.

Possibly the noise I made was much less than it sounded in my nervously sensitive ears. The place was so weirdly still. Even the fog itself seemed petrified, standing thick and heavy, so that it needed a mental effort to thrust one's hand through it. Anyhow, when no response came I could not bring myself to repeat the knock. Instead I stood up on the step and tried to peer into the room. Immediately inside there appeared to be a dark curtained-off recess; but, as the curtains did not quite meet, the opening between them permitted a diagonal view into the interior beyond. I could see the soft glow of a fire showing above the back of an intervening lounge chair; but the room seemed unoccupied. Possibly, I thought, my host had fallen asleep in that huge chair beside that fire. After debating what course to pursue I tapped on the glass again, more loudly. The hollow, glassy rattle seemed to reverberate suddenly at my back. No doubt the illusion was caused by some high parallel wall behind me, invisible in such a night; but, coming from behind like that, the echo so startled me that involuntarily I pushed the glass door open, and stepped just inside the room.

My first glance showed me there was something wrong.

There had been a struggle in that room. One of the heavy curtains had, I now saw, been half torn from its suspension; a table inside the recess lay overturned, with a draught screen toppled against its upraised legs. The room itself was in great disorder, a jumble of displaced furniture, some chairs broken, with white shattered fractures showing oddly, and almost everything in disarray, or standing at unwonted angles. Somehow it was horrible to view all that evidence of violent motion in its present almost frozen stillness. Only one thing appeared to be in its normal place – the massive oak table, covered with books and writing materials, which stood opposite the fire. As I regarded it in wonder a sudden crackle came from the fire, and a flurry of gassy flame lighted up the shadowed end of the long table. Then something else caught my eye, something that protruded beyond the far end of that table – a human foot. Yes, a human foot, with the firelight now flickering brightly on the patent leather of the upraised toe.

IX

How long I stared at that shoe I cannot tell. I must have been waiting in the hope of seeing it move. There were moments when I could have sworn it did move. It must have been an illusion, created by the spurts of firelight playing intermittently on the polished toe as the fire began to break through. Emboldened by the illusion of movement, I crept round the other side of the table and found – well, instant proof that the foot had not moved, that it would never move again.

The body lying there on its back, one foot doubled awkwardly underneath, and with the arms extended, palms upward, was that of Mr. Ponsonby Paget. On his white pleated shirt front there was a dark red circle, and on the grey, thick-pile Indian carpet, a puddle of crimson.

It was quite clear to me he was dead. I had attended police courts and inquests too often, and heard too much about the symptoms and appearances of death not to be assured of that. And the moment I was assured of his death I started off to rouse the house.

Once outside the room I found the house in total darkness, and in haste went blundering and fumbling about, seeking the back stairs to find the servants' quarters. For though I knew Ponsonby Paget to be a widower I was unaware of what relatives might form his household, and judged it safer first to establish contact with some domestic. As it happened the servants found me rather than I them; for as I stumbled up the service stairs, a man in shirt and trousers, holding a candle in one hand and a poker in the other, appeared at the top.

'What do you want?' he cried shakily.

'Hush,' I motioned to him. 'My name is Chance. Come and show me where the telephone is – something's happened.'

As he stared down at me uncertainly some figures in white appeared behind him, huddled together with scared faces.

'Come at once,' I urged.

'Are you the gentleman Mr. Paget was expecting?' he asked.

'Yes.' Then to reassure him I added, 'You were to give me supper.'

'That's right, sir; it's laid in the morning room now,' he said, as if I had merely mounted there to ask about it.

'Oh, you fool, send those women back to bed and come at once.'

But he was all right by the time I got him down. Indeed, from the manner in which he surmounted the shock of finding his master dead, he was either a man of good nerve or had small affection for the deceased. With some relief I learned from him that Mr. Paget had no relatives in the house. My first act was to ring up the local police, which did not take long, and my second was to get on to the *Record* with the news, asking them to keep space for further particulars. One is not a good journalist for nothing. While I waited for the police I wrote furiously, knowing that already in the office they would be hunting out the obituary and the stock half-tone block of the murdered man.

The weather conditions did not delay the arrival of the local police. First one came in, off his beat apparently, and he took over charge of the room. On his heels came an inspector and two others, accompanied by a doctor. To the inspector I presented my card and told my story. But all on edge though I was to get away to my paper, he refused permission. Indeed, he seated me in a chair against the wall, with one of his men pretty well standing over me, while the doctor examined the body.

I could hear them talking together, but did not catch what passed. When the medical man came across and had a look at my coat sleeves he shook his head to the inspector after giving me a grim smile of apology.

'Must have been drenched,' he said, turning to the inspector. 'I'll tell you this, Green, the hand that sent that knife to the heart was expert – accustomed to the use of it. He struck upwards, not downward as is the natural inclination.'

The inspector was nosing about among the *débris* of furniture, clearly looking for some signs of the murderer's presence. Nothing was being disturbed, I saw; he used his eyes only, while the rest of us watched. In a very short time we saw him stoop swiftly and fish out something from beneath the overturned screen. I could see it was a light-coloured walking stick, and after examining it thoughtfully for a moment he came across to us.

'This seems out of place in a study,' he said. 'I wonder if –' He checked himself and said, 'Dr Dunn, how tall was the man who used this stick?'

The doctor took the thing in his hand. All at once he started rather violently.

'My God!' he whispered.

'What?' the officer said in surprise. 'What is it?'

'Oh, I see what you mean,' the doctor stammered hurriedly. 'You think this may have been left by the criminal?'

The other nodded.

'Must have been at least six feet to use a stick of that length comfortably.'

'At least,' agreed the doctor rather eagerly, trying it at his side, 'if not a bit over.'

How impatiently I listened as they talked on. Would they never let me go? The provincial editions, and the home editions of my paper were already out My only hope was now for the 3 a.m. London edition. That I must catch.

At last, when I had reached despair, the inspector, after taking counsel with his chief on the phone, and then verifying my identity by referring to the *Record* office, let me go. But in the police car only. And it was still early morning when they set me down at the office.

I found myself almost famous, the printers on tiptoe for my copy. And when my job was completed the saturnine Matheson informed me that Babbington would want to see me later. Lord Babbington was the proprietor of the *Record*, and seeing the surprise on my face Matheson grunted.

'It is not often that keeping doubtful company leads to so great a distinction,' he said.

*

It seemed to me I had not been ten minutes in bed that same morning when there came a furious knocking at the door. A note was slipped in, and on tumbling half awake out of bed I found it directed me to go at once to Ealing to assist McNab, who had been sent there to investigate on the paper's behalf. As I dressed, the clearness of the day outside made me look at my watch: it was close on noon. I had slept for nearly five hours, and the fog had gone. It was only then that I had time to think of poor Ponsonby Paget as a human being whom I had known and liked, and not as a sensational case which I had to report. But I can say that I thought of him with a personal sorrow all the way to his house.

There was little difficulty in knowing which that was once I reached Tookworth Avenue. A constable stood at the gate to prevent the scores of curious sightseers from entering the grounds. I observed, too, that a rope across the drive now prevented anyone from entering that way. This was a precaution that appeared to fascinate the onlookers, for they craned their necks and pointed at the drive beyond the rope. But nothing was on the path except the wheel tracks and footprints of many who had come and gone before the rope had been placed there to stop them. On the lawn press photographers were mighty busy getting the deceased's residence from every sort of angle. My friend, the Ealing inspector, I found inside the hall, reduced now to little more than doorkeeper since the arrival of the big men from New Scotland Yard. He nodded to the officer to let me enter.

'Inspector Snargrove wishes to see you,' he said, beckoning. 'Come this way.'

Snargrove I knew by repute. So far I had been too busy with the fact of the murder to theorise on its motive. But I had taken it almost for granted that it was the work of some burglar, or prowling vagabond, who, like myself, had come on the unlatched window. To hear, however, that the local police had called the Yard in at once dispelled the notion that this was a case without complexity.

The Ealing inspector tapped softly, as if at a sick room door, and popping his head in to announce me stood aside.

Inspector Snargrove, a magnifying glass at his eye, was on his knees closely examining the wall opposite the fireplace. As a greeting he waved me to one side without speaking. Another man stood with his back to the fire, close to McNab, who was seated. Except that the body had been removed the room appeared to be untouched since I first entered it. Neither McNab nor the thin man with the sharp ascetic face of a priest took any notice of me, both being intent on Snargrove. So I also turned to watch him.

The detective was peering at certain dark spots showing on the plain, grey wallpaper, about three feet from the floor. There was a series of these spots, disposed regularly in sets of three, close together, the one in the centre slightly higher than the other two beside it. Each set was separated from the next by about two feet. The spots varied in density, those nearer the inner door being fainter.

Before I had ceased to wonder Snargrove pocketed his lens, rose to his feet and came across. He was a burly man with a drooping moustache, was rather high in colour, and had eyes of the cold grey-blue so frequent in men of his complexion.

'I think,' he said as he took a chair, 'we are now able to put a few questions, a few intelligent questions, to our young friend.'

The man with the thin-lipped, priest-like face sat down also. McNab motioned me to a small chair next to his own. Snargrove turned towards me pleasantly, producing from his pocket the report I had intended for the *Record*.

'Your notes have been very useful, Mr. Chance, very useful so far as they go. Still, from my point of view, they leave several details uncertain.'

'All I know is at your disposal.'

'Good,' He waved his powerful hand. 'Mr. Freely's affair.'

The thin-lipped man referred to nodded curtly. His questions were quick and snappy. One somehow had to be quick in reply. Snargrove gave one time to think, but Freely didn't.

'Mr. Paget expected you last night?'

'Yes, he had asked me to dine with him.'

'What hour was fixed?'

'Eleven.'

Mr. Freely lifted his eyebrows. It was as if he meant to disconcert me. I recounted the telephone talk I had held with the dead man.

'He was anxious to have you here?'

'Oh, yes.'

'Hm, how are you so certain of that?'

'Well, I remember he swore to himself, quite softly, when he thought I couldn't come. And I never heard him use an oath in any circumstances before.'

'He was agitated?'

'Very much.'

'Did you gather there were to be any others present?'

'He mentioned none, and I certainly expected to find him alone.'

'Mr. Chance, if a decanter of whisky and two glasses were set out on this table, would you take it that one of the glasses was meant for your use?'

'No.'

'Why not?'

'Mr. Paget was aware of my habits. When I first went to his club he pressed a drink on me.'

'And he never did so again?'

'Never. He was a man who remembered little things very well.'

'You reached here about one, the officer says?'

'Three minutes past by my watch.'

'You were so anxious to see Mr. Paget that you entered even at that hour? What made you so determined to see him?'

'I debated the question of entering with myself when I got here, and finally walked round the house to see if any room showed a light. I was anxious to show Mr. Ponsonby Paget that I had not failed him without an effort.'

Mr. Freely came over to me.

'Hold up your left hand,' he said, fingering in his pocket.

When I held up my hand half resentfully he examined it closely through the lens he had brought out. It struck me as stupid to look at my hands after all the time that had elapsed.

'Thank you. Now tell us what first attracted your notice when you entered the room.'

'The torn curtain and the overturned chairs. Then I saw a foot projecting from behind the table.'

'It frightened you, and you gripped the table?'

'Startled me, not frightened; I saw the foot before reaching the table.'

'You are mistaken, Mr. Chance. You did not see the foot till you stood at the table. Although the room was lit the body lay in the shadow at the far end of the table.'

'I do not recall gripping the table, though.'

Mr. Freely smiled.

'Don't be so eager to deny that. It is a fact which serves to clear you of any complicity in the crime. Look here.'

He led me to the farther side of the big table, and, removing a newspaper, revealed four chalk marks on the outer edge of the polished wood.

'These are the four fingers of your left hand. The thumb is underneath. Excellent impressions they are, just because you gripped hard, and your hand became suddenly clammy. The man who made that impression came on an unexpected sight, in fact he broke into a cold sweat. Compare the whorl in the middle finger and the lines making a half circle as if to avoid contact with the double transverse line behind the first joint – they are your marks.'

Freely was certainly right, as I had to admit on making the comparison; but I had no recollection of ever having gripped that table.

'We had a reason for demonstrating this to you, Mr. Chance. Your profession, with its acquired habit of observation, makes you a more reliable source of evidence than we usually get, but not – er – as you see – infallible. Be careful about the answer to my next question.'

He paused for my nod of assent.

'James Brown, the butler, says the key of that door always remains in the lock inside. When you left the room to summon help was that door locked or not?'

It was humiliating to me not to remember, but I did not, and, after a pause, said so.

'A pity,' Freely commented, 'but quite natural while the one thought of getting help occupied your mind. However, here is something easier.' He stepped over to the table, lifted from it the walking stick I had seen the Ealing inspector find beneath the screen, and held it out. 'Is this your stick by any chance?'

'No, I never use a stick.'

'Look at it. Have you seen it before, with Mr. Paget for in-stance?'

It was a long stout oak stick of the ordinary kind, with a plain rather grimy handle.

'Never. It would be too long for Mr. Paget,' I remarked; 'and not half smart enough.'

'Capital! That corroborates the butler, who scoffs at the idea of his master possessing such an article. It was almost certainly left by the criminal.'

Mr. Freely's satisfaction was very manifest, and Snargrove nodded agreement. While he replaced it a knock came at the door, and an officer entered carefully carrying a square of white paper on the palm of his hand. Freely directed him to put the paper on the table. From the five smudges I could see on its upper surface I divined they were imprints of the dead man's fingers.

'Better settle this at once, eh, Snargrove?'

For answer to his confrère's question the inspector rose and approached the table. McNab remained where he was, elbows on knees, his face between his hands and his brow furrowed, obviously lost in thought. More than interested in the proceedings, I took up a position on the side of the table opposite the two Scotland Yard experts. When one is a journalist one becomes hardened to possible rebuffs. But they did not seem to mind my watching them at all.

It was now that I observed on the table an array of articles which my experience in the law courts told me the police called 'exhibits'. A queer lot they were to be brought into connection with each other! At the far end of the row was an overcoat with fur collar and cuffs; next to it a pair of dress shoes, followed by a little heap of broken glass, a plain envelope, a decanter half full of what looked like whisky, then a wedge-shaped splinter from what seemed a hand mirror, and, last in the row, the stout oak stick already mentioned.

The two Yard men began on the little heap of glass. With a pair of forceps Freely lifted and set out each piece into one or two separate places, and when he had finished I saw they now formed the remains of two tumblers. Snargrove, watching, took a small box from his pocket. But Freely upon reconsideration shuffled one or two pieces from the remains of one tumbler to the other heap. Then the inspector dusted the whole with grey powder from his box. Waiting a minute or so Freely began to go over the powdered surface, delicately, with a soft brush. The result amazed me. It was like watching a photographic plate being developed, for fingerprints came up on the glass as if by magic.

'Got him!' Snargrove murmured. 'Got him: this is the glass he used.'

Freely stood up and, after a glance at the paper with the dead man's imprints in black, nodded assent. I could see myself those fingers on the glass were different, even in size. They left untouched the other glass, which had evidently been Mr. Ponsonby Paget's.

But it was a disappointment when they returned to their seats, for I was curious about the other 'exhibits', especially so in regard to what the envelope contained.

'We are now almost in a position to reconstruct the crime,' said Snargrove, settling himself comfortably. 'Call James Brown, the butler. I've one or two supplementary questions yet to put.'

The butler seemed a trifle nervous with his hands as he entered. In the excitement of our first meeting I had scarcely looked at him. But I took note of him now as he stood in front of Snargrove. He was in the early fifties, stoutish, puffy under the eyes and with the smooth mask-like face peculiar to his calling. There was no hint of nervousness, though, in the bow he made to the inspector.

'You have said you admitted no visitors to this room last night?' Snargrove began.

'Yes, sir, that is so.'

'Did Mr. Paget ever have visitors you had not admitted?'

'Frequently.'

'Late at night?'

'More often than not, sir.'

'You could hear their voices?'

'When I went round locking up, or as happened sometimes when the bell rang for me to serve refreshments.'

'Did you ever happen to hear a woman's voice?'

'Oh, yes, sir, quite often.'

Snargrove nodded.

'Of what class were these ladies?' he next inquired.

And as the butler hesitated he added quickly, 'Come, a man in your position must know how to "place" people by their appearance or their voices.'

'Well, they were of all classes, from ladies' maids to – well, to the lady herself, as you might say.'

'And did you ever form any notion as to their business and why they came so late?'

Brown moved uncomfortably for a moment.

'Well, sir, it was generally understood – in the Room I mean – that they came on business connected with the paper, and so naturally they did not wish to be seen.'

At this reply I saw McNab glance swiftly up at Brown's face. He too, I know, was asking himself if this mask-like butler was capable of the irony his answer implied. Snargrove also caught at the word.

'Naturally, you say. Do you mean they came to supply Mr. Paget with gossip for the *Eye Opener*?'

But Brown was not to be drawn. The flicker of light died from his eyes and like a man who had said more than he had intended his face became wooden again.

'That I don't know; I never heard they did, sir.'

Snargrove gave a laugh – to my ear of bluff carelessness.

'And how about the men who came, Mr. Brown?'

'There never were any, leastways so late as that.'

'So if a man was here about midnight last night you would regard it as exceptional?'

'Indeed yes, sir, very exceptional indeed.'

'Thank you, that will do.'

'And now,' Snargrove said when the door closed softly behind the butler, 'we can proceed to the reconstruction.'

To me there was something appalling in the cold, slow, unruffled deliberation of these men. For all they knew the murderer might with every minute that passed be putting another mile between himself and pursuit. Yet here they were, slowly and methodically thinking it out; and, to judge from McNab's attitude, they might have been at it for hours. All the same at Snargrove's words McNab looked up alertly.

'Go on, inspector,' he said.

X

Inspector Snargrove began his reconstruction of the murder in a quiet, even tone.

'Last night,' he said, 'Mr. Ponsonby Paget sat where I am now. He was expecting someone who did not come. That person was not Mr. Chance. The deceased, knowing his abstemious habits, would not have got a glass ready for Mr. Chance's use, nor would he, as James Brown, the butler, has said he did, have directed the decanter to be refilled. Mr. Paget became very uneasy as the time passed and his expected visitor did not arrive. He opened the French window leading into the garden. Why? Not perhaps to look for his visitor there, but because from there he could most quickly and conveniently see if the fog still held. He wondered if the person had been delayed by, or gone astray in, that fog. Therefore that person was neither a neighbour nor, probably, one familiar with the neighbourhood, but one who had to travel some quite considerable distance. It may or may not be symptomatic of Mr. Paget's nervous condition that he left the window unbolted. But his uneasiness assuredly went on increasing as the night passed. He left the house by the front door, and walked for some considerable time, presumably in an attempt to find the person who he must have concluded had lost his way. That he did this on the smallest chance of lighting on him reveals the anxiety he now felt. He returned alone, re-entering by the front door.'

At my exclamation of surprise McNab touched me.

'Hush!'

But Snargrove was quite mild about it.

'The overcoat he wore is kept in the cloakroom beside the front door, Mr. Chance. The coat is still damp. Soaked fur retains moisture a long time, especially in muggy weather, such as has prevailed, if *well* soaked. So he was out some considerable time.'

'He was a considerable time in town yesterday,' I said dryly.

'Not wearing this coat, Brown asserts. Besides, there's the grit and mud on his dress shoes, and these he certainly did not wear in town.'

After that crushing retort I kept a respectful silence.

'He returned alone,' Snargrove resumed, in his former dreamy tones, like a man retelling something seen in vision, 'replacing the coat in the cupboard where we found it. Why do I say alone?' Snargrove said with his eyes on me. 'Because of what that decanter tells me. When I cross-question it, at first its testimony seems to say he did not return alone. But a little careful questioning gives us the truth. Its measured capacity is one quart, and it was filled to capacity by the butler after dinner last night. Now one pint two ounces are gone. Who consumed that amount? We have the broken pieces of two glasses, both of which were used last night. But note this: that used by the criminal has but one set of clearly defined traces of the right hand fingerprints. That is, it was but once used, and its capacity is a half-pint.'

Snargrove's eyes glittered brightly as he looked round his audience. He pointed to the second broken glass, the fragments of which Freely had not brushed.

'I am going to say that if the fingerprints on that glass, the glass used by the dead man, were exposed, they would show that the glass had been used more than once.'

Freely, rising hurriedly, produced his powder and the little brush, and set to work on the glass.

'Assume that is so till we know,' the inspector continued. 'The inference will follow that the two parties who used these glasses used them at different times. Notice this well! This stranger took his whisky in one gulp. Does a guest do that? I think not. Neither, on the other hand, does a host go on helping himself while his guest's glass is empty. And if I am right about his glass that is what Mr. Paget did – if the two men drank together.'

'You're right, Snargrove,' Freely announced. 'He took up and put down this glass five times at least.'

Snargrove waved a hand.

'That settles it: the man who used the other glass is the man who had already killed Ponsonby Paget, and he used the glass put there for someone else who never came.'

All this close reasoning was startlingly impressive and convincing to the mind. The detective-inspector drew a deep breath through his teeth.

'And now,' he said grimly, 'let us have a look at the murderer.'

Freely returned to his seat. As for me, I hung on Snargrove's words, startled by his tone of certainty.

'He crept in by the French window while his victim sat where I now sit, with his back to that window. Mr. Paget had given up all expectation by this time, and sat low down in his chair so that he was hidden from the man who examined the room from behind the curtains. This man was tall and dark, well under middle age, of exceptionally powerful build, but lame. After a glance around the room he concluded from seeing the lights left on that it had been only temporarily vacated. He must therefore be quick and take what lay to his hand. He had just emerged from behind the curtain when Mr. Paget rose from his chair and approached the table to replenish his empty glass. The stopper found lying on the table beside the decanter tells its own tale. It tells us that at the precise moment he was about to lift the decanter he heard a noise, probably the intruder's awkward attempt at stepping backwards behind the curtain. Thinking it might be the delayed guest, or Mr. Chance here, Mr. Paget hurried to the alcove. The intruder could not get away in time, and his lameness made it certain he could not finally get away at all. Mr. Paget seized him; there was a struggle, the curtain was torn, and the small table and the draught screen were overturned. Mr.

Paget raised an outcry and held on. Though a foot shorter, his weight, and the other's lameness, enabled him to hold his own. The struggle carried round the room. In the end youth told, and the older man, in the act of being thrown, clutched desperately at the other's hair. Only then did the murderer draw his knife. He was a man who knew how to use a knife. But before he could use it Mr. Paget saw what was coming and, dropping his hold, started back, stumbled, fell here.' Snargrove moved across to a spot on the carpet on which a little circle of chalk was drawn, and indicated the spot with his foot. 'He was trying, you can see, to put the big table between them. He was too late.'

The inspector stepped to the place marked by the dark crimson stain. For a moment he stood regarding that stain. Then approaching the table with the exhibits he picked up an envelope. From it he very carefully shook a few strands of dark hair into his palm, and as he looked at them said:

'Freely, he was not one of your chronics. The habitual criminal whose outfit includes a weapon, carries a revolver, not a knife of the sort used here. Your type of criminal has a prejudice against the sight of blood; and in addition he knows all about fingerprints. But this man, though unaware of the danger of fingerprints, was a fellow used to the sight of red. He was probably a soldier, an ex-service man, to judge by the length of this hair. A bit of a fop too' – Snargrove touched the splinter of the mirror – 'young men carry that sort of thing now. Ten years ago that would have meant a woman in the case!' He laughed shortly. 'This chap whipped it out to see if his face had got – well, splashed. The glass had got cracked in the struggle and this splinter dropped out. Something scared him then. Probably some noise, real or imaginary, for he left in a mighty hurry, before he had time to recover his stick, which was only out of sight under the overturned draught screen, at the spot where he was seized by the murdered man.'

Inspector Snargrove, his eyes brightening, nodded satisfaction.

'Yes, it ought not to be a long hunt, Freely. A regular amateur in crime, though not in killing, this fellow. Why, look at that' – he wheeled round dramatically, pointing to the smears on the wall opposite - 'who but an amateur would think of wiping his fingers on the wall! In the whole of my experience I never saw anything like it – never.'

At this juncture McNab looked up, and, nursing his left knee in his clasped fingers nodded his agreement.

'Nor have I. That's what makes me wonder.' He whistled meditatively for a moment. 'But, after all, these smears tell you little.'

We were all now looking across at the marks on the wall.

'Yes,' Snargrove agreed, 'that is so. The dragging of the fingers downward, and the rough canvas surface, destroyed the finger-prints, if that is what you mean.'

'Partly,' McNab rejoined. His eyes narrowed. 'You say he was a tall man. If so he must have gone on his knees to put those marks where they are. He may have gone down to do that, of course, but it bothers me to think why he took the unnecessary trouble. You say he was scared too. There again I'm in a diffi-culty. The marks were made by the right hand of a man going towards the door – those nearest the door being fainter. But if he was scared by anything at all his natural impulse would make him run for the exit, the window by which he had entered, which was that French window at the other end of the room. But as a fact he made for that door leading to the interior of the house.'

'The scare possibly came from the garden,' Snargrove said.

'Quite – if there was a scare at all. By the way, you have examined the path for footprints?'

Snargrove smiled.

'We have not – it is only in works of fiction that criminals leave footprints on a brick path.'

McNab ignored the gibe.

'Suppose there was a scare, inspector, did the man take the whisky before or after he had wiped his hands on the wall?'

Snargrove smiled still more indulgently.

'After, otherwise the glass would carry traces of blood. Wiping his hands on the wall was sufficient to remove the stains at just the points where the fingertips made contact with the glass.'

'Then if he stayed to drink the whisky he must have discovered his scare to be a false alarm, and did not leave in such a hurry after all?'

Snargrove thoughtfully licked the end of his moustache in between his teeth, and then frowned as if he did not like its taste.

'And yet,' McNab continued, 'he takes nothing, except the whisky – not even his victim's watch and chain, which glittered in the light before his eyes, ready to his hand!'

'He was an amateur in burglary but not in killing, as I read him,' Snargrove said; adding significantly, 'Like most amateurs he bungled.'

'What's your theory,' Freely asked bluntly, turning to Mc-Nab.

'I've got none: it fair beats me,' McNab admitted, 'to account for all the – the – phenomena.' He turned to the inspector. 'I'll allow, Snargrove, that some of your inductions were masterly in certain details, but in the total I find your reconstruction does not carry complete conviction. There's the matter of the walking stick for example.'

From the surprised look on Snargrove's face it was clear he plumed himself on his deductions from the stick.

'Well, what about it?'

'You infer the murderer was lame because he used a stick. Put that into logical form and see what happens: *All lame men are men who use walking sticks*. Is that what you say?'

The inspector after a moment nodded assent.

'That's about it.'

'Very good. Here then we have a walking stick. If the conclusion you draw from it is sound, it should be capable of conversion into this other complementary proposition: *All walking sticks are things that are used by lame men*. Which is a manifest absurdity, since many who are not lame use walking sticks. There's the fallacy for you, arising from the fact that the predicate in your proposition is an undistributed predicate. Therefore such a proposition can only convert into this proposition: *Some walking sticks are things used by lame men.*'

'Quite so, and I say this one was.'

'But why? Just because you *want* to believe it. I defy you to give any reason in logic for that belief.'

Snargrove, reddening at the gills, pursed out his lips.

'Logic! What is logic?' he asked contemptuously.

The retort that came must have been as little expected by him as it was by me. Perhaps the previous sneer about bungling amateurs had stung more than appeared at the moment.

'Logic,' said McNab coldly, 'is the science which teaches foolish men a respect for truth not theirs by nature; it trains our ignorant minds to take account of all the facts, and not merely – like lawyers, policemen and politicians – those facts which suit their case.'

Snargrove went quite pale – more pale than Freely himself. But I will say this for him – although he may have been a poorer logician, he had a better control of his temper than McNab. McNab called logic a science, but he was as touchy about it as if it had been a religion. Indeed to him it was a religion. So in the silence that followed his rude retort I made a mental note never to speak disrespectfully of logic in his presence. And the next moment I was admiring the amazing way in which discipline told on Inspector Snargrove.

'What are the facts to which you allude?' Snargrove asked calmly.

'Besides those I have already mentioned there's this. You say the murder was not done by the man Ponsonby Paget waited for. He never came, you say. Then, doubtless, a letter of apology or explanation has come in. No? Odd, surely, one would have expected a letter of apology or explanation by first post from a guest who had failed to turn up.'

Freely looked over quickly.

'Oh, I don't know,' he said pointedly, 'bad manners are not so uncommon as all that.'

McNab smiled as he took the thrust.

Sir,' he said, turning to Snargrove, 'for classifying you with lawyers and politicians just now I apologise humbly.'

'That's all right,' the inspector said with brusque awkwardness. Then turning to Freely he added, 'We'd better be moving now.'

McNab must have seen that he had mortally offended Inspector Snargrove, and he stood up eagerly.

'Before you go, inspector, I beg you to consider one possibility overlooked so far in this case. Was the light on or off when those hands touched that wall? It's almost incredible the man knew of the blood on his hands. If the light was off, was the man who left the traces of his bloodstained hands on that wall not feeling for the switch? He was going in its direction, crawling – he was certainly crawling – along the wall, anxiously feeling for something. Why did he crawl? Because the furniture was all scattered over the floor. He was afraid of falling over something, and making more noise, or more likely, getting hurt. And, if he was in the dark, consider how that fact explains more than the bloodstains. He did not see his hands, and so of course did not observe what he was leaving on the wallpaper. But this would explain, too, the fact that nothing was taken, or could be, till he found the switch; and the darkness would also account for the fact that he left his stick behind. The room was in *darkness*, man.'

Snargrove laughed.

'That it wasn't. You are forgetting the mirror. He would hardly take out a mirror in darkness. Besides, Mr. Chance found it lit up.'

Yes, but *not* lit up by the man who crawled along the wall, and who, as the marks show us, never reached the switch.'

'I beg your pardon, you are –'

But McNab threw up his hands on recognising that Snargrove's mind was closed.

'Oh, man,' he cried with a weary sigh, 'do not bother to beg my pardon; it would be more to the purpose if you didna' beg the question.'

And he turned his back on Snargrove.

The inspector wheeled round.

'You go your way, I go mine,' he said challengingly.

'We'll see who lays him by the heels.'

When we in turn left the room we found Freely trying for fingerprints on the glass of the French window, and Snargrove himself busy inside the roped-off portion of the drive. That anything could be got there seemed to me incredible. The footprints on the drive, which was spongy after the days of soft rain and fog, were numberless. While McNab watched I tried idly to pick out my own of the previous night, and soon saw how impossible it was. So I turned to see if on McNab's face there was reflected anything of the futility I felt Snargrove's examination to be. But he was not looking at the inspector's broad bent back. He seemed to be occupied in much the same way himself. I waited as patiently as I could, till after a time he perhaps became conscious of me as a disturbing presence and straightened himself.

'You needn't wait,' he said. 'I won't be coming yet. There's still something I want to ask James Brown, the butler.'

XI

On the following Wednesday, after returning to the office from the inquest, which was adjourned for seven days at the request of the police, Matheson asked me to go round to the Adelphi to remonstrate with Francis McNab.

'He seems to have fallen out with Snargrove,' Matheson said disagreeably. 'The *Record* will suffer for it. This will never do. Snargrove has turned uncommunicative.'

He lifted a police bill with the usual heading, and handed it to me.

'Take that round to him; it is all Snargrove has seen fit to give us about the case. Nothing more than is to be read on every hoarding. Show him what he has done. And you can add that it will be difficult for Lord Babbington to secure him special privileges for his work if he becomes – er – *persona non grata* with the authorities.'

While Matheson was laying it off I read the bill:

'*WANTED. Young, dark, well dressed man, about six feet in height and of strong build, but walks with a pronounced limp. Known to have been in Ealing on the night of Monday, 15 January. Any information should be sent to New Scotland Yard or to the nearest police station.*'

'McNab won't like this; it's contrary to his own theory,' I said.

Matheson pricked up his ears.

'He has a theory, then? What is it?'

'He hasn't said.'

'But he thinks Snargrove wrong?'

'Astray – like a lost sheep.'

Matheson ruminated for a rather long time. I knew just what was passing in his mind: he was thinking of the possibility of working up a stunt on the Ponsonby Paget case, supposing the paper took a line at variance with that taken by the authorities. In other words, he was thinking that even if a break with the police were inevitable it needn't be unprofitable.

'Tell him,' Matheson said at last, 'this paper will back him in any reasonable line he cares to take.'

'Against the police?' I asked.

'Against anyone,' he snapped.

I found McNab in his eyrie overlooking the old river. 'Matheson says he'll back up any attack you make on our police methods,' I announced.

'Does he? Well, I'm not proposing to begin one. The police do their best, and that more often than not is pretty good.' He walked up and down for a little. 'A fine thing if I were to attack the police!' Stopping, he eyed me quizzically. 'Look here, you once asked me why I took up this kind of work. The true answer is that it's in my blood – my father was a policeman.'

'Oh, I didn't know.'

He nodded.

'Yes; though he ended a county inspector he was once a humble village constable who did fine work in the matter of some Irish Fenians just before I was born.' McNab looked down thoughtfully. 'Still, of course, this Snargrove isn't the police; we must not commit the fallacy of arguing from the particular to the general.'

I seized the moment to produce the police bill.

'Matheson wants to know if you wish to write him anything on this,' I said.

He read it through, making a running commentary:

'"*Young, dark, well-dressed man*" – ay, all that's because his hair was kept well brushed. They've had the microscope on it. At what age do men cease to use a hairbrush?'

'"About six feet in height" – that's an inference from the length of the walking stick.'

'"*Walks with a marked limp*" – that's the stick again, a *non sequitur*, I think.' He looked up at me in disgust. 'Man, the thing fair reeks with fallacies.' Then he thrust the bill back on me. 'No, tell Matheson I've nothing to say.' And with that he bundled me with the police bill outside.

*

When, however, the day of the resumed inquest arrived I went round, at Matheson's request, to see if McNab would

accompany me to the court. But he met me with a point-blank
refusal.

'I've washed my hands of that case,' he declared shortly.

'Well, of course, it is a rather difficult case,' I admitted.

He met the remark with a snort.

'Matheson,' I continued, 'is keen about it. He will give you
carte blanche as regards expense, if you are sure you can make
a big splash of it on *Record* lines. But he won't stand a penny
piece, he says, if all you can do is to say "Amen" to what Snargrove says.'

He wheeled round on me.

'Is that likely?'

'It's not what I gathered from what you said to him at Ealing.
Still, as you now refuse to get on with it I suppose, after deeper
thought, you've changed your mind.'

'Look here, Chance,' he cut in. 'I'll at least go out with you
to hear the evidence offered at the inquest. It's just possible
Snargrove may have modified *his* notions.'

That was all I wanted.

We arrived at the court rather early, and to pass the time
went into the small ante-room in which the various exhibits
connected with the case were laid on a table. While we were
there Snargrove came in to post a constable in charge of the
productions. He affected not to see McNab.

The little court was crowded to excess by the curious public.
But, after I had repeated my evidence as already recorded, I
secured a place at the press table. In the small gallery at the back
of the hall I saw McNab's intent face as Inspector Snargrove
gave his evidence in the presence of a hushed court. Before that
evidence – unaltered in any particular of vital importance –
had closed, however, I was startled by a change of countenance
in McNab. Seen against the dark woodwork of the gallery his
face had previously looked pale, worn and harassed – the face
of a man disgusted and, disagreeing with what he heard, yet
unable to say why – but now there was a complete change. His

face, still pale, had become – it is the only word – illuminated! His dark eyes shone like lamps. Catching sight of me; he rose, made a gesture towards the door, and left his place. My heart began to thud. Something big had happened. I got up from the table. There was no real need to wait for the verdict, it would come through on the tape later. After Snargrove's evidence the finding was a foregone conclusion – wilful murder by some person or persons unknown. I hurried out.

McNab stood in the corridor waiting for me, with his eyes shining. Seldom have I seen a man so eager. Beyond all doubt he had lighted on something startling and unexpected. And knowing the kind of man he was I felt certain it was no mare's nest but something that threw fresh light on the perplexing case.

'Just let us have one more look at the exhibits,' he said, taking my arm.

We passed into the ante-room with a nod to the policeman guarding the door. He gave little heed to us, for with out-stretched neck and awestruck eyes he was trying to catch the evidence then being given by the great detective from the Yard.

McNab almost pounced on the walking stick, examining it all over, top and bottom. It trembled in his hands.

'Ye heard me suggest the room was in darkness when those hands with blood on them marked that wall?' he demanded, his voice vibrating in suppressed excitement.

'Yes, I did. You were wrong, of course, for the room was brilliantly lit when I entered.'

He shook his head with decision.

'I was not wrong, lad. You see this stick? Examine it well and tell me what you make of it.'

I took the stick and examined it narrowly.

'Describe it,' he ordered.

'It's a common, cheap, heavy, oak stick. Except that it must have been used by a very tall man it is not different from others of its kind,' I said, wondering and mystified, for I had expected something big.

'There is a difference, though. Look! Hold it out straight as if you were walking. Do you see the *sole* of it bevelled towards what you may call its heel? A stick you used would be bevelled slightly on the side next your right leg. Because you are right-handed it would sooner or later get worn down on the nearest side. Similarly in the case of a left-handed man his stick would have at bevel towards his left leg. For no man holds a walking stick quite perpendicular; it is always closer to his flank than to his boots.'

'But this is neither,' I interrupted, turning up the end. 'It is worn, very much worn, not at either side but right across the heel.'

'Precisely. I said that man did his fell work in darkness. I was right. He did. This stick proves that.'

To me it seemed McNab had gone off his head, for all his assured tone. I watched him anxiously as he stood eyeing the wretched stick, now in his hands again. There was an expression of rapture on his face. In fact, he looked like some professor reverently handling the body of some vile but uncommon reptile. What to make of it I did not know. It was one of those moments when thought is paralysed. Some vague remembrance of Moses and the rod that turned into a serpent came to me. Then McNab looked up and began to talk just like a professor starting a lecture.

'Here,' he said, 'we have a demonstration of the value of the logical method. In spite of Inspector Snargrove's presentation of the case, and in spite of your own confident evidence in support, I just could not believe the room was lighted up when those marks were put on that wall. No, that I could not believe. Such an act was devoid of sense. And all actions have some sense traceable in them somewhere. So as a reward of my fidelity I come on the amazing truth.'

He was as maddening then as any long-winded, fossilised professor.

'Don't see how that stick can tell you anything,' I said to hurry him up.

'No? Well, it quite transforms the case. A queer man that! But the rope is already as good as around his neck.'

He replaced the stick on the table, and as it were, awoke from his ecstasy.

'Must see Matheson at once,' he said in a new tone. 'Money will be needed – lots of it. But, Lord, it will be worth it to his paper! This is a case that will make a noise in the world, Chance.'

He began to make for the door. I stopped him, eager enough now.

'Tell me more,' I urged.

But he shook me off.

'You bat! You unbeliever! It's all before your eyes. If you can't see, it will be a good discipline for you to wait.'

Again I seized his coat. But he broke free.

'No, no! Matheson must be the first to hear of this.'

Then he fairly ran for the door.

XII

But for the officer in charge of the exhibits I should have caught McNab before he got down the steps. For I had no mind to undergo the discipline of waiting to learn what the startling discovery was. The tantalising refusal to tell me I owed to the evidence I had just given, which happened to support Snargrove's theory. But the policeman at the door stopped me. Recalled to a sense of his duty, I dare say, by McNab's dash past him, he became uneasy, and detained me till he had counted and scrutinised all the exhibits. That needn't have taken very long, but by the time he had finished scratching his head over them McNab was beyond reach.

When I got to the office I heard McNab had been closeted with Matheson for the last twenty minutes. That, I thought, settled my chance of hearing more. Matheson would be sure to order McNab to say nothing. But just as I was resigning myself to the situation the chief's phone rang sharply, and the order came through to send me up the moment I came in.

When I entered it was to find Matheson at his table in the hunched-up, thoughtful attitude I knew so well. McNab on the hearth rug, his story apparently finished, stood fiddling with a cigarette. Matheson, unlike McNab, cared nothing for the niceties of a criminal case, and McNab, unlike Matheson, cared nothing as to whether or not a case would make a rousing stunt for the paper. I knew therefore that I had been called in not by McNab but by the chief, so that he might be sure the affair was worth the *Record*'s money. And that told me two things. First, as I already knew that Matheson wanted McNab to take up the case, I saw that the case must have taken on an unexpected aspect; secondly, that it seemed likely to cost more than Matheson bargained for.

But for a time neither of them even glanced at me. McNab, having unloaded his mind, stood at his ease, breathing out a cloud of smoke, and looking more than ever like a doctor who has completed the successful diagnosis of some perplexing case. Matheson, though, seemed doubtful. He twisted uneasily in his chair, looking down at the notes he had evidently made of what the other had said.

'If one could only be sure.'

'Sure of how much – all?' McNab inquired.

'Well, less would do. But some indubitable facts we must have.' He pondered heavily for a moment. 'Perhaps if you were to recapitulate the absolute certainties in the case it would help us to a decision.'

I could see McNab stiffen as he listened.

'If you will only back a certainty,' he said tartly, 'you'd better drop this and wait for the Derby.'

It was good to hear someone speak like that to Matheson; but I thought McNab rash if he wanted the paper to take up the affair. Yet Matheson, fingering his notes, replied quite mildly:

'Didn't you say you were certain the police were on the wrong scent?'

'In my own mind; but there's nothing absolute in that.' Matheson grunted.

'Then just enumerate any other points on which in your own mind you are equally certain.' He glanced over at me to add in quite another tone: 'Attend, please; this is where you come in, Chance.'

McNab threw his cigarette into the fire.

'First,' he said, 'it seems a certainty to me that Mr. Ponsonby Paget that night expected a visitor whom for some reason he feared. It is Snargrove's view that this visitor failed to come, and that the deceased went out to look for him. But on the latter point the balance of probability surely is that it was Chance for whom he scoured the roads that night. For some reason unknown, Ponsonby Paget felt compelled to face his visitor, otherwise he might have evaded the visit by an absence from home. I regard his dread as proved by the anxiety he showed to secure Chance's presence. Naturally, then, it was for Chance he searched, for Chance who had never before been to the house, and who might well, on such a night, be stumbling about in search of it.

'The next point is still more certain. Those two whisky glasses show us that the host expected but one visitor. But the visitor did exactly what Ponsonby Paget tried to do when he rang up Chance from his club: he too arranged to have another person present. And he succeeded where his host failed.'

Matheson looked up.

'What reason have you for that conclusion?' he asked.

'The list of exhibits is before you. A blind man does not carry a mirror. Neither did Mr. Ponsonby Paget. It follows that the walking stick and the mirror belonged to different persons. It is thus established that two at least were concerned in the murder.'

Here I felt bound to intervene.

'But,' I burst in, 'how do you know there *was* a blind man there at all?'

A smile flickered from McNab as he saw me agape with incredulity.

'That stick is a blind man's stick,' he said. 'It is worn away across the heel, as you saw, just where he held it well out in front of him to feel his way. If you doubt it, stop the first blind man you meet and examine the end of his stick. Yet,' he continued, 'the walking stick alone might have told me nothing without those marks on the wall. Those marks were, and are, simply inexplicable unless the man who made them did not see what he was doing. Therefore, one of two things: either the room was in darkness or he was blind. But you yourself, Chance, asserted the room was not in darkness when you entered it a few moments after the murder had been committed. Now –'

Again I had to cut in.

'Not so fast, McNab. You say I entered a few moments after the murder. That is news to me.'

'There are two facts that "time" the deed. First, we must conclude that it was at a late hour, long after you were expected, since the man went out to look for you. That act implies a high degree of prolonged nervous strain, for really it was long odds against finding you. The man was fairly desperate before he went out. But better than that is the witness of the fire. You said in your evidence before the coroner today that you were startled by a sudden crackling from the fire which then burst into flame, and revealed a foot lying where the table had previously cast a shadow. That crackle of coal was significant. It is only newly added coal, expanding with the heat, that crackles like that. So unless we are to suppose that the murderer thoughtfully mended the fire before leaving, that coal was added *before* the murder was committed.'

This reasoning carried conviction. It staggered me to think I had been so close to the criminal. But just as I found my voice Matheson cut in impatiently.

'Let's get back to the blind man, if you please.'

I knew what Matheson was nosing after: more sensational and exclusive matter for the *Record*. McNab turned to him.

'Only two facts remain which I can regard as certainties,' he said. 'The first is that the blind man is innocent.'

With my eyes still on Matheson I saw, and understood, his disappointment. Indeed, as a journalist I sympathised with him there.

THE EALING MURDER
HUNT FOR A BLIND MAN

What a provocative bill that would have made! And Matheson was good at bills. When he had anything exclusive to put on them he did them himself.

'Hm,' he almost grunted, 'let's hear why you so conclude.'

'A review of the known facts forces me to it. First there's the medical evidence. The job was so neat – one stroke under the fourth costal rib. By a miracle a blind man might have been so neat. And miracles sometimes happen. But remember the smashed and scattered furniture! That took my eye the moment I entered the room. Had the dead man made all the fight implied by that confusion? I asked myself. If so his body would have borne the marks of it, and he would not have been knifed so neatly by anyone. Now, with a blind man present, I can account for what I saw. Most of that confusion at all events could result from a blind person's frantic blundering about in an unfamiliar room among furniture he could not see. Further, those marks on the wall tell the same tale – a frantic and useless effort to get away. But they got him down at last. Yes, and took him away with them by force.'

As McNab stopped speaking and began to pace the room with rising excitement, I believe our presence was forgotten. His kindled imagination was seeing the successive events that followed the murder. But the practical Matheson drew him back to earth.

'By force,' he said after moment, 'where is the evidence for that?'

McNab wheeled round impatiently.

'Lord, man, are you still forgetting that stick! Have you considered what a walking stick is to a blind man? It is what your eyes are to you. No, take that as settled, he did not go willingly without his stick. He was carried off by someone – oh, yes – but someone who may very well have been unaware he was blind, and who supposed the blind man would be certain to know him at sight.'

'You mean he was an acquaintance?'

'I do not. For in that case he would have known he was blind.'

Matheson sat up.

'So you mean the murderer was a person of distinction – a public man?'

McNab, I remember, did not reply. He stood gazing dumbly into vacancy with his hands thrust deep in his pockets.

'There are things in the case I cannot fathom, though. Why didn't they finish off the blind man when he was on the floor against the wall? He was certainly not an accomplice. One cannot visualise anyone bringing a blind man as an assistant in murder. Therefore he was there by accident. He stumbled in at the garden window – just as Chance himself did later on – probably while the man was being murdered. There must have been a cry, you know. Something that told him something untoward was happening; and he went forward to help, fell, and got the man's life blood on his hands. What happened when he felt the fluid was *warm*? But, Lord, how he must have startled *them*! Ay, but what have they done with him? Where is he *now*? That is the new mystery.'

He withdrew his hands, and turning to us smote one fist on an extended open palm with great violence.

'Matheson, the Acton Green affair was nothing to this.'

'Of course, in that affair it was only the social position of the guilty man that attracted interest.'

McNab nodded.

'And in this case we have that interest too, and others as well.'

Matheson pricked up his ears. But I knew it was not because someone had come knocking at the door. Several times in the last half-hour people had knocked at that same door, and he had paid no heed. He said:

'I don't exactly see how the – er – social status of the guilty man is evident in the present case.'

McNab, pausing as he walked about the room, opened his eyes in surprise.

'No? Why, that to me is so palpable that I took it for granted. You don't see it? Well, consider this. You know Ponsonby Paget and his paper. The most popular man in England they called him. He was – with the masses. But he had his enemies. Big ones! In his paper he shot only at the biggest game – eh? The smaller fry were not worth his powder and shot. Well, we needn't look in the East End, or even in Suburbia, for the man who killed him. And he was sure the man who stumbled into that room would recognise him. Och, I've no doubt you've published his portrait in your own paper often enough.'

Matheson's face lighted up.

'Go ahead, then. We'll be ready to insert his portrait again – when the time comes. The *Daily Record* is behind you,' he said rising. 'In the interests of Justice that man must be unmasked.'

*

And McNab at once began to set his machinery in motion. In the corridor outside, where I waited for him after Matheson had dismissed me, he gripped my arm.

'You are to work with me,' he said. 'I stipulated for that. But nobody is to know,' he added. 'You're to act as go-between, you understand, between me and the *Record*.'

This was better than I had hoped.

'Right,' I cried joyfully, shaking his hand.

'Here's your first duty, then. Find out if any report has recently come in of a blind man missing from his home. Bring me round all particulars.'

'That won't take five minutes. If you wait –'

'No! That is the point. Not a soul must guess for whom the information is wanted. And that's not all. Look out too for any item that may come in reporting the finding of the body of some unknown man. And, if these news items haven't already appeared, don't forget I want them before publication.'

The second request startled me. McNab had stirred the imagination by his conjectures on the blind man's share in the tragedy. It had moved me to think of that man stumbling innocently by the same entrance as myself into that room and getting caught in the whirlpool of crime.

'You don't think –' I began.

But he cut me short.

'What I think will keep,' he said. 'You go and get me what I want to know.'

It took me longer than five minutes to get the information he desired in the way he ordered. For I could see that if I had to go on repeating the request for possible news of a missing blind man, or the discovery of a body, questions would be asked which would be awkward to explain away.

The thing might even become a joke against me, and be bandied about among the staff. So I had to think out a plan, and set it in motion tactfully. But I did elicit the information that no such reports had come in since the date I gave. About five o'clock I went round to the Adelphi to tell McNab. He seemed to be working out notes on the case, for his table was littered with foolscap, and I observed a piled-up quantity of the *Eye Opener* on his left hand. He looked up eagerly.

'Nothing come in yet,' I said. 'Nobody missing and no body found.'

'Sit down.'

'McNab, you don't really think they'll do away with this blind man now?'

A snort of indignation came.

'There's nobody, it seems, would miss him much. Queer that nobody's asking for him. Does that tell you anything?'

'Possibly he got back to his home.'

'And said nothing?'

'They'd have done him in before now, wouldn't they? Why haven't they done it already?'

He turned on me.

'You offer a fine field for unprofitable speculation there. Why does a parrot always eat from its left hand? The point is that they have not, and as long as he remains alive he is likely to prove very useful to us. For after all, Chance, there are not so many blind men in England, and of homeless ones still less, thank God.'

'You speculated long enough before Matheson.'

He laid down his pencil.

'Now don't get huffy. I said unprofitable speculation. I'm ready enough to speculate where I have data on which to work. On the question as to why he wasn't finished off along with the old gentleman I have none.'

He glanced at me quizzically.

'That doesn't content you?' he asked, feigning indignation.

'Well,' I said, 'it isn't true. You must have formed *some* theory as to why the man's life was spared that night.'

'Half a dozen! Here's the best of them, and if you can choose between them it's more than I can do,' he cried in a sudden burst of impatient disgust. 'First, it's possible they turned squeamish, especially if there was a woman in it. She would be for cajoling him into silence. A woman's weapon is not violence but guile. Second, they may have discovered he was blind after they got him down on the floor near the door, and so knew he could not be sure as to what exactly had happened in that room, or even, if he had lost his way and strayed in, in whose house he was. Again, they could have no grudge against him, such as had moved them to murder in the case of Ponsonby Paget. Thirdly, the condition of the room points to the fact that at first the blind stranger was attacked. That scrap of human hair, whoever it belongs to, tells the same tale. Yet they evidently changed their minds about him. Why? Chance, can you visualise that scene! Suppose you had strung yourself up through black hate to the point of murder, and unexpectedly found yourself, in the midst of your deed, confronted by a stranger. The first instinct, with your weapon still in your hand and your blood up, would be to attack him. But think! When you had him on the floor, and saw those sightless eyes turned on you, straining to see, fearful of your blow, yet not knowing where, or when, it was to fall. What then? Could you do it?'

'No; it must have been that.'

'Ay, maybe. We cannot tell. But I can tell you this, Chance' – the impatience had dropped from his voice and he spoke with the utmost solemnity – 'little as he may dream of it now, if they once discover how dangerous he is to them his fate is sealed. Blindness will only have bought him a respite.'

*

It was only on that first occasion that McNab talked so freely with me on the case. In the course of the next few days he turned much less expansive, and it seemed the affair so gripped him that he must go like a hound with his nose on the scent, looking neither to right nor left. On the few occasions on which he did speak at all, I had the fancy that he was merely using me as a whetstone to stimulate thought, or focus certain ideas floating in his fertile brain. For, careful as he had been to warn me against talking to others about the case, I must here say that in his irritating, Scotch fashion he made doubly sure of my prudence by telling me no more than he could help. And even then he broached the matter in the most roundabout way. One day he said:

'I suppose your paper has representatives in different parts of the country?'

'We have our own correspondents in most places, if that's what you mean.'

He nodded assent.

'Well, ye see, the other day a car knocked down a plumber in Maida Vale, and I'm particularly, anxious to trace it.' He looked up at my exclamation. 'What is it now?'

'Have you abandoned the Ealing case then?'

'Oh, no; but this affair in Maida Vale – I'm sure it was Maida Vale – has upset the equanimity of my mind, you see. It must be settled first, and I've thought your correspondents might help me.'

'What can they do?' I asked in disgust at what seemed a desertion of the momentous Ealing tragedy for a petty accident in Maida Vale.

'Report to you the presence of the car in their locality. The car, you see, has certain well defined characteristics.'

'Oh, well, if you give me a description I'll see that it goes into tomorrow's issue.'

'But that's exactly what I don't want it to do, the car's chief characteristics being removable. My notion was that the description could be sent out privately, and so we could cover a large area. It's a case in which I'm particularly keen to beat Snargrove,' he added.

'Is Snargrove in this too?' I asked, surprised.

'He is that. But whether he found traces of the car when we both examined the drive at Ealing I cannnot say.'

'Ealing? You said Maida Vale just now.'

'Did I? Well, it was one or the other. But you'd better be careful to call it Maida Vale to your correspondents.'

Then I comprehended.

'Damn you, McNab,' I cried, irritated, 'why do you trifle with me like this?'

'Oh,' he said coolly, 'you're very young, and I put it like that just to impress you with the need for caution.'

Caution! But I sat down again, relieved to find he had not abandoned the big case.

'You recall that day at Ealing,' he resumed, 'When we came on Snargrove examining the drive and I joined him while you looked on, pitying us both?'

'The road had been trampled by scores that morning,' I said defensively.

'True. It was all trodden by sightseers – women mostly – too curious to mind the mud. Still, I found something there. Nothing to do with footprints, you know.'

'You found a clue?' I cried, starting up. 'Tell me!'

He said nothing at first. I could see it was something big, from the way he looked at me. And he had kept it to himself all the time. I never knew a man like McNab for keeping a thing till it was ripe.

'What sort of clue was it?' I demanded.

'An amazing one. The wheel marks took my eye first. I was idly wondering why there were so few. Then I remembered that no vehicles had come to the house that morning, which was Tuesday, since the gate was closed by the police, and that since there had probably been none on the Sunday, such wheel-marks as showed very likely belonged to the Monday's traffic. It was quite easy to count three marks – a studded Dunlop, the criss-cross of a Michelin, a third with grooved tyres much worn on the tread, but with the pattern quite discernible at the two sides of the deep impression made in the soft road. Besides these three there was a plain unpatterned track, too narrow in the tread to be made by a tyre, which zigzagged slightly as if from the stride of an eager horse. 'Four tradesmen, three of them prosperous,' I said to myself, 'called at the house on Monday.' Merely as a matter of routine I went to verify this at the house. Brown could not tell me much, and took me to the kitchen, where the domestics put their heads together. There was disagreement at first, and a rather hot dispute began between a housemaid and the cook as to whether the greengrocer's man had, or had not, called. But when I got it into their heads that I was not interested in tradesmen who called on foot, or on bicycles, there was general agreement that three motor vehicles only – the laundry, the general stores, and the baker – had been to the house. As I made a note of the names and addresses I said, 'And whose was the horse-drawn van?' Then came the surprise. There was no disagreement about the horse van: no such vehicle had been to the house. I tried to dispute this, but found that on that point at least they were all quite positive.

'It is queer how a trifle will vex a man. I took Brown out, almost by the scruff of the neck, to let him see those narrow wheel tracks which, being far more visible than any of the others, spoke of a vehicle heavily loaded. Then just as I lifted my finger to point them out to him I saw the strange thing.'

McNab paused, and ceased twiddling his thumbs.

'A car is heavier than a man, and therefore makes deeper marks on a moist road. But a horse is also heavier than a man, and hoofs cut deep in pulling a weight. Well, in between those narrow ruts there were *no hoof marks*. Not one in the whole length of the drive, Chance. Not one. To tell you the truth their absence struck me dumb, for this was no handcart, the wheel marks were too far apart for that to be conceivable. What I said to the butler I don't know, but when he had gone I made a close inspection of those same tracks.'

McNab opened a drawer, extracted a paper and handed it over to me.

'That is what I found.'

On the paper there appeared two upright lines two inches apart, and close to the line on the right there was a circle about the size of a shilling.

'That,' said McNab, 'is the brass cap of a number .8 cartridge which this tyre had picked up, and which became embedded in the solid rubber. Very firmly embedded it was, for when dug out it brought away a clean-cut disc of rubber. In the soft earth of the drive that hole left a protuberance which for neatness might have been stamped out with a baker's biscuit mould. You see that tyre was solid rubber, but it was on no horse van, for there were no hoof marks. Well, there is only one type of car that answers to these facts, and on this particular one that hole appears on the outside edge of the offside back wheel of a Trojan car. That is why I want a copy of this drawing to be sent out to all your local correspondents.'

'But Matheson will want to put this in the paper, probably with a drawing of the wheel showing its exact position,' I said. 'It's irresistible, a thing like this. I'd put it in myself if I were in his place, especially in so sensational a case.'

McNab lifted his eyebrows.

'Sensational – a plumber knocked down in Maida Vale!'

Then I saw the reason for his earlier pretence. Matheson assuredly would not trouble about an accident in Maida Vale which had not even got into the press. I was so thinking when McNab, laying his hand on my arm, spoke in a quiet, confidential tone.

'It was this car that stood somewhere behind the house, that night, when you stumbled about the garden or were maybe already in that room. You understand, Chance? This car which no one saw, which none of the servants knew of, is the car that carried off the blind man.' His grip tightened. 'If they keep him we have them,' he whispered with eyes aglow.

*

And it was only when I caught myself in the midst of this eager hope of McNab's that I realised how intense was the interest I felt in that blind man's fate. His would be a story worth telling once we found him. But it wasn't only as a journalist I wanted him. The human element was in it too. The man himself as McNab had pictured him, unconscious of the sudden death that hovered over him, aroused one's sympathy.

Well, news came at last. News that I had indeed planned and schemed to receive, but had ceased to look for by this time. For in my concern with posting up the local correspondents I had almost forgotten that news might come in independently. This news item was ticked off by the tape machine about 6 p.m. and was laid on my desk with other items from the same news agency. As soon as I had read it through I put on my hat and took it round to the Adelphi. How did I know I should find McNab at home that night? I cannot tell. We always seem to be at home when bad news comes knocking at the door.

McNab was in. He looked up quickly at my entrance, divining I brought news, and supposing, no doubt, that something about the car had come in from one of our correspondents.

'We are too late, McNab.'

'Too late?' he repeated, a sudden shadow coming on his face. 'Read this.'

I laid the flimsy bit of paper before him on the desk. As his eyes took in the first words I saw him stiffen suddenly, pass a hand over his eyes with a quick gesture, and then go on reading. Over his shoulder I followed the words again:

Man Found Dead. Rye, Sussex. At a lonely spot near Stone, Isle of Oxney, the dead body of a man was today discovered among some bushes close to a hayrick by a farm labourer proceeding to work. The body is that of a man in the early thirties, clean-shaven, with dark hair and refined, regular features, and it is regarded as curious that though well dressed nothing was found on him which could establish identity. The cause of death was not apparent, and is so far unknown.

McNab sat looking fixedly at the slip of paper long after he must have finished reading it. Then a sigh came.

'So they've done it after all,' he said.

'I had ceased looking out for this.'

'It was always a probability. Pass me that timetable.'

The pages whirled under his deft fingers.

'Charing Cross to Ashford... 9.15 Appledore... Yes, we can just do it, Chance.'

'You are going to Stone?'

'You too. I'll need you. Phone Matheson now.'

I was more than ready for the expedition. Then as I stepped to the phone a thought pulled me up.

'McNab, how can you identify this man? I mean, how can one tell a man has been blind after he is dead?'

McNab, already stuffing some things into a handbag, looked up.

'From the track of a car, if we find any in those lanes,' he said. 'If a small disc shows in its tread this dead man was blind. Yes, and by God, the man that did this thing shall die too, because he was strong and had no pity.'

BOOK THREE

Statement by Dr. Dunn

XIII

This is a voluntary statement. It includes all the facts within my knowledge regarding the Ealing murder, and covers the time from the night of Monday, January 15th, when Alexander David Kinloch came to my house in Albany Road, Ealing, till the 26th day of April following, when I saw him for the last time.

Kinloch was brought to my house by a constable about 8.30 on the date given. The officer said he had found him loitering, and that he claimed to know me. He pushed him forward for inspection. The darkness of the night was intensified by a thick fog, and I requested the constable to put his lantern close to the man's face. The moment this was done I recognised Kinloch. He looked in a deplorable condition, his clothing torn and spattered with mud, and himself nervous and shaken like a man labouring under strong but suppressed excitement. But as soon as the light was thrown on his face it was demonstrated to me that something had happened to him since we had last met. He was different. The next moment I saw what had happened. The glare from the officer's electric torch went full into his face, and yet he stared back into it with unwavering eyes. When the officer thrust a walking stick into his hand I didn't need to be told what had happened: the man he had brought to me was blind.

Kinloch had been an old friend of mine, though I had heard nothing of him for some years. He had come to me that night for help. That he came unwillingly I deduced instantly from the fact that he had not sought me out earlier, but had put it off till he had fallen to the state in which he stood before me, in the last extremity of want.

He was with me about four hours. But he left my house without receiving any help from me. We disagreed on a matter unconnected with this case. We had often disagreed before. Indeed, it might be said that to disagree was part of our friendship. But no previous disagreement had ever made any rupture in our relations to each other.

When he had gone, however, I sat down filled first with perplexity and then with remorse. For a long time I sat bewildered by the suddenness of the rupture. Had he become more touchy? I asked myself. Had I failed to make allowances for the hammerings of misfortune which he had endured? Or was the change in myself? Which, I asked myself, has the worse effect on a man's character – prosperity or adversity? Then the remorse came when I saw I had taken a too high-handed line with a man who had come to me unwillingly and ashamed. I want to make this clear. Many men I have met who eye and appraise a new acquaintance from the standpoint of their own interest and advantage. Kinloch was not of that sort. He never tried to make *useful* friends. And then, just when I was thinking with increased shame that he certainly had not made one in me, I heard the telephone bell ring up in my bedroom. It was a welcome interruption; a night call on the most trivial case would be better than being left to my present thoughts. I remember glancing at the clock in the hall as I passed through to mount the stairs: it showed twelve minutes to two.

But it was not the plaintive voice of some long-suffering attendant on a querulous patient that awaited me on the other end of the wire. The voice of the station sergeant came, gruff and hasty:

'Tookworth Avenue, number 15, case of stabbing. Quick as you can go, sir.'

'Ambulance?'

'No.'

Knowing from this what instruments and dressings to take, I packed a bag and ran. At the entrance gate of the house which I recognised as that of Ponsonby Paget as soon as I sighted it, I met Inspector Green and two constables approaching as quickly as myself from the opposite direction.

'Not Ponsonby Paget?' I said.

The inspector nodded breathlessly. We entered together.

In the long oblong room into which we were shown by a white-faced maid we found a constable and two men. Ponsonby Paget lay on the floor near his writing table. But as soon as I got down to examine his wound I knew he was beyond my help. The position of the wound was clearly revealed by the puncture showing on his pleated shirt, and the stroke from the knife was one that must have gone through the arch of the aorta. No need to tell the inspector the man was dead. Green whispered to me to have a look at the two occupants of the room, who appeared to have been detained there by the constable in charge when we entered. One was an elderly man, who turned out to be the butler; and the other, a young, fair-haired fellow, seemed rather restless and excited. But a cursory look was enough to show me that neither could have administered that wound within the previous half-hour and got rid of the traces from their persons. It was in fact a mere formality to look at them. So Green took it, for he had already taken his keen eyes elsewhere.

Then the shock came. Green, who had been poking delicately about among the wreckage of furniture, pulled out a walking stick from beneath an overturned table. After looking at it narrowly he brought it across to me, and held it out, putting some questions to me. But the moment I had it in my hands I recognised the stick. It was Kinloch's stick. It was the stick the policeman had handed back to him on my doorstep a few hours earlier. And of course I remembered it the better because Kinloch had not put his walking stick into the hall-stand when I led him in. A blind man and his stick are inseparable, and I had seen him with it lying across his knees all the time he had been in my study. So I inferred that Kinloch had gone to call on Ponsonby Paget after I had failed him.

What I said and did while the stick was in my hands with Green and the journalist looking on, I do not know; but I got away somehow. And the next I remember is finding myself sitting in my study in the dark. My whole thought kept revolving round one fact and its consequence: I had practically turned Sandy Kinloch out of my house; he had found his way into another, and now a man lay dead in that house. And I who had, as it were, pushed him into that room had been called into it to witness the consequences of my act. That was the awful thought that obsessed me. Kinloch had been a man of kindly nature, with something of more than average capacity for human sympathy, I argued. Yet hardship hardens, and I had seen traces of bitterness in him that night. Not that I thought his was the hand that had given that expert thrust to the heart. No; such a blow could only by a miracle come from a blind man's hand. Still he had been involved in the affair; there was the stick to prove as much. However innocently he might have got into that room he was in danger, and – this was the thought that kept recurring – I had pushed him into it as really as if my hand had gone to his back.

The inquest on Ponsonby Paget still further disturbed my peace of mind. It is true, that, when after giving my own medical evidence I stayed on to hear the verdict, nothing came out against Kinloch. What did come out from the butler's evidence was that the dead man appeared to be constantly in touch with a considerable number of very dubious people. And there might have been comfort for me in that but for one fact. All along I had cherished the hope that Kinloch's stick might have got by accident into that room. He might have lost it, or had it taken from him, I argued. The criminal might have brought it into the room, or even the dead man himself, for it was certainly proved by the police that he had been, unknown to the butler, out of the house after he had dined that night. But this possibility was dispelled by what I saw in the ante-room to the court. For among the exhibits, and preserved between two botanical glasses, there was shown something found in the fatal room – a wisp of black hair which I was able to certify had been violently torn from someone's head. Still, nothing came out then to connect Kinloch directly with the murder.

Of course I was aware that the police do not disclose all they know at an inquest. So when I met Inspector Green a few days afterwards I made a cautious reference to the case, trying to get him to talk. He did not prove to be communicative. The chief, he explained, had called in Scotland Yard, and he himself was no longer working on it. I knew that even so he would know a good deal of what was going on; but I dared not risk appearing too curious about this particular case. Green's reticence I put down to his irritation or disappointment at being elbowed out of a big case by the Yard. Yet, though polite enough, he was certainly rather short with me.

Thus denied any inside knowledge of what was going on, I had to rely on the newspapers. They certainly were full enough of the case. I took them all and read everything. It was a case that excited more than the masses. People hardly talked of anything else. At every turn, in train, bus, street or restaurant the wildest rumours circulated, the most far-fetched theories as to the cause of the murder, and its perpetrators, were advanced. My own patients, I found, wanted to discuss the Ponsonby Paget murder with me – even the old maiden ladies whom I had never before known to show the least interest in anything in heaven or earth beyond the symptoms of their own, mostly imaginary, diseases. My nerves suffered badly.

'Doctor,' one of them sighed, 'we may all be murdered in our beds.'

'Well,' I said, exasperated, 'it's quite a good place to get murdered in.'

That was a patient I lost.

Then in the outside world beyond Ealing interest in the case began to slacken. This could be detected from the newspapers. Progressively the space allotted to the Ealing murder grew less. Presently one of my papers one day had no reference to it. A little later and the case had dropped out of several – it seemed for good. After that I told my newsagent to stop my extra supply. Soon I found myself – no, not ceasing to think of the Ealing tragedy, but able to think of other things as well.

One morning, on leaving the hospital, I ran into Inspector Green. He had been in about some road accident, he told me.

'Nothing doing on the Ponsonby Paget affair?' I said, so much at ease now that I could refer in an off-hand way to the case.

'No, not much to tell,' he said. 'Of course you know the Yard took it over.'

When I saw he was now willing to talk of the affair, I inferred that he had got over his sense of injustice at being pushed aside when the Yard was called in.

'It has dropped out of the newspapers,' I remarked.

'Except the *Record*.'

'And you fellows have dropped it too, without exception,' I said banteringly.

He looked back at me humorously.

'I wouldn't say that, doctor. The police never give up a case, you know.' He sighed softly. 'Queer case, wasn't it? It wasn't as if we had nothing to go on; the room was scattered with traces – even to first-class fingerprints. Hardly ever seen a case with so many good exhibits – seven, no less.'

'Eight,' I corrected him promptly.

Green shook his head.

'Wrong, doctor. I remember the number well, for I remember saying to myself there was one for every day in the week.'

'Eight,' I persisted.

'Oh, but no. Listen, here they are: overcoat with fur collar, pair of dress shoes, broken whisky glass, the decanter, the paper of fingerprints, the envelope with the wisp of black hair, and the wedge-shaped splinter of a mirror. Seven, I think.'

'Yes, seven,' I admitted, but –'

'But what, doctor?' Green turned in surprise.

I felt vaguely uneasy. I'd rather he had forgotten any other item than that walking stick.

'You've forgotten the stick,' I blurted out.

Green, after a moment of discomfiture, in which he stared at me in a comically intent way, laughed most heartily.

'Fancy me forgetting the stick – me, who found it,' he said.

And I laughed too. It was a relief that the stick could be forgotten. Evidently Green, at least, attached little importance to it.

'But what was I saying?' he resumed thoughtfully. 'Oh, yes, I was saying I'd never known a case with so many apparently promising clues; and yet' – with a shrug he threw out his hands in a gesture eloquent of helplessness – 'there were so many people to whom these same clues pointed. You heard the butler's evidence, didn't you? About Ponsonby Paget's numerous nightly visitors, I mean. Well, with all sorts coming in secret to see him Snargrove's job needs time.'

'Snargrove still on the case, then?'

'Why, yes, of course he is. And I don't envy him. Trying to trace a score of those visitors who for reasons quite unconnected with the murder don't want to be found.'

We had reached my house by this time; but the inspector had opened up a new vista for thought, so I paused with my hand on the gate.

'Mostly women, Brown said his visitors were.'

'Yes, doctor, women – from the lady's maid to the lady herself. But they all came on the same errand – to sell him society scandal for his paper.'

'I see. Snargrove is after them all, then?'

'Got to. And they're not coming to meet him halfway, as you might say,' Green nodded, sweeping his hand in a parting salute.

*

It was the feeling of security I had received from my talk with Inspector Green that led me to reply to Selwyn & Smith's advertisement. But for now knowing that the authorities were busy tracing those women I should have been too cautious, without knowing much more about Selwyn & Smith than I did when I went to see them. This is the notice I found in a chance newspaper, picked up while waiting in a house:

ALEXANDER DAVID KINLOCH will hear something to his advantage by communicating with Messrs Selwyn & Smith, Devon Chambers, Chancery Lane.

One peculiarity of the thing caught my attention. For it was mighty queer, I thought, that they should, as the wording implied, be unaware that he was blind, and yet know his full name. Was it a bait set to catch him? For several days I did nothing – nothing except read the successive reappearances of that advertisement each morning. I did not know what I could safely do. On the sixth day the notice had disappeared. That troubled me. Had something happened? Two more days and, finding ignorance unbearable, I went up to see Selwyn & Smith, determined to find out if anything had happened, but resolved to be very cautious.

'You are advertising for one Alexander David Kinloch,' I said, on being shown into the manager's private room.

Mr. Spencer, a little round-faced man, looked up, eyeing me narrowly, over the top of his eyeglasses at the end of his nose.

'Are you Mr. Kinloch?'

'What if I am?' I replied defensively.

Mr. Spencer's eyebrows lifted.

'We shall certainly require proof of your identity,' he said dryly.

'For what purpose?'

He got nettled by my wariness.

'Come, come, sir,' he said, 'let us have no more of this fencing. Your question is not reasonable. For all I know you may have wandered in off the street, after seeing our advertisement, to impersonate Mr. Kinloch.'

Well, when I heard that I knew at least that it would be some advantage to be Kinloch. But when he saw me hesitate his hand went to the bell, and it was clear he no longer took me for Kinloch. Hastily I placed my card on the desk and said:

'Will you give me your word that it really is for something to his advantage you want him? You see,' I added lamely, 'I want to find him myself.' He had been scanning my card while I was speaking, and now stared hard at me.

'And will you give me your word to the same effect, doctor?'

'That I will. Indeed, sir, if I could be certain you meant him equally well, I'd leave you happier than I've been for many a day.'

The fervour with which his question had made me speak seemed to surprise him. His manner changed.

'I am a busy man,' he said, 'and since it is clear we both mean well by the young gentleman, I do not understand why you beat about the bush. You say you want to find him. So do we. What do you know about him? We had almost concluded he must be dead.'

'No, he is not dead, at least he was alive on the 15th of January when he called at my house in Ealing.'

'Dear me, if only I had known! Strange he didn't see our advertisement.'

'It would be stranger if he did. Kinloch is blind, Mr Spencer.'

'Blind – oh, how sad! Dear me, not totally and permanently, I trust?'

'Totally, but not, I hope, permanently. That is one reason why I am so anxious to find him. He suffers from *corneitis*, a form of blindness once regarded as incurable, but not so since the war.'

Mr. Spencer was deeply interested, and while he sat polishing his eyeglasses I explained that Kinloch had not come to me about his sight but because I was an old friend, that I was not an oculist, and had inquired into the new treatment for *corneitis* only since learning of my friend's affliction. I wound up by saying that I was ready myself to bear all the expense of taking him to Edinburgh for treatment by the famous surgeon whose war experiences had taught him how to perform this new miracle of ophthalmic surgery.

'Well,' he said, 'that's very good of you, very good. Still as to expenses, Mr. Kinloch ought to be able to meet them himself.'

I almost laughed.

'It's very evident you know little about Kinloch,' I said. 'He's quite destitute. He hasn't a penny, and so even if he had his sight I doubt if he'd have seen your advertisement. You see,' I felt bound to add, 'he came to my house that night in rags almost, a broken man, and – well, we quarrelled. It was all my doing. I don't want you to take me for what I am not; and it is the base truth that I let him go away unhelped. That is why I want to do something for him now – something beyond price, beyond all his hopes.'

Mr. Spencer bent forward and touched my knee. 'Dr Dunn,' he said, 'I understand your feelings, your mental distress, and I am sure if you can do this for him it will more than make amends, without meeting the expenses, which he does not now need you to do.'

'Not need me –' I said.

'Did Mr. Kinloch ever mention the purchase of any shares to you?'

'Yes, some worthless shares which another of his friends swindled him into buying,' I said bitterly.

The little man smiled.

'I'd like to be swindled in the same way,' he said. And he went on to tell me the story; a complicated story it was, but the gist of it seemed to be that Kinloch, a babe in financial affairs, had been induced by someone to put his every penny into the worthless shares of some tea company. Then the unexpected had happened. Some financial genius had evolved a scheme to get the output of tea restricted, with the result that an artificial scarcity was created and prices had soared. But Kinloch, who had left his holding in the hands of Selwyn & Smith when he discovered he had been swindled, knew nothing of the sudden rise in their value.

'And you mean he is rich now?' I asked.

'Rich is a relative term,' he replied, 'but at least I'll venture to assert he is comfortably off.'

Well, I left that office keener than ever to find Sandy Kinloch. And I fancy what Mr. Spencer had heard about him from me made him keener too. But there were difficulties in the way of which Mr. Spencer knew nothing. It would have been better if I had told him something of the Ealing murder. But I had kept silence on that subject; it was not my secret, for one thing; and, for another, I was too wary to blurt out such a confidence to any man at a first meeting. Yet, as things turned out, it would have been wiser to have risked a little in the way of frankness with Spencer. For in his new keenness he began advertising again for Kinloch, recasting the words in consequence of the facts I had supplied, and now inserting the thing in the papers read by the masses. The only paper of that type I had kept on taking in was the *Record*. It I still saw because it never ceased hammering away at the Ealing murder. And the moment I read Mr. Spencer's latest advertisement I felt we were in for trouble. It ran thus:

ALEXANDER DAVID KINLOCH, last seen at Ealing on the night of Monday, 15 January. Will any person in a position to supply information as to his present whereabouts kindly commu-

nicate with Messrs Selwyn & Smith, Devon Chambers, Chancery Lane. Liberal reward.

Then the mistake I had made became clear. I should either have taken Spencer into my confidence or at least have supervised the terms in which the new advertisement was to be recast. All the way up to town I kept hoping against hope. But my first words with Spencer seemed to make disaster certain.

'No replies yet?' I asked, inwardly praying for his assent.

'But yes – three,' he said almost cheerfully.

'Three!'

I was aghast. It was almost as if the earth had begun to tremble under my feet.

'Oh, don't be too hopeful. None of them were very promising, I fear.' Mr. Spencer polished his glasses meditatively. 'You see,' he continued, 'all three came to make inquiries about our young friend.'

'You didn't tell them anything?' I interjected.

'Dear me, no! But they were rather troublesome. I had to point out to them that they had misread our notice: we desired to *receive*, not to *give* information.'

'Do you know who they were?'

'No, and I didn't trouble to inquire. An offer of a reward brings all sorts buzzing in, as we know from experience. Still,' he continued, 'these three didn't exactly conform to type, so to speak. That's why I saw them, and wasted my time.' He paused. 'You don't know if Mr Kinloch had a judgement summons out against him?'

'No. Why?'

'Well, one of them, a burly, fresh-complexioned and muscular fellow with a heavy moustache, looked as if he might be connected with the law.'

'Connected with the law?' I said in sudden apprehension.

'Oh, well, I don't necessarily mean the criminal side of the law. Debt, you know. And this fellow did look as if he might be a bailiff's man.'

Swift as light there had come back to me the memory of a man who tallied with the description Mr. Spencer had so off-handedly given – the Scotland Yard man at the inquest, Inspector Snargrove. But who could the others be?

'And the two others?' I said.

Mr. Spencer stroked his chin reflectively.

'Well, one was a tallish, rather hawk-eyed fellow with a very close clipped black moustache, who held himself – well, rather like a soldier out of uniform. Thought he might be an old comrade of Kinloch's. And the third man – he hasn't been gone more than half an hour – was wiry too, but clean-shaven. Unlike the others he did not look as if a uniform would fit him. Looked rather like a medical man; and he was certainly a fellow-countryman of yours.'

The last two men I could not 'place' at all. And I think it was the uneasiness that inability roused in me that made me there and then resolve to take Mr. Spencer into my confidence. So, after a hurried moment or two of thought, I said:

'Since they didn't tell you why they want Kinloch I'd better tell you –'

Mr. Spencer with a hasty ejaculation shot out his hand, cutting me short.

'They didn't need to,' he said. 'I guessed it – from what you told me of Mr. Kinloch's financial circumstances – they were all after money; the bailiff's man, the old comrade of the war, he was either after a loan from Kinloch or seeking repayment of one; and the Scotch doctor – nosing after an unpaid bill, eh?'

He laughed. But I shook my head.

'Much more serious. Kinloch is innocent, but –'

'Oh,' he cut in again, 'of all the witless –' He broke off to search for his eyeglasses which had fallen to the floor.

Utterly taken aback, I stared in silence. After fumbling about a little he sat up rather red from stooping, and went on as if he had not heard me. 'Of course the bailiff's man said he would find the means to open my lips at the proper time. But it was easy for me to show him that if I had the least notion where Mr. Kinloch was I would hardly be offering a reward for the information.'

So that was it! At last I understood. Spencer did not want to know lest he should have to tell. My respect for him went up. He was as honest as I had been stupid.

'They will come back, though – these men,' I said.

'Oh, no doubt,' he replied, cheerful again, 'but not till we discontinue that advertisement.' Then, as if to make sure I understood, he added knowingly, 'I have paid in advance for quite a series of insertions. Foolish, perhaps, for the notice will possibly be appearing for some time after we have found Kinloch.'

*

But as the days slipped past and nothing was heard of him I began to think we had heard the last of Kinloch. The frequent visits I paid to the office in Chancery Lane were always blank. Spencer, however, was invariably confident. When pressed for his reasons all he said was:

'Doctor, money never goes long a-begging. Never has this firm advertised like that in vain. Sooner or later it draws a response.'

One day later he surprised me by a question:

'Doctor, do you ever look behind?'

Not comprehending, I merely re-echoed his query, and he beckoned me to the window.

'Look there – that man in the grey overcoat and black bowler on the opposite pavement, sauntering.' And as I peeped out he put the question: 'Ever seen him before?'

I could not recall the burly figure:

'Ah – there – you see!' Spencer cried.

For the man opposite had just taken a swift glance up at our window, and catching sight of us moved on again, affecting interest in the traffic.

'He blundered that time,' Spencer murmured.

'Who is he?' I asked, not liking this at all.

'Oh, I thought you'd better have a hint you are being shadowed, doctor. He's been seen out there waiting for you on your last three calls. If you've been up to anything – well look out.'

After that I ceased my calls at the office, and we arranged that Spencer would telephone or wire if he wanted me.

For, if I was being shadowed on Kinloch's account, it would be well to let it be supposed from ceasing my visits to Selwyn and Smith's that we now had no hope of any reply to the advertisement.

And, indeed, hope on my part had sunk into despair by this time. Yet in the end Spencer's confidence was proved right. One morning my telephone rang, and as soon as I picked up the receiver Spencer's voice sounded in my ear:

'That you, doctor?'

There was elation in his voice. I knew something had turned up.

'Yes, what is it?'

'News.'

'Not –'

In my surprise I was almost betrayed into an indiscretion.

'Hush. Come and see me. It may be a hoax.'

When I reached the office he laid this scrap of writing before me:

If Messrs Selwyn & Smith will send someone to Mr. Keiller, now staying at the Aberlundy Arms, Gart, Argyllshire, they can obtain full information about Alexander Kinloch.

'Well?' Spencer queried as soon as I had finished reading.

'This is no hoax,' I asserted.

'You think this Mr. Keiller knows something?'

'I think this Mr. Keiller may turn out to be Kinloch himself. Anyhow, this was written by a blind man. You can see how he used the parallel rulers to guide his pen. See, each line is straight in itself but rises towards the right because the ruler was not set straight across the paper.'

'Are you sure?' Spencer asked. 'I wouldn't care to go far on a wild goose chase.'

A closer scrutiny of the handwriting increased my conviction. I had never seen Sandy's handwriting since his blindness; and I was aware what a difference is made by blindness. But even now, although all individuality is taken out of writing so slowly and painfully achieved, I could detect in the formation of certain letters a resemblance to his former hands. These I indicated to Spencer.

'I'll tell you what,' I said finally, 'I'll send you an old letter of his and you can judge for yourself.'

'Right,' he said. 'In any case I can't go before tomorrow night.'

Neither could I, since I had to arrange for a man to look after my practice. But that I did arrange before returning to Ealing. And apparently Spencer convinced himself from the letter I sent when I got home, for next morning a wire reached me:

EUSTON MIDNIGHT TONIGHT

The rest of the day went in making preparations for getting away. Unusual preparations they were to me. If the truth must be admitted, I was keenly ashamed that Spencer had to prove to me I was being shadowed. And yet, though a medical man is a trained observer, his line of observation lies in another world than that of a man in Spencer's position. I loathed the notion of peeping round corners, turning round to watch who might be behind me, or pausing at shop windows to see who passed. And in fact, even after he warned me, I never did one of these things. But that day I took precautions. And with the result that never have I approached any railway station by a route more

circuitous than I reached Euston by that night. In fact I began
by undressing, turning out the light and getting into bed at
10.15. There I lay for three quarters of an hour, when I rang up
the hospital and so alarmed a night nurse with inquiries about
one of her patients that I got myself summoned to an urgent
case. At the hospital door I left the taxi standing for ten minutes
while I soothed the nurse, and then returned to tell the driver
to come back in an hour when the operation would be over.
After that I passed through the building, and getting away by a
back exit, took the 11.25 to Paddington. From there a taxi down
Marylebone Road landed me on the Euston departure platform
at three minutes to midnight. Spencer was there, standing near
the ticket collector at the gate. He had booked to Glasgow.

'For a novice, a first-rate performance,' he said approvingly.

He saw I did not comprehend.

'Look,' he said, 'if there is anyone on your heels they're not
close enough this time.'

The ticket collector had just shut the gates with a rolling clash.
And I had been the last man to enter.

*

Night was closing in as our train drew up at Gart. All the
afternoon, ever since we had left Callander, behind, and while
the engine patiently nosed its way round the flanks of mighty
mountains, and over hissing torrents, we had talked of Kinloch.
For Spencer was now as eager to hear about him as formerly
he had been unwilling. This surprised me at first. Then I came
to see the reason: in his profession, unlike my own, one must
know either nothing or everything about a case. And now that
he could no longer honourably say he knew nothing it was safer
to know all. And that is what I told him then, as the train labori-
ously climbed among the hills. But, nearing Gart, we had fallen
silent as I watched the lights twinkling brightly from cottage
windows down in the valley. My thoughts had turned on our
approaching meeting with Sandy Kinloch.

Stiff with our long journey, and cold in that sharp northern air, we took our directions from Gart's solitary porter, and made our way to the 'Aberlundy Arms'. A long, whitewashed, two-storey house, as soon as I discerned it in the dusk I knew the sort of hotel it was – busy perhaps in the fishing season and in summer, but likely to be quiet enough now. So it proved. The landlord, a big tub of a man, rosy of face, but obviously lazy and soft, gaped with surprise when we entered with our bags.

'Come to see Mr. Keiller,' Spencer greeted him briskly.

The big man, recovering, shut his mouth to open it again for speech.

'Ay, I was thinkin' somebody ought to turn up afore long. Losh, gentlemen, I'm right glad to see ye.'

'Anything wrong?' I asked sharply.

He turned to examine me before replying.

'Och, no. No catastrophe, if that's what you mean. Not a bit of it, sirs. He's just been' – dropping his voice to a confidential whisper – 'drinking a bit. A blind man, ye ken – it's no quite safe for a blind man to get verra drunk.'

My heart sank. I heard Spencer's voice as in a dream.

'Ah, and is – is this Mr. Keiller frequently the worse for drink?'

'Hoots, no, not him. Not once have I seen him fou. That's just what bothers me. He seems to have something upsettin' on his mind that robs my whisky of its natural effect.'

'Take us to him,' Spencer said brusquely.

'Say nothing at first of my presence,' I whispered to him as we were led down the passage.

The landlord threw open a door at the far end.

'Gentleman inquiring for you, Mr. Keiller,' he called out as if to a deaf person.

At first I thought the man had shown us into an empty room; but as I peered about in the gloom I saw a face lifted from the table at which a man sat with outstretched arms. It was Sandy Kinloch. I knew him as he turned his sightless eyes in our direction. Thus it was I saw him next, sitting alone in the dark like a hunted animal.

'Good evening, Mr. Keiller. We – we have come to see you on business,' Spencer said.

'Business?' Sandy echoed hoarsely.

'Yes; if the landlord will switch on the light for us.'

'I'll bring ye a lamp,' the big man said, reluctantly going out.

I slid into a chair close to the door as Spencer took a seat opposite Sandy.

'We are searching for a Mr. Kinloch really,' he said.

'So I thought! And, it's not difficult to guess your business with him,' Sandy interjected.

'You surprise me. I thought Mr. Kinloch alone would know about the tea shares.'

'Tea shares?' came blankly.

'Yes; about tea shares.'

There was a moment's silence, and then Sandy burst into wild laughter – laughter that was, however, quite mirthless and which stopped as abruptly as it started.

'Excuse me,' he said, 'but your pretence of being here about tea shares was more humorous than you could know. As it happens, Kinloch did put a lot of money into tea shares; and he let them lie with the agents, because they were worthless.'

'Worthless!' said Spencer. 'My dear sir, do you suppose I'd come all this way about worthless shares?'

'No, I don't,' Sandy rejoined. 'That's why it's easy for me to tell why you have come. Let's have done with pretences: I am Kinloch, and you are a policeman. And it's not for tea shares you want me but for the Ealing mur –'

I smothered the last word by kicking over a small crockery-laden table by the door. But I was just in time, for I saw the advance light of the lamp which the landlord was carrying along the passage. He entered, much perturbed by the crash, to find all three of us on our feet. He surveyed the damage with dismay.

'Och, sirs,' he cried, 'hae ye been quarrellin' already? If ye'd waited for the lamp it maybe widna' hae been so expensive.'

'Macfarlane,' Kinloch almost shouted, 'who are these men – what do they look like?'

In the light of the lamp now set on the table I saw Sandy's face glisten with beads of sweat. The landlord, trying to soothe him, examined us with a critical eye.

'They're no that ill-lookin', Mr. Keiller,' he pronounced, 'nothing out of the ordinary. I've seen better, and I've seen waur.'

'But do they look like policemen?'

'Polismen?' Macfarlane laughed the suggestion to scorn. 'Them polismen? Losh, no; they're no' near big enough – for this district onyway, unless they were to go about in threes or fours.'

He winked across to me as if to convey his apology for this libel on my physique. At last I mastered my feelings sufficiently to speak.

'Sandy,' I said, going over to him, 'Sandy, lad.'

He started violently, and his feverish hand came out to seek my own.

'Peter!' he whispered. 'My God, Peter – you here? What have you come here for?'

'Just to find you, Sandy.'

And while he gripped my hand I turned to get rid of Macfarlane, who was lingering on.

'Is this a private sitting room?' I asked.

'No, sir, though it's just as good as one at this time o' the year, for there's naebody by mysel' to come into it.'

'Let's have a quite private one, then,' I said to him meaningly.

He replied, stiffening at my tone of voice, as he turned to go:

'Certainly, sir; but, mind you,' he said, lifting a forefinger warningly, 'it's an extra, with use of the piano.'

Of all the incongruous things I have ever heard, this mention of a piano at such a moment remains unexcelled, even by a patient under an anaesthetic. Spencer even smiled. But Sandy seemed stimulated to the pitch of lightheartedness by the word. At least that was what I supposed when he began to hum the refrain of a Scotch ballad:

'Roy's wife of Aldevalloch,
Roy's wife of Aldevalloch,
Wot, ye how she cheated me
As I cam' ower the brase o' Balloch

Did she? Or did I cheat myself?'

He shook his head wearily, like one who repeats a question he had already found unanswerable. I could have answered it for him! And that without knowing the story. For, as I said to Spencer later, if there was one of these women in it there was not much doubt as to who had done the cheating.

Kinloch was in a much healthier mental condition next morning. When I went into his room, the daylight streaming in by an east window as he sat up, it was possible for me, while we talked, to see his eyes fairly well without letting him know what I was up to. The scarification certainly was severe. Before the war his case would have been called hopeless. But now I wasn't sure. So I resolved to avoid all talk of the Ealing affair till he had been seen by Fyffe, the Edinburgh specialist. The first thing was to get him into a healthier, happier condition. And for that I had set great store on the news Spencer had to give him. But that morning he seemed to have forgotten Spencer.

'You haven't yet told me how you found out where I was,' he said.

'Spencer let me know.'

His face showed wonder.

'Spencer – I thought he was a mental case you were in charge of.'

'Why?'

'Well, from his nonsensical babble about those shares.'

'He'd heard you mention them, no doubt.'

'He was right about your being here.'

'That's true, though how he knew –'

'He was right about the shares also. You can sell for forty-one shillings today.'

'Hmp – for the lot, I suppose.'

'No, each. Mr. Spencer, as a partner of Selwyn & Smith, knows what he is talking about.'

'Selwyn & Smith!' he cried. 'Oh, I don't know.'

I could see he believed me. A faint flush swept over the pale worn face. He was silent for a long time, and I wondered into what queer world his thoughts were speeding.

*

It was on a Sunday morning that I first talked openly to him of his eyesight. Spencer having finished his business had gone. Kinloch was not so elated over his news as we had expected. To me it was clear that Sandy, as the landlord said, had something on his mind. But I put no questions. I was not there, to gratify my curiosity but to help a friend. So on that Sunday morning while the hills behind re-echoed the church bell, I suddenly took the plunge, as tactfully as I could.

'You mind that man at Bethsaida, Sandy – him that was blind and had his eyes opened?'

'Yes,' he said after a slight pause. He was very quick with his ear, and maybe my voice was not under perfect control.

'You mind how they asked him if he saw anything and how in his delight he cried out, "Yes, I see. I see men as trees walking"? He was so content with only that – to see men dimly like walking trees.'

'Content? He – he went on his knees, if I remember.'

'So he did. Most of us would not, I suppose, be content with so little.'

His hands clenched as I watched him.

'God – how little you know,' he burst out. 'To see men as trees, even to distinguish the light from darkness – promise a blind man that, and he will go down on his knees to you too.'

Well, I could not promise him even as much as that, but I talked to him of Fyffe's operation.

He shook his head hurriedly.

'No, no. Things like that don't happen, Peter. The world isn't made like that. Think of my luck with those shares. Luck isn't showered on a fellow like that.'

'Sandy,' I said, 'I wouldn't call you a lucky man. Precious little you've had up to now. But sooner or later there's such a thing as compensation – a levelling up of things – long overdue in your case, I think.'

He said no more.

And all I need say here of what followed is this: the operation for *corneitis* was performed by Sir Donald Fyffe in Edinburgh, and one week later Kinloch got his first glimpse of the light again, that light which he had not seen since he was buried by a high explosive during the advance on Remy in the last six weeks of the war. It was in the sitting room, the quite private sitting room which I had insisted on having, that the first experiment was made. I removed the bandages, in semi-darkness, with only a glimmer of weak lamplight in the room. But when I saw Sir Donald had made another success – well, I felt like making use of that piano after all.

Yet the first use, the very first use, to which Sandy put his eyes made me think he had gone crazy. He whipped off his jacket and looked at the lining, staring at a spot just below the collar. The queer thing was that there was absolutely nothing to stare at, so far as I could see in that light. Yet he shook with excitement. After a little he said as if to himself:

'Now when was that done?'

'When was what done?' I asked.

He held out the jacket.

'See, someone has clipped out the centre of the tab with the tailor's name and address on it. That was clever – damn clever. "Wot ye how she cheated me... Roy's wife of Aldevalloch..." Really *smart*, you know.'

Hearing this, I trembled for his sanity, thinking that in the shock of his recovery his mind had become unhinged. For the coat had been in no way damaged.

In the next few days, however, his physical improvement grew so steadily that I began to think of my practice. Indeed, had he become equally well mentally I should have returned to Ealing much earlier. But he did certainly show symptoms of mental unrest not at all to my liking. And into this I knew I must probe before I went. That the trouble had a connection with the murder I did not doubt, and to diagnose a woman behind the trouble was still easier. But it was the latter belief more than the former that made me broach the matter with the utmost circumspection.

We had climbed up the hills and were sitting among the bracken and gorse, with a wide prospect down the valley.

'You'll get better every day here,' I said. 'The air is like wine. A month or two –'

'I go next week, Peter,' he interjected.

'Go next week – where to?' I asked, amazed.

'Town.'

'To London?'

He nodded assent without looking at me. Following his long condition of sightlessness he hadn't yet recovered the habit of looking at those he was speaking to, I noticed.

But I was horrified by his intention.

'London isn't safe for you – yet,' I said meaningly.

'Oh, surely a little smoke won't hurt,' he replied, thinking I had referred to his eyes.

When I said nothing he did turn his face my way. Then I said:

'I meant – the Ealing affair.'

He in his turn was thunderstruck. For a moment he could say nothing.

'So you know about that,' he said at last. He began to breathe quickly. 'Well,' he added, 'if you know much about it you know I had no hand in it.'

'No, Sandy, you hadn't; but you had – well, a stick in it, so to speak.'

'Dunn,' he cried, 'do you mean to say you have known this all along, and have never once spoken of it?'

'You said nothing to me, Sandy; and I force no man's confidences.'

He didn't like that. Pulling up a strand of the dried bracken he began to twist it round his finger mechanically, his thoughts elsewhere.

'Peter,' he said after a while, 'I owe you more than can ever be repaid. Few men can ever have done so much for another as you have done for me; but there's things about this affair I cannot tell you, for there's – there's someone else to whom I owe more even than I owe to you.'

'Roy's wife, I suppose.'

'You can if you like,' he said, taking the gibe in the same quiet tone.

This put me on the high horse instantly.

'And what kindness might ye owe to her?' I inquired, adding in pretended haste, 'But perhaps the question is indiscreet.'

I rejoiced to see his colour rise.

'My debt there is like what I owe you, Peter,' he replied patiently, 'in this, at least, that it is more than I'm likely to be able to pay her.'

'If ye'd said pay her *out*, it would be understandable.'

In the old days this would have been the point where we would have quarrelled. And even then, seething with indignation over his foolishness, I myself would have been ready enough for a quarrel. But Kinloch still held himself in check. Instead of firing up he said nothing. And for a little, as I saw his eyes fixed on the outstretched valley at our feet, I thought he meant to say nothing at all to my outburst. Then he turned towards me, and I knew he had been considering not the landscape but what he might reply to me.

'Peter,' he began almost wistfully, 'there was a time when I could have agreed with you about that. About paying her out, I mean. There was a time when I hated her. Really hated her, you understand, exactly as I now hate the man whose murderous attack on me she stopped. I would have scoffed at the notion of being grateful, for even when she carried me away I knew it was all done to save not me but him. At no time did I have any illusion about that. But there was a time when I behaved like a cad in that house. You remember that night I came to your house? What did you think of me – that I had become coarser, less scrupulous, harder? Yes, you did, and it was true too. Insensibly I had taken on the colour of my surroundings. For two years I hadn't, as you might say, touched a clean hand till you took mine that night. Yet it was not you who lifted me out of that pit, much as you've since done. It's only as I look back that I see what life with her in that lonely house really did for me.'

'And how,' I asked pointedly, 'did this happy home come to be broken up?'

'The old woman who came to do the housework found out I was there. One night to get rid of me she came back with a cock and bull story about having seen some man wandering about the common as if watching the house, affecting to believe him to be Stella's husband. The trick would have failed but for the fact that it coincided with a newspaper item about an impending arrest in connection with the Ealing murder. We thought we had been traced and had to fly, and fly far. But even then, Peter, that girl was fine, you understand. Broken as she was by the old woman's imputation on her honour she first got me out of the house and then herself returned to prepare for our long journey and if necessary face the unknown man we suspected to be really a policeman – face him while I sheltered in that haystack.'

'And all this she did for you out of a pure disinterested kindness? You never came to doubt that, did you?' And to rub the question home I began to whistle the tune, 'Roy's Wife.'

He flushed at once.

'What if she did cheat me?' he cried. 'Hadn't I been trying to outwit her myself?'

'And you lost.'

'As I deserved,' he rejoined. Then, after a minute of silence he turned to me, bending forward. 'Peter, I told you I behaved like a cad in that house. That was true. But the most caddish thing came at the end. We had travelled here by night in her little car, sleeping in it all day in some out-of-the-way corner of a field or in a wood. It took us five nights to reach this place. Then, before I let her go away, I made her kiss me.'

'Ah, here enters the love interest,' I said sarcastically. 'Is it possible the hussy spoils this very romantic story by refusing?'

'No,' he said quite seriously, 'she didn't refuse. At first I thought she was going to. But when she did –'

'You knew she wasn't –' I helped him out.

'But when she did,' he went on, 'I found her cheek was wet with tears.'

It wasn't what I had expected to hear. And, though I felt it would have been saner to scoff, I somehow couldn't find the right words in which to do it. His childlike notion that the woman had cried over his brutality in making her kiss him simply turned me dumb. There was nothing left that I could usefully say. But this extravagant notion of Sandy's prepared me for what was to follow. And for what followed at once I certainly needed preparation.

'What made you communicate with Selwyn & Smith?' I asked. 'You didn't remember they held the shares?'

'No,' he said. 'I thought the police were behind that advertisement and I wanted to give myself up.'

'To give yourself up! What for – the murder?'

'Yes.'

I could scarcely believe my ears. Of all the silly, quixotic acts ever recorded this seemed the maddest. Give himself up indeed! Yes, but the very foolishness of it gave me the measure of this unknown woman's hold on Kinloch. Cleverly indeed she had done her work, abandoning him at Gart just when he was sufficiently bewitched to make him keep his mouth shut, or even, if it came to that, to play the part of willing victim. And as I perceived this, it was not only anger I felt, but something like awe, that a woman could so dominate such a man as Kinloch.

'You see,' he went on, 'to give myself up seemed a way out, an escape from life. I had got rather tired of life before, you know. My hold on it was purely parasitic – just an existence, a crawling about in the dark.' He looked over at me with something in his eyes that glowed. 'But you have made all the difference, Peter. You have given me back my interest in life, and now I can see how mad it was to think of giving myself up like that.'

This was so far satisfactory. But it was still far short of what I wanted.

'But,' I said, 'to go to London with the police on the lookout is just to give yourself up in a different way. They'll be on you like hawks, from what I've seen.'

'I'm not afraid. And I've got to find her, now that I can do something,' he said stubbornly.

'But are you sure she wants to be found?'

I had him there, for he looked more sure she did not from the way his face fell. To push home this discovery I went on:

'Was it her name you took when you came here?'

'I don't know her name,' he admitted.

'Then it was to hide your own name from her you called yourself Keiller?'

'No, she knows my name.'

'No doubt! And all about you; while you only know as much about her as she chose to tell, which seems to have been nothing.'

Then a thought burst in on me.

'Why, you don't even know what she looks like, for of course *you've never seen her.*'

'No,' he admitted, 'if you were to place her photograph in front of me I wouldn't recognise her.'

'And you don't even know so much as her name, or where she lives, or what she looks like. Why, man, the search is hopeless – needle in a haystack is nothing to it.'

After that I let the matter drop, for I saw he was weary. We descended the slope and passed through the pine wood almost without speech, even when we came out on the highway at the bottom of the valley, where talk would have been easy.

*

It is unlikely that I would ever again have reverted to Kinloch's project had he himself not done so a few nights later. We were sitting by the fire, smoking an after-dinner pipe. I was to leave Gart next morning. He began by desiring my advice, showing great deference to my opinion. Of course I knew he was merely trying to smooth down my ruffled feelings. But when he went a step farther, and proposed to tell me his plans, I cut him short. What he meant to do, where he intended to go, were, I told him, things it was safer to keep to himself. That he had some plan of action, some wildcat scheme for finding the lady I already divined. But it did not interest me; and, in view of his confessed ignorance of the most essential facts about her, I knew he must fail. Had he been willing to help the police to lay the man by the heels the situation would have been simplified. For I did not doubt now, that, provided he came forward voluntarily, he could, with the help of Spencer and myself, clear himself from complicity in the murder. But this he would not do. He would not lift a finger to help the authorities till he knew how the man's arrest would affect the woman, a position which put him on the wrong side of the law, and which might well jeopardize his own safety if the police got their hands on him. It was this that filled me with an exasperated despair. For he knew his danger by this time. He had been poring through his tinted glasses, longer than was good for his eyes, over a file of old newspapers in which the fullest details of the murder, and the various theories as to its perpetrator and his motives, were given. So I firmly refused to listen to his plans for finding out where that woman had gone. But it was only at Gart Station, while waiting for my train to start, that I told him why I refused.

'You see, Sandy,' I said, 'if anybody should ask me where you are, or what you are doing, I can truthfully say I know nothing.'

What I had in mind now that I was about to return to London was the difficulty experienced in getting away from it. And I had not forgotten the man who had watched me in Chancery Lane, nor the three who called at the office there.

'Oh,' he said hastily, 'of course I can't expect a friend to lie for me.'

'Certainly not,' I said. 'He has no right to undertake the duty unless he can do it really well.'

It was good to see him smile back as he gripped my hand. I think he understood.

But it saddened me to part with him, not knowing what his plan was for finding the lady. Yet it was some satisfaction that we had parted friends, in spite of great provocation, given and received.

BOOK FOUR

The Second Narrative of Godfrey Chance

XIV

That a man should remember his successes in the hour of failure and his failures in the hour of success – this I have heard Francis McNab say was the one sure way to keep a level head. He regarded both success and failure as very severe mental temptations, the one inclining us to take too rosy, the other too black a view of our abilities. But he himself, I always thought, emerged better from success than from failure. A mere check he could surmount. Indeed a check stimulated him, whetted his appetite and all that. But in his investigations into the Ealing murder it was not one check he met with, but a succession of them with, at the end, a rank and final failure staring him in the face.

That journey to Stone, near Rye, proved to be but the first of a series of false scents. We had set off on the hasty journey confident that we were on the right track. And we reached Stone in time to see the body of the young man found by the estate worker identified by relatives who, indeed, had travelled down by the same train as ourselves. That the deceased had not been blind, and could have no possible connection with the Ealing affair, these facts were placed beyond doubt inside half an hour.

That was a failure out of which McNab emerged shaken. What he was thinking of as we returned to town I cannot say, but if it was some former success one would never have guessed it from his face. It was both grievous to me and astonishing to see the settled gloom with which he gazed through the window while our train flew across the Weald of Kent. Only now and then I stole a look at him, and as for speaking to him – well, I hope I know when to keep silence. But what a relief it was when the train left the fresh, green fields and orchards behind, and climbed up into the cavernous darkness of the Sevenoaks tunnel! Here, at least, in that murky gloom, was the right environment for us. There was just this difference, though: the train every second was moving on to daylight, but I doubted if Francis McNab saw any daylight ahead of him. Yet for all that, after our return, I did not doubt that he began at once to cast about for another scent. Occasionally in the days following, I took him an advertisement for some person missing; sometimes, in fact, quite a crop of such notices. But of course every day that passed lessened the likelihood that any of these had a connection with our case, and soon almost every one of them could be eliminated, as the person advertised for had disappeared at a date much later than that on which the murder took place. How often he must have found himself barking up the wrong tree in those days!

McNab's darkest hour while on the case came, it seemed to me, on a day I well remember. For ten days I had been away on some work at Manchester. And for several days before that I had not been round to the Adelphi, for it did really pain me to see McNab at a loss. And so even after my return I might not have gone round so soon but for the message I received that he expected me. Of course I hurried off at once, hopefully. I found him pacing up and down his room overlooking the river. This restlessness revealed to me, without the need for words, the exact state of his mind. Obviously he was not then engaged in recalling his former successes. On the contrary every symptom showed that he was chafing and fretting over his present failure in a very human way. And as I remembered his saying that the world was crowded with men just not good enough for their jobs their ambition had made them take on, I suspected that he was just then including himself in the ranks of that ignoble army. Francis McNab was no all-over superman. But some qualities he had in super-excellence, and one was his tenacity. He never acquiesced in defeat. The new way under defeat and failure is to 'cut one's losses', to console oneself by saying it is no use crying over spilt milk, and so on. But none of these modern phrases, masquerading as wisdom, and meant to comfort the ineffective and the unsuccessful, did I ever hear on his lips. Defeat stung, rankled and reproached him.

Much of this passed through my mind as I stood with my back to him, looking out on the river, waiting for him to speak. And at last I heard the restless steps behind me cease.

'Chance,' he said, 'what do you consider the greatest enemy of Justice?'

'Justice?' I repeated, turning round.

'Yes, Justice, the blindfolded goddess with the sword in her hand who does not know where to strike.'

'Oh, some say the lawyers,' I replied flippantly.

'And others the police. They're both wrong. It's Time, the old fellow with the scythe in his hand, who strikes at everybody and all things.' He came over and stood beside me at the window, looking down upon the traffic on the Embankment. At least his eyes rested there. 'Time fights hard for the criminal. Clues are destroyed by time, traces vanish, evidence is blotted out, things alter, and people's relations to each other. Why, the mere lapse of time is held to lessen guilt: "It's so long ago," people say.'

'Is that what you think they'll say about the Ealing murder?'

'No, it hasn't come to that yet, thanks to the *Record*, for keeping the public agog with expectation, but' – he broke off, sighed and shook his head helplessly.

'The *Eye Opener* isn't letting the murder drop out of sight, either,' I said. 'This week's number gives the winning design in the competition for the memorial to be erected over the grave in Kensal Green. Have you seen it?'

'Over Ponsonby Paget's grave?' McNab inquired as if he had not been listening.

'Of course. It's a fine thing, a life size reproduction in white marble of the female figure on the cover of the paper; but with one significant difference – the two pennies no longer cover the eyes, which are now wide open and uplifted as if in an appeal to heaven. A fine touch, don't you think, to remove the two pennies, the only *earthly* details on that figure.'

'Well, he was a man, they say, who saw all things in terms of money. And of course he won't be doing that now,' McNab said in a way that reminded me of Matheson. That irritated me. Besides, I felt a trifle huffy over my offhand reception after so long an absence.

'The trouble is,' I said petulantly, 'you didn't like Ponsonby Paget. If you had you might have had more to show for your ten weeks' work on the case.'

It was a stupid speech, and McNab eyed me reproachfully for it. Then he said:

'You don't care much for Matheson, do you? Oh, I know you never say a word against him. But don't you find your prejudice affects your work?'

'Certainly not,' I declared. 'If it did I couldn't stay on. A journalist does his best irrespective of likes and dislikes.'

McNab nodded.

'So do some others, my lad, who are not journalists. And I don't need to admire Ponsonby Paget to sharpen my wish to see his murderer hang. So let's have tea.' He rang the bell.

When Janet, the old housekeeper, had departed, I tried to explain the anxiety which had possessed me, an anxiety which I shared with Matheson himself.

'The paper has backed you to win,' I said, 'and after what it has said about the police it would be a bad knock if they should prove to be right and get home first.'

This I said with a sigh, intending both to sting and stimulate him, for I could not forget it was now over a month since we went to Stone.

'Well,' he replied calmly, 'the police have great advantages.'

'You mean their fingerprint register?'

'That and a lot of other things – their organisation and well-knit system, and their numbers, their familiarity with the methods and haunts of the habitual criminals and so on. But they're at a loss in this case for all that. Why? Because the man we are looking for hadn't got his fingerprints on the Scotland Yard register. He does not belong to the criminal classes. This deed of his was an exceptional incident in his life.'

McNab became more animated as the tea progressed.

'That is not a rare thing, Chance. There are many who are what you might call one-act criminals. Any policeman will tell you what a troublesome problem they make. And they would be a more trying problem for the law than they are but for one fact – the fact that in their inexperience they are apt to make mistakes. Take this case. That room in Ealing was scattered with evidence. We had a table, you remember, almost loaded with exhibits. Snargrove at once pronounced the murder to be the work of an amateur. He was quite right. But – mark this – the man did not follow up the "mistakes" left in the room by making others afterwards, as Snargrove expected he would. Once he got away from that house he left no traces and gave no sign. There was no bungling. And when we know that he had to carry a blind man with him, and dispose of him somewhere, surely it is obvious to you that we are dealing with a man of remarkable talent and resources.'

'Yes,' I agreed, 'that seems clear. Still there were clues left in that room.'

'Not by the criminal. Those marks on the wall were made by the blind man; the stick was his too. And for all we yet know the fingerprints on the glass may be his also, and that shred of hair as well. The one thing, in fact, which could *not* have been the blind man's is that splinter of looking-glass. That man was a genius in organisation. Just think. He had the deed all carefully planned, and it would have gone off pat but for the unexpected entrance of the blind man. And you can read both his alarm and the blind man's innocence from the fact that the murderer left no trace of his own but many of the other's presence. He could not foresee and provide for the presence of that blind intruder, yet even in that terrible moment he made no blunder that gave *himself* away.' McNab prodded me with a stiff forefinger. 'Now, Mr. Godfrey Chance, do you begin to see the niceties of this particular case?'

'One thing I can't see – why you concentrated on finding this blind man instead of going straight for the actual murderer, as Snargrove is doing,' I replied.

McNab waved towards the window.

'Look out there and tell me what you see,' he commanded.

A good deal was visible from that lofty window as I went over, cup in hand.

'There's the river,' I said, 'and four barges sliding down it on the ebb tide, and there's two trains crossing the bridge, and numberless motors whirling along the Embankment, besides a stationary tram with a bunch of people struggling to get in, and a stream of pedestrians flowing into the Underground from the foot of Villiers Street.'

'Good! Now, look here! One among all these people has just stolen a banana from a dealer in the Strand. He has it concealed about his person, he is hurrying away in the train now out of sight, I suppose, or on the barges or in the trams or taxis or on foot, and he will certainly vanish utterly unless we find him in time.'

I stared at McNab. He seemed quite serious. But he was like that, even when, as now, he tried to be humorous.

'What else do you know about the man?' I asked.

'Nothing. The dealer didn't see the banana lifted – only missed it off the bunch.'

'Has the dealer issued a description of the banana?' I asked, not to be outdone in affecting seriousness.

'No. It would be useless, for the man will eat it at the first quiet moment and so destroy the evidence against him.'

'Looks hopeless.'

'Ah, but there's a postman, among these people, who knows who took the banana. That both narrows the field of search and speeds things up.'

It was easy to follow his argument.

'So you went for the postman – in other words, the blind man. But after all, though it is as easy to pick out a blind man in a crowd as a postman, you haven't got him yet. And you are sitting here doing nothing.'

'Not doing nothing.'

'Well, only talking to me about the case.'

'That would be doing nothing.'

In certain moods McNab, as will have been observed, could be extremely irritating.

'What else do you think you're doing?' I demanded.

'Besides lighting this cigarette I'm listening for a ring at my door bell.'

'Oh, you expect someone.' Then, gathering from his tone that it was no ordinary caller, I cried, 'Someone connected with the case?'

'Yes. Someone who can tell us a lot about the case.'

That was a big enough surprise for me. But more was to follow. As I stood still in astonishment McNab crossed to his desk and opening a file extracted something from it which he laid on the table before me. It was a photographic print about six inches square, evidently an enlargement from a group of soldiers, for the shoulders of two other men showed on each side of the print. The face of the man thus picked out of the group yielded what seemed a good likeness. Under an open, unlined forehead the eyes showed clear, dark and well apart, with a hint of the cheek bones showing, after the Slavonic type, and though the nose was straight and well proportioned there was something of delicacy, if not weakness, in the smiling mouth.

'Who is it?'

'The postman,' said McNab.

'What – the blind man?' I cried.

'In other words, the blind man.'

That sent my eyes to the print once more, and I crossed to the window to get a fuller light on the face of the man we had hunted for so long. Things had evidently been moving during my absence. If this thing in my hand was a photograph of the blind man, McNab had certainly succeeded in picking his post-man out of the crowd that moved on and changed so swiftly, I thought, looking down for a moment on the Embankment.

'That's right, my lad,' McNab's voice came, sarcastically humorous, 'take another look at the ugly old bridge. A lot of water has run under it since you were last here.'

'How did you get it?' I asked, holding out the portrait.

'I'd have got it sooner except for your blundering. But there's no time to tell you the story now,' he replied, as he looked again at his watch.

Things had not only been happening; things, I saw, were about to happen. The restlessness which I had taken as a symptom of failure, the talk which had seemed idle trifling, and this slow pacing about the room which I had assumed to come from a sense of depression and defeat – all this took on a new meaning now. Every moment he was expecting something was about to happen. Someone was about to ring that bell. How often I had rung it myself. How familiar its sound was to me – an old-fashioned handle you pulled. You could hear something like a chain grate against wood as you pulled it, and then the subdued tinkle in the distance. Like McNab himself I began to listen. There were, of course, a dozen questions I wanted to put. One was, under this strain, irresistible.

'Who is it – is it really the blind man – is it him you expect?' I asked.

He shook his head.

'I don't know. Wait and we'll see. He has only a few minutes left.'

That characteristic reply sticks in my memory. It roused the maximum of curiosity and gave the minimum of satisfaction. And that was what McNab liked to do when he was 'out' with me.

Ten more minutes passed. They passed in silence. For I did not risk expulsion by probing him with any more questions. The memory of how he had got rid of me after the inquest at Ealing when he made his great inference from the walking stick was too vividly reawakened now that I held in my hands the portrait of that stick's owner.

Then just as McNab was glancing again at his watch, the shadow of a frown on his face, he looked up sharply, lifting a hand.

The next moment there came a quick, decided ring at the bell.

XV

The bell had not ceased before McNab, slipping across, shoved me down on the low window seat, and then seating himself at the other end said quickly:

'Not a word from you, Chance. Remember, not a word, however great the temptation. If you want to say anything, put your thumb into your waistcoat pocket.'

Taking the photograph out of my fingers he laid it face downwards on the small table standing close to the window seat on which we now were seated.

I nodded understandingly, my eyes glued on the door. At last it opened, and the old housekeeper's voice came wheezily:

'Dr Dunn to see you, sir.'

McNab rose when his visitor had advanced to the centre of the room. But his welcome was hearty enough.

'Glad to see you, doctor.'

The doctor did not seem equally glad to see McNab, and his eye travelled doubtfully to me. He clearly was trying to remember where he had seen me before. As McNab drew a chair forward he explained me.

'Mr. Chance, doctor. I think you've met already – at Ealing on Monday the 15th of January,' he said casually.

While he spoke the doctor was looking me straight in the face, and I, naturally, was looking at him. Recognition of me sprang into his eyes, and then something else – something like fear.

'Sit down, doctor,' McNab said pleasantly. 'I'm glad you have come.'

'You expected me?'

'You or another. As I said in my note to you I needed someone who could answer certain questions bearing on the night of Monday, 15th January.'

'Well, I was called in by the police on that occasion,' Dr Dunn conceded.

As he spoke McNab took up his former position beside me on the window seat. Between him and the doctor stood the little table, on the dark polished surface of which the white back of the photographic print seemed like a sheet of paper placed there for taking notes. As for our visitor it was easy to see his discomfort. Indeed, as he sat in that high backed chair fronting the window, he seemed all on edge, rather like a patient in a dentist's chair. Indeed, he made the very picture of a man visibly bracing himself up before the dentist began to pull out his teeth. A battle of wits it was going to be. I sat up at the thought.

'I am a very busy man,' he said defensively.

'Of course you are,' McNab replied, 'after your recent – holiday was it? – your practice will have its arrears. Patients, I'm told, never take kindly to a locum, however good he may be. Still, you were wise to come; it may save you not only time but trouble later on.'

'So you said in your note, which, I own, roused my curiosity,' the doctor nodded, making an attempt to be at his ease.

But, quite in the dark as I was as to what McNab wanted with his visitor, it was clear enough that he had roused in this same visitor an emotion which would more correctly be called apprehension than curiosity. I found the situation tremendously exciting now. Ten minutes earlier I had misread things so badly that I had been sure the case was at a standstill. Now I had in a moment been made to realise that in my absence things had been happening; that events were moving with swiftness and momentum. For quite abruptly as I sat looking at those two men facing each other across the little table, I perceived that this meeting was a decisive moment, probably the turning point in the whole case. And the fascination of watching the two men in this moment of crisis can be imagined. Neither seemed over keen at first to come to grips, the doctor being obviously on the defensive, with McNab like a keen-eyed boxer circling round an over-cautious opponent, weighing him up and looking for an opening.

Then with unexpected suddenness McNab struck.

'And when,' he asked, 'did you last see Kinloch?'

The doctor's brow furrowed.

'Kinloch?' he repeated thoughtfully. 'Kinloch? I seem to recall the name, but I cannot exactly –'

Like a flash McNab picked up the photograph lying on the table between them and held it out before the other man's eyes. And into those eyes there came, in swift succession, surprise, recognition, horror, dismay.

'My God!' he faltered.

McNab smiled with satisfaction.

'Thank you very much, Dr Dunn. This, then, is quite a good likeness of the man. That was exactly what I wanted to be sure of.'

Dunn looked up sharply.

'What for? Why do you want to be sure of that?' he asked.

McNab tapped the photograph in his hand.

'This man is being looked for in connection with the Ealing murder. It would be useless to furnish the press with an unrecognisable portrait.'

Dead silence followed. The doctor seemed to be slowly considering the consequences which would follow the publication of the photograph. Indeed, I was myself engaged in thinking how I could induce McNab to give the picture to the *Record* as a first day's exclusive. Then Dunn in his turn picked up the print after fumbling over the attempt once or twice.

'He's – he's altered considerably since this was taken,' he said. 'I doubt if he could be identified by this.'

'You recognised him quickly enough,' McNab reminded him.

'Quite; but I remembered him like this, you see.'

A frown darkened McNab's face.

'Blindness can't make all that difference,' he said aggressively.

'Ah – so you know that too – that he was blind? Well, blindness alters a man's face very much. That perhaps you did not know. A sighted person's face is continually altering, reflecting, as it were, the varied emotional impressions of what the eye sees from one moment to another. But when the eyes see nothing, the face muscles cease to be flexible, and the face becomes still, rigid, the man's whole expression in fact is altered, even the shape of his face becomes different.'

The doctor appeared to gain confidence now that he was speaking on a matter in his own line of business. When McNab remained silent, and seemed to be pondering over what he had just heard, Dunn bent forward and in his turn tapped the photographic print on the table.

'You can do what you like about publishing this, of course, but I can assure you that if you set a photo of the blind Kinloch beside this one you would yourself refuse to believe that both were pictures of the same man.'

Thus were the tables turned on McNab. He sat looking at Kinloch's photograph with grave eyes. His features could not have been more set and wooden if he himself had been blind. At last he looked up.

'In that case,' he said, 'I'm compelled to a course I wished to avoid. I must force you to tell us where this man is now hiding.'

The other shook his head with decision.

'I can't do that.'

'You mean you will not.'

'No; I mean just what I say. You see I had the foresight to anticipate that such a moment as this might come. So I refused to hear his plans.'

'His plans?'

The doctor crossed his legs and sat back at his ease.

'Yes. It must be clear to you I can't be forced to tell what I don't know.'

'Quite. But I have a notion, doctor, that it would be useful if you would tell what you do know.'

The rueful sigh which accompanied this brought a smile to Dr Dunn's face. He certainly looked top dog now, and his attitude and manner showed he was quite conscious of the fact. He leant easily, almost condescendingly, forward towards McNab.

'I'll tell you this much at once,' he said confidentially. 'Don't waste your time on Kinloch. In the first place I have a conviction you will not find him – he seemed absolutely sure about that. And in the next place he'd be no use to you if you did find him, for he is innocent of all complicity in the murder; and though present when the murder was committed, he was blind and saw nothing – nothing that would help you.'

McNab's eyebrows lifted in incredulity.

'Yet he doesn't want to be found?'

'He does not – more's the pity. But that makes no difference in the fact. Do you think I'd be taking a hand in this if he were guilty?'

Dunn spoke sharply with some heat. To the question so earnestly put McNab did not reply.

'Yet he does not want to be found,' he repeated.

'Looks black, I admit.' The doctor hesitated.

'Unaccountable, if he's innocent,' McNab commented, incredulity in every syllable.

'You think so? But what if there is a woman in the affair?'

McNab looked up quickly, as if the suggestion had startled him.

'Ah – a woman? Well, that might make a difference in the way one has to interpret Kinloch's present action.' He paused before adding: 'But we have no evidence, not a shred of evidence of any woman being connected with the affair.'

Here I ostentatiously thrust my thumb into my pocket; for I wanted to remind McNab of the wedge-shaped splinter of glass found in the room. But he took no notice of me. Indeed, as I told him afterwards, I might as well have put it in my mouth. And as the doctor sat silent McNab resumed consideringly, 'Yes, if I knew there was a woman in it I could understand Kinloch's action. I might, indeed, be ready to agree with you as to his innocence, for I've observed that when a man does a thing of exceptional silliness there's usually a woman behind him – if you can see her.'

Dr Dunn tapped the table emphatically.

'There *is* a woman here, a very clever one. You can take my word for that. Indeed, you'll have to take my word for it, for I doubt if you or anyone else will ever get a glimpse at her.'

'Go on, please,' McNab said, rising to his feet in his restlessness.

But Dunn seemed alarmed by the other's eagerness. He shook his head.

'Perhaps I've said too much already. I've a duty to Kinloch, you know.'

'Oh, so that's the way of it?' McNab cried, stopping short. 'And isn't it odd that so many of you should find it their duty to stand between a criminal and justice! Here are you, doctor, sheltering Kinloch, while Kinloch is sheltering this woman, and the woman is sheltering the actual murderer.' He looked Dunn quizzically up and down. 'I trust, doctor, you don't encounter so many barriers between yourself and a necessary surgical operation – so many barriers erected by friends of the patient – as you are now helping to erect between the hangman and his operation on this man's neck.'

Dunn, flushing up to the eyes, rose with a sharp indrawn breath. At first my thought was that he was going to resent McNab's gibe about the hangman. But regaining self-control he said, referring to McNab's burst of anger:

'At least, sir, you make it easy for me to perceive I have not said too much.'

The stiffly uttered words restored McNab's good humour.

'Oh,' he replied as the doctor picked up his hat, 'you have said quite enough to be going on with. You have cleared up the situation wonderfully. You do not think so? Well, let me assure you that within a week I expect to lay my hands first on Kinloch, then on the lady, and finally on the man behind her.'

'In consequence of what I have said?' the other asked, staring.

'Almost entirely.'

After a moment's cogitation Dunn shook his head with evident relief.

'No,' he said. 'That's impossible.'

'And to prove to you that I believe you when you say you do not know where Kinloch is I'm going to tell you how I'll do it,' McNab resumed. 'You recognise it would be a dangerous thing to tell you if I thought you were in touch with Kinloch, don't you?' And when Dunn nodded assent McNab continued: 'Very well, here's the proof I believed you when you assured me you did not now know where he was. This is how I will find him. I have only to co-ordinate the facts within our knowledge, group them in sequence and make the necessary deductions.' From the manner of his speech and the protracted way in which he approached his point McNab must have been aiming at Dunn's nerve. He had stepped close up to the doctor too, so that now the men stood face to face. The doctor's eyes narrowed as Mc-Nab's forefinger touched him on the chest masterfully.

'Your practice at Ealing was in the hands of a locum for three weeks. You left hurriedly on the 3rd of April. Your patients did not know you were going. Will you tell us where you went and let me verify? No? Then I say you went to see him. Up to shortly before you left you had been paying frequent visits to a firm in Chancery Lane who were advertising for Kinloch. It was a good notion to keep on advertising for him after you knew where he was. The ruse served for a time. But your sudden departure and prolonged absence let me comprehend the trick.' McNab nodded. 'You tell me you have never seen the woman, and I suppose I may take it you are still less likely to have seen the man? Good. It was on or about the 3rd of April you found him. But the murder at Ealing had taken place on the 15th of January. Where had Kinloch been in the interval between that date and the day on which you reached him? In hiding somewhere alone? In hiding, yes; but not alone. In such circumstances a blind man must have had someone to look after him – someone who was in the secret. That would be either the man or the woman, if not both. I conclude it was the woman; and I will tell you why presently. But you found Kinloch alone when you arrived on the scene, therefore the place, wherever it was, where you found your friend, was not the place where he had been so long concealed. Am I not right? You won't admit it?' McNab laughed.

'But I will go further. I will hazard the guess, doctor, that whoever brought Kinloch to the place you found him – and someone must have taken him – dumped him down there and vanished in a mighty big hurry. Ah, I see from your face I'm right. Of course they did! It was hardly safe to risk being seen by people with eyes who could supply a description. Not so would they waste the mighty stroke of luck that had come when the only witness to the crime turned out to be a blind man. Everything done subsequent to the murder proves that they knew how to take full advantage of his blindness.'

McNab touched the motionless Dunn again.

'Doctor, did Kinloch tell you where he had lived before you met?'

'He did not.'

'Because he did not himself know. It would be some remote place, to lessen the chance of accident, or of his finding out where he was, until he had been worked upon sufficiently, and won over, to keep his mouth shut. That part of the business would be left to the woman, eh? And she didn't need to be even personally attractive in this case. She might be even hideous, for a siren tongue would be enough here! Anyhow, her blandishments did succeed.' Dunn seemed surprised by McNab's conclusion.

'I do not follow you there,' he demurred.

'But you have so far agreed?'

'I say nothing about that.'

'Quite. Your lips are sealed, are they not, by a promise to your friend? Still, you did say something about his having plans.'

'I told you I had refused to hear them.'

'Ah, but think how significant it is that he should have plans at all. Plans are simply means to some end. And, though you may be ignorant of the means he meant to adopt, you may yet be quite cognisant of the end at which he aimed. Indeed, it is not unlikely that you refused to hear the plans simply because you disliked the end towards which they were directed.'

Whether this was meant for a shot in the dark or not I could not tell, but I saw Dunn shift uneasily and look away.

'I thought,' he said evasively, 'you were going to tell me how you proposed to lay your hands on Kinloch.'

'Patience! That is the point we have almost reached.'

McNab seemed in no hurry. He kept us waiting while he took out his cigarette case and selected a cigarette carefully, as if it had been a cigar. For myself, though I was free from the doctor's very manifest disquiet, I at least shared in his impatience.

After a whiff or two McNab picked up Kinloch's photograph and looked at it narrowly.

'Here, then,' he said, 'we have a young gentleman with plans in his head. Plans to what end? I ask myself. Not for the arrest of the murderer certainly. For in that case the quickest way would be to put himself in touch with the police and tell what he knows. This he had not done – a neglect which, by the way, will count heavily against him if the police get their hands on him. So directly, at least, his plans do not centre on the man. Yet they ought to, for you, doctor, assured me he was innocent of all complicity in the crime. You were even indignant about it. And as I look at this photograph I appreciate your heat. It is a good face, frank, open, honest, the face of one whose every instinct and impulse should put him on the side of justice. What, then, has occurred to pervert his natural instincts and inhibit the reaction such a man must show to such a crime as the Ealing murder? I can think of two causes. Either this man afterwards became demoralised by his war experiences so that this photograph, taken before he left for France, no longer truly represents him, either that, or he has become infatuated and morally blinded by some woman. Both war and women are forces which can and do demoralise men.'

I think McNab at this point laid down the photograph of Kinloch at which he had been again looking, for he ceased speaking; but my eyes were all the time on Dunn. I could see his emotion fire under McNab's words. His hands became clenched.

'The question is,' McNab resumed, 'which was it in this case
– war or a woman?'

'A woman,' Dunn burst out. 'Yes, a woman, by God, infatuated by her – yes.'

'Then his plans undoubtedly centred on finding her again.
Take that as settled. The question now arises: how is he to find
her? Mark his handicaps. He never saw her, and we may safely
assume she did not supply him with her name and address when
she left him. And she left him at a place which was not that
where she had lived with him and where there must necessarily
be someone who could supply information about her.'

'Far, far from there,' Dunn whispered uncontrollably.

'That you cannot know,' McNab asserted provocatively.

'Can't I? You forget Kinloch could judge distance from the
time spent on the journey.'

'But they might have been travelling in a circle, covering the
same ground again and again for the express purpose of deceiv-
ing him.'

Dunn hesitated, obviously tempted to refute McNab's confident assertion, yet afraid to risk more words.

'Well,' he said at length, 'there was one point Kinloch knew
they did not pass twice.'

McNab shook his head.

'A blind man couldn't possibly tell that,' he said with decision.

'Couldn't he indeed?' Dunn broke out in impatient derision.
'You think so? But if blind he is not deaf, all his other senses are
unimpaired. Could he not, for example, tell that he once, and
once only, went down a long hill with a sharp right-hand turn
before passing through a village at the end of which he heard the
sea close on the left side, so close that the spray came into the
car, the noise of the surf on a shingle beach mingling with the
notes of a bugle high up on his right? And couldn't he tell from
feeling the sun on his left cheek that the sea was to the south?'

'He heard the sea?'

'Certainly, but only for about five minutes, and it was the only time he heard it. So they weren't doing circles there anyhow.'

McNab sighed gently.

'A sharp fellow, Kinloch. Wish I'd got my hands on him.'

Dunn shook his head.

'That wouldn't help you. They were sharp too and took care his knowledge was confined to things that did not matter. Why, he was ignorant even of the name of the village where they lived.'

'Village? Nonsense. A lonely house, if you like, in its own grounds, but not a village,' McNab contradicted.

'A village it was, though apparently lonely enough, shut in by gates – he knew that much – at each end, and up among hills.'

McNab in his turn shook his head.

'They'd never try to conceal him in a village. Couldn't be done, as you would know if you had ever lived in one. Villagers are mighty inquisitive about strangers. A blind man too, he'd be seen daily from the house opposite.'

'A village it was,' Dunn reiterated impatiently. 'But there wasn't any house opposite. At least there was, it seems, a good half-mile of common between the houses on each side.'

McNab pondered for a moment and then looked up slyly.

'You won't send me hunting for an imaginary village, doctor. It's Kinloch I'm after, as keenly as he himself is after the lady. I'm going to find him too, and with my assistance he in his turn will find her.'

Dunn looked disconcerted.

'Without me,' McNab went on, 'he is unlikely to find her. The odds are too heavily weighed against him. He doesn't even know her name. That in itself would be enough to deter most of us from beginning the search. But when we add to this the fact that the seeker is blind –'

From Dunn there came a sharp, inarticulate little cry.

The interruption appeared to take McNab by surprise. He ceased speaking and gazed thoughtfully at the doctor.

'Go on,' Dunn said.

'Add to this the fact that the seeker is blind,' McNab repeated, 'still this other fact remains, the fact that in spite of all these handicaps he had formulated some precise plan. He had when you spoke with him some notion of how she might be found. Therefore I conclude he knew something about the woman. Indeed, when one thinks it out, he could scarcely avoid learning something, closely associated as he was with her for a considerable time. I myself, for instance, formed the opinion that the people concerned in the murder of Mr. Ponsonby Paget belong to what is called the higher social classes. Kinloch's ear would at once enable him to tell me if I am right. Her voice, its inflection and tone, her vocabulary would proclaim her class. And, however much the woman was on her guard, she was bound to let slip many other things from which a man of even mediocre intelligence would infer much. I am not suggesting that he might learn anything so definite as her name and address; but it is exceedingly unlikely that Kinloch would not hear something about her tastes, habits, the places she liked, the cities she knew, the streets with which she was familiar, and even, being a woman, the shops she favoured. That sort of thing. Very well, now I put myself into Kinloch's shoes, and ask myself how, if similarly handicapped, I should set about the business of finding her.'

McNab took what seemed to me, at least, a long time before he found an answer to this last question. He stood quite still, fronting Dr Dunn, but, I am sure, without any consciousness now of either the doctor's presence or my own. How Dunn felt I cannot say, though he stood there almost as rigid as McNab himself. As for me I dared scarce let my breath go. For I saw that McNab meant to catch the elusive Kinloch while the latter was out in the open searching for the lady. And then, just when I was beginning to fear that McNab's imaginative insight had been set too stiff a problem, his eyes unclosed.

'There's just one way open to him,' he said.

'Well?' Dunn almost whispered, his eyes dilating apprehension.

'Obviously he can't go about looking for her.'

'Well?' Dunn repeated, a tremor in his voice.

'He will wait in some road or street he has heard her mention more than once, wait for her to come along. He's sitting there now, a blind man with a Braille book on his knees, reading aloud to draw attention to himself.'

It was amazing to see how Dunn received this announcement. His face suddenly cleared. He laughed in an explosive way that left one in no doubt of the genuineness of his mirth. And the laugh was one of those good-natured but contemptuous guffaws that hurt like a blow. I felt my face flame with anger. But McNab did not seem in the least put out.

'You don't agree with me, doctor?' he said quite calmly but with a tincture of surprise that invited a reply.

'I do not,' Dunn declared bluntly. 'A more forlorn hope I never heard of.'

McNab wandered over to the table, and picking up the Kinloch photograph again looked at it thoughtfully.

'You know your man, of course. He never risked his skin in a forlorn hope, did he?'

'Oh, Lord, he did heaps of silly things,' the doctor cried impatiently. 'He's got enough shrapnel that went deeper than the cuticle to prove it, but that was in the war, in action. This is quite different. Why, he might sit waiting for her till the crack of doom. And even if she did happen to come that way, why, do you suppose, should she take the least notice of him, even if she saw him, if she doesn't want to?'

'I don't suppose she will dare to speak with him, however much she may want to, but, after all, Kinloch will have decided his course not by what I think but by what he himself thinks. And if the woman has worked off her wiles on him, put a spell on him, as I gather is the case, sufficiently well to keep his mouth shut – if this is so then Kinloch will act under the belief that she has a tenderness for him; he will be convinced she would not pass him by without a word when she sees him sitting there.'

Dr Dunn picked up his hat as if to hide what was almost a grin of incredulity.

'It's plausible,' he said, 'but preposterous. No need to fear you will find my friend and drag him into this ugly business.'

'No? Man, doctor, if you saw enough you might well go down on your knees now to pray that I might find him first.'

McNab spoke earnestly as Dunn was moving towards the door.

'First?' he asked, turning round. 'What do you mean by first?'

'Before the other man finds him,' McNab nodded. 'You don't seem to see that Kinloch has himself gone back into this ugly business – gone back into it after being got out of it. Why? Ah, you know I'm not so sure that Kinloch is mistaken if he thinks the lady has developed a tenderness for him. That sort of thing does happen. You will know the story we in Scotland tell about the woman who went out for wool and came home shorn.'

Dunn at the door shook his head.

'You're too fanciful for me. She needn't have left him if that were true,' he said, offering McNab his hand.

'There were probably a dozen good reasons why she had to leave him. And mark this' – McNab held on to the other's hand – 'perhaps to her the strongest reason of all was that she saw herself beginning to care for him.' ... McNab hesitated for a breath or two. 'You seem to care something for him yourself, doctor, if one may judge by all you have done and said. Very well, that ought to help you to believe in the possibility that another may do the like.'

Dr Dunn left, forgetful of my presence in the room. At any rate he didn't trouble to say goodbye to me. When McNab returned after letting him out he threw himself as if exhausted into the big, low Minty chair.

'You didn't get much change out of him,' I said.

'Did I give him anything to change?'

'No. On the contrary you seemed to succeed in taking something from him.'

'What was that?'

'A load off his mind.'

McNab, not at all stung by my sarcasm, crossed his outstretched legs and lay back with a prodigious yawn.

'That was one of the things I wanted to remove,' he said. 'But it wasn't the only thing I got.'

This took me aback. I had to consider for a moment.

'Then you were just bluffing as to how you meant to get your hands on this fellow Kinloch?'

He sat up with a jerk.

'You don't think he thought that?'

'Heavens, no! He's quite a simple soul. He took it for gospel truth.'

He sank back in relief.

'So it was, Chance, gospel truth. I intend to work the West End for Kinloch tomorrow, and I expect to find him exactly as I described. But what puzzles me most is why Dunn laughed as he did when he heard my scheme. A little amusement I could understand. But he was almost mirthful. Why? I want to think it all out alone. All he said, Chance, and all he didn't say. But above all I want to apprehend why Dr Peter Dunn thought my scheme so very amusing. But come round here tomorrow about noon; I shall have the machinery in motion by then. And tell Matheson I shall be keeping you busy all day.'

So, though there were many questions I wanted to put, I left him alone with the question he had put to himself, about Dunn's laugh, which he found strange. Even clever men, I'm told, have their stupid moments. Anyhow I was sure this was one of Francis McNab's moments of dullness; for a more wild-cat scheme by which to discover a missing man I had never heard.

XVI

On going round to the Adelphi next day I found McNab busy with the telephone. When I entered he turned with the receiver at his ear and motioned me to take a seat. He did a lot of listening after that; but occasionally his voice responded to someone.

'Yes, sergeant. That's exactly what I mean – any peculiarity about the man. Eh? ... No, anything that would make him seem in any way different from the usual blind man, anything exceptional about him that would catch the eye of an attentive constable.'

A long pause followed.

'Oh . . . He noticed that. Howley is the constable's name. Sharp fellow, yes. All right. Is he on duty now? ... Comes off for dinner at one? Ring me up when he comes in.'

He hung up the receiver and turned to me.

'That means we have a whole hour to wait. More time lost. And it took longer than I thought,' he remarked, offering me a cigarette.

'What did?'

'Getting round all the stations.'

I was astounded.

'Mean to say you're going to look up all the blind men in London?'

'No; only those who have a pitch for reading, and even among them only those who have appeared inside the last month.' He took so deep a pull at his cigarette that I saw the little red ring run along the paper. 'Seen three already. None of them the man we're looking for. But several possibles remain.'

That reminded me and gave me an opening.

'McNab, how did you come to know about Kinloch? Remember, so far I've heard nothing of that.'

He regarded me almost with reproach in silence.

'Do you know what Matheson calls you, Chance?' he asked.

'No.'

'Matheson calls you my jackal.'

'Like his rotten cheek!'

'It is, my son, for as a jackal you're a rotten failure.'

The unexpected sledgehammer blow knocked me speechless. As I sat there tingling McNab, producing his pocket-book, extracted a press cutting.

'Didn't I trust you to bring me all advertisements for men missing since the 5th of January?' he demanded. 'How did you come to overlook this?' As he spoke the telephone rang, and laying the slip on my knee he jumped to his feet and crossed the room.

At first as I read the slip I was quite sure I had passed it on to him. It was headed Alexander David Kinloch, which explained why the name had seemed vaguely familiar to me when McNab had startled the doctor with it the previous day. But as I read my heart fell again, for in it were the words, 'last seen at Ealing on the night of Monday, 15 January.' And these were words I could never have forgotten. Yet I felt certain I had given McNab a cutting headed with Kinloch's name. Then I saw just what had caused me to miss this advertisement for Kinloch. I had read no further than the man's name and, knowing that I had already passed the thing on, assumed that its terms remained unchanged.

When I had finished my fervent excuses McNab emitted a grunt of indignation.

'Fortunately I didn't entirely trust to you, and had a look at the papers myself. But possibly you can now see something I did get out of Dunn yesterday. Of course after seeing that advertisement you missed I had the office of that firm kept under observation. And we were soon able to establish the identity of the professional-looking man who called there more often than anyone else. The discovery that he was an Ealing doctor formed a coincidence. But it might well be no more than a coincidence, just as it might be a mere coincidence that this man Kinloch was last seen in Ealing on the night of the Ealing murder. For, after all, a man who intended to disappear on some particular date would not be likely to postpone his purpose just because a murder chanced to happen on the day he had chosen. And of course I had no means of compelling this firm, Selwyn & Smith, to disclose the nature of their business with either Kinloch or Dr Dunn. Therefore what I had to ascertain was, first, whether Dunn's repeated visits to that office had any relation to Kinloch, and, secondly, whether this Kinloch had any connection with the murder. As it happened the second point got settled first, in my own mind anyway.'

McNab produced from his pocket-book the two advertisements for Kinloch, the one I had seen and the one I had missed. Passing them to me he said:

'Look at them and observe the difference. Read together they are significant.'

Alexander David Kinloch will hear something to his advantage by communicating with...

Alexander David Kinloch, last seen at Ealing on the night of Monday, 15 January. Will any person in a position to supply information...

The difference was obvious, the second being much fuller. But when I indicated this McNab showed impatience.

'The significant difference is that the first is addressed directly to Kinloch and the second is not,' he said. 'The second also offers a reward!'

'Well, they would hardly offer him a reward for reporting himself so that he might hear of something to his own advantage,' I objected.

McNab glanced imploringly up at the ceiling.

'In the first the advertisers address Kinloch himself. They hope he will see and read the notice. In the second they no longer expect him to read it. Isn't it quite clear that after the publication of the first advertisement some information has reached them about Kinloch? There's the "last seen in Ealing" to prove that. But what else reached them? Have they now learned either that Kinloch was never taught to read or that he cannot read for some other reason?'

'Because he was blind!' I cried.

'Ah, that possibility is what seemed to bring this Kinloch into closer contact with the murder. If so, all the chances were that I had got the name of the blind man for whom we had been seeking. Then I turned to the first point, which was to ascertain if Dunn's visits to Selwyn and Smith had any connection with Kinloch. This was less easy, for I had absolutely nothing to go on. So I took a shot in the dark, by assuming that what is true of nine-tenths of the blind men in England at this moment would be also true of Kinloch, namely, that his blindness was contracted during war service. Furnished with his full name I went to the War Record Office. Inside half an hour we had traced Kinloch to the seventh battalion of a Scottish regiment in whose ranks he had been thrice wounded. I also got a note of Dr Dunn's war record which showed that his time had been spent in the General Hospital at Boulogne. Here was a possible point of contact between the two men – the thrice wounded soldier and the hospital doctor. Slender as this was, I pushed on with it, ultimately securing the group photograph taken at Hamilton before the battalion left for the Front. And yesterday you saw what happened to Dunn when his eyes fell on Kinloch's face –'

A sharp ring of the telephone interrupted McNab, and in a moment he had the receiver at his ear.

'Yes, it's me, sergeant … All right. Yes, Howley had better speak with me himself… Enderby Gardens you say? Where's that? Kensington? Off Campden Hill Road? Yes … against the garden railings on the north side under an overhanging tree – that right? Good! Now when did you first notice him? … Not more than three weeks ago – you are sure? … Right! Now how does he differ from the usual type? Ah! … only sits there from eleven to one and from three to five ... Yes, that's odd. Eh? ... No, thank you, constable. No questions to him till I turn up, please.'

Ringing off, McNab turned, rubbing his hands.

'I've a notion,' he said softly, 'that you and I will be looking at this Kinloch inside the next thirty minutes.'

*

On our way to Enderby Gardens McNab explained the part he had assigned to me. While I listened I saw he had chosen the one part most easy for me to play. As a journalist I was to interview the man suspected of being Kinloch, getting him to tell his story for my newspaper – the sort of thing I could naturally do to the life. By the time we had settled the details our taxi was turning into Campden Hill Road. Dismissing it at the corner we walked along into Enderby Gardens. And at once we saw our man. He was sitting against the railings on a short three-legged campstool, the usual large volume on his knees. He was visible at quite a distance because the garden side of the square seemed less used than the other which carried the main stream of pedestrians. With a blind man there was less need to take precautions about examining him. So we passed slowly and had as good a look as his bent head permitted. On reaching the far corner McNab stopped.

'That man,' he said, 'is not impossible at least, as the others I saw certainly were.'

'Seems older, more worn than the photograph.'

'He would be. It's eight years since that was taken, and pretty bad years for him. There's his shabby clothes to be discounted too. Go and talk to him. I'll observe from here, for the blind have abnormal hearing and we must raise no suspicion.'

So I sauntered back to him.

'Afternoon. Doing well today?' I asked affably.

His head jerked round. The face was not unlike Kinloch's – harder and thinner certainly. The eyes I could not see, for he never raised them towards me, though I saw they were shut.

'Not particular,' he replied, beginning to rub his fingers as if they were stiff.

'Been at this long?'

'Goodish bit. Five years since I got myself blinded over there in France.'

'What were you before the war?'

He stopped his rubbing.

'Here, is this a game? What you gettin' at?'

It didn't seem worthwhile pushing things further, for Kinloch certainly did not belong to this poor fellow's class. And it was more from pity that I explained the questions were put on behalf of a newspaper interested in disabled soldiers.

'If you could read my card,' I said gently, 'you would see I am on the staff of the *Record* and that my name is Chance.'

A sudden queer, startled cry came from him. The book on his knees fell to the ground.

Stooping forward I picked it up.

'No harm done,' I reassured him.

'You'll – you'll excuse me a-hollering out so,' he stammered breathlessly. 'W – we – have to be very careful with them raised letters. They've only to get a little damp for the fingers to push 'em flat, and then there's no readin' of 'em.'

The explanation seemed natural. And yet I was puzzled. For I could have sworn the cry came before, not after, the book fell. Of course he may have cried out because he felt the book slipping from his knees. Besides, why should the mention of my name startle him: he never could have heard of me before.

'Where were you before the war?' I repeated.

'What was I before the war? Why, a bricklayer is what I was. And a good un, mister, sure as me name is Dick 'Ollins.'

'You seem to be quite good at the Braille too.'

'That ain't no catch. Good or bad, nobody listens, really. And you just think, mister, on the wages what bricklayers is getting these days, now I'm out of it. But, there, I never 'ad much in the way of luck – not what you'd call luck.'

His tone had turned lachrymose, almost a whine. I could tell what was coming. Hastily I planked down half a crown on his book and with a mumbled wish for better luck soon went off to rejoin McNab. I felt sorry for McNab. Once more his hopes were doomed. And great was his disappointment as he listened to my report of the interview. For he stood regarding Dick 'Ollins, whose monotonous reading was again audible, regarding him with an expression of misery mingled with despair.

*

That night to cheer him up and divert his mind I took him round to the Little Theatre. It was the Grand Guignol season, but for all that my effort failed. When we got back to his flat, his spirits still clouded, he sat staring in silence at the large woodcut of one John Knox by name, which hung over the fireplace. McNab's walls were hung with old prints of criminal trials and criminals, but the place of honour went to this one, which depicted a long-bearded man with terrible eyes and a Scotch cap on his head.

But it was a thinking cap McNab had on his own head that night. At last he broke the long silence.

'Chance, I'm not at all satisfied about that man.'

'John Knox?' I said, for lying back in his chair he still stared up at the portrait.

'No, Dick Hollins. I'm not satisfied that is his name, and still less that he ever was a bricklayer. Why does he sit there from eleven to one and from three to five only? That's a peculiarity that even the constable on the beat noticed, and it hasn't yet been explained. It may be he moves to another pitch, but that is not the custom. And a bricklayer! Did you observe his hands? Oh, yes, I know; it must be years since he laid a brick, no doubt. But I'm not thinking of the whiteness of his hands, but of the slenderness of his fingers. A pickpocket perhaps. A bricklayer – no!'

'He doesn't seem to be the man we're looking for, anyhow.'

'No, he does not seem to be,' McNab agreed.

'But then if he were Kinloch he would hardly want to seem that. Anyway,' he nodded, 'we'll try to make quite certain about him tomorrow.'

And the next morning McNab assuredly did his best. When I called for him about ten I was told by the housekeeper he had left word that I was to wait his return.

'He's had to go round to the Yard,' Janet confided in admitting me.

'Scotland Yard?' I said in surprise, wondering if something fresh had suddenly developed.

'Ay, Scotland Yard,' Janet assented, flicking imaginary dust off a chair before I occupied it. 'It's a verra queer name to give to a place in the heart o' London.'

'Your master told me once it's because there's more brains to the yard there than in any other English mile.'

'Did he so, Mr. Chance? Well, that's no what he tell't me when I asked him.'

'What did he tell you?'

'He said it was called Scotland Yard because it was so full of inquisitive old women.'

'That would be when he was annoyed with the Yard.'

'Or with me,' she grinned, shutting the door.

Left alone I began to wonder what had taken McNab to the Yard that morning, and whether he would return satisfied or annoyed with them. But I had not long to wait before hearing the metallic click of his latchkey in the outer door. And a glance at his face revealed his satisfaction. He only thrust his head inside the room, but I saw he was pleased with the Yard that morning.

'Ah!' he greeted me. 'You've come. Good! Taxi at the door. Come on; I can explain on the way.'

And before we reached the corner where Enderby Gardens joins Campden Hill Road he had made me familiar with my part.

'We have a trick to play on him. But if he turns out to be Kinloch he must suspect nothing or the game is up.'

'And what if he turns out to be Dick Hollins?'

'Then it won't matter what he thinks. If you are convinced he is Dick Hollins that is all the better, for you are to talk to him as if you had no doubts. You talk to him as you did yesterday, like a press man. The only difference this time is that I am coming close up to inspect him. That's all, I think.'

We left the taxi at the corner and walked along the short bottleneck entrance that brought us opposite the gardens. From the pavement on the south side, much the more frequented, we could see the suspected Dick Hollins crouching on his three-legged stool, his book on his knees. He was, indeed, visible for a considerable distance, for the pavement had but few pedestrians, mostly nursemaids and their charges strolling towards the entrance to the gardens to which our man had his back.

For perhaps twenty minutes McNab studied the man from every angle, as we passed up and down, and if he detected anything strange or unusual in him it was more than I did. When we paused finally exactly opposite him, his voice came quite audibly across the road, and McNab stood with his ear turned to the voice, closing his eyes, as I noted, like someone striving to hear a distant melody. Whether he detected any falsity in the man's voice, or a pronunciation of a word that was too refined to belong to a genuine bricklayer I could not tell. It all sounded just right to my ears.

Hollins was reading from the book of Psalms, awkward pauses in his voice, as he fingered away at his raised letters.

Here is the passage exactly reproduced as he read it:

Wy . .. 'op ... ye so . .. ye 'igh 'ills?

This .. . is .. . th' Lord's ... 'ill ... in wich ... it pleas ... eth ... 'im ... ter ... dwell.

To me it seemed all plain, straightforward Cockney. And yet as I watched McNab listening I saw something like the ghost of a smile appear on his face. And since I could not suppose him likely to be pleased to discover that Hollins was as genuine as he looked, I felt certain McNab's ear had taken in something suspicious to which I had been deaf. My eye went again to Hollins. A queer figure he made, sitting hunched up on his stool, his chin elevated so grotesquely while he read that I might have thought him impudently regarding us through half-closed eyes, had I not known he was sightless.

Quietly McNab took my arm.

'Now for the "close up". Talk as yesterday. But mark this: when I go behind him you are to get his hat off somehow. Knock it off if you can't think of some pretence. You can be clumsy enough. Then till I am finished with his head, retain the hat, pretending to brush off the dust. When I am done, get him to read aloud. But above all he must have no suspicion of my presence. Got that?'

McNab finished by a gentle push, and I stepped across the road to where the blind man sat.

'Morning, Mr. Hollins. You don't remember me perhaps,' I added as he hesitated over my greeting.

'Yes I do. You're the newspaper gentleman again.'

'You don't forget voices then?'

Mr. Hollins chuckled.

'Not when they comes into me ears along o' 'arf a crown as yours done yesterday.'

McNab stepped behind him like a cat.

'And your fingers are as good as eyes, aren't they? I'd like to try what my fingers make of those letters. May I?' Giving him no time to reply I bent forward and with the hand I did not lay on his book, lightly swept off his hat. With an apology for my clumsiness I stooped to pick it up. And then while pretending to flick the dust off I watched McNab. He was holding something close to the man's head. I saw what it was – a small wisp of dark hair. Then I understood why he had been to Scotland Yard. This was part, at least, of the hair found in the room at Ealing. The comparison lasted but a second. Almost as soon as

I realised McNab's purpose he had the wisp back into its glass tube and out of sight. I replaced the hat. McNab gave me a curt nod.

'Better let me see your own fingers at work,' I said. 'Do you mind?'

'Mind? Of course not. I'm often asked to do it,' Hollins replied, putting up his hands to readjust the position of his hat. The act made me smile, for every man has to do that when another puts a hat on his head, even when that other is his wife. This act McNab had apparently counted on, for in a flash he had placed a sheet of paper, taken from where I never saw, upon the volume on Hollins' knees. But the moment the blind man's fingers went back to his book he instantly detected the interposed paper, drew his hands away as if he had been stung, and his sightless eyelids lifted.

'What's that?' he whispered, lowering his hands, gingerly, to feel. McNab, however, had already flicked away his sheet of paper.

'Felt queer it did – all spongy like. Ain't been no water dropping on the book, 'as there?' Hollins queried, bewildered.

'Must have been something on your fingers,' I said. 'There's nothing on your book.'

'It certainly feels all right now,' he admitted.

What Hollins read to me I do not know. My eyes followed McNab, who was walking lightly away. But I had to wait till the reader stopped, for he must have no suspicions. Somehow or other I took leave of Hollins, his blessings following me after I slipped another half crown into his hand. McNab was waiting round the corner. He seemed pleased with himself.

'That, I should think,' he said, 'is the first time a man's fingerprints have been *taken* from him without his knowledge.'

But adroitly as the trick had been worked I knew McNab's quiet elation must spring from something other than a sense of his own cleverness. To have taken the fingerprints of Dick Hollins without Dick Hollins being aware of what had happened would never have brought that gleam into McNab's eyes. Only a very decided advance achieved in a troublesome case could have done that, I reflected as we hurried away. At the corner of Bayswater Road McNab hailed a passing taxi. While we stood waiting I found my voice.

'So the blind man isn't Dick Hollins?'

'No, no more Hollins than you are Holofernes,' McNab said.

'But if he is –'

'Hush!' He cut me short as the taxi swung in to the kerb.

XVII

There was no mistaking the certainty in McNab's voice. And the suddenness with which I perceived he felt assured that the disguised man was Kinloch left me breathless. All the way along Bayswater Road I kept trying to get a grasp of this fact and what it would mean in the development of the case. For, if McNab were right, we were on the eve of many discoveries.

How he had penetrated the man's disguise I could not imagine. The man's voice sounded, as I have said, genuine Cockney to my ear. And the comparison of his hair with the wisp found in the room at Ealing, exactly alike in shade as McNab may have found it, was far from conclusive evidence. Dark hair is not so uncommon as all that. And the fingerprints could not be the basis of his certainty, for he had not had time to examine them, much less compare them with those left on the broken glass found in the room after the murder. To make the comparison McNab would have to visit the fingerprint bureau at Scotland Yard.

It will be recalled that McNab considered the fingerprints on the broken glass might possibly be those of Kinloch and not – as Inspector Snargrove held – those of the murderer. On this question I found myself, to my regret, again forced to agree with Snargrove's view, though for other reasons than those which had weighed with him. My argument was that Kinloch being blind would be ever so much less likely to find the tumbler on Ponsonby Paget's table than the murderer, who had eyes to see it. But this quite rational view McNab brushed aside by saying that though he could not see the whisky or the glass I must remember Kinloch was a Scotsman and still had a nose. This, of course, was mere jesting, the sort of thing he said when he for some reason wished to conceal from me the real grounds which had forced him to a specific conclusion. All the same I saw that, if McNab now went to Scotland Yard with a set of fingerprints the duplicates of those already on their books in connection with this case, he was likely to be met by questions which could not be turned aside by a jest. Where had he got those prints which were those of a man wanted for the Ealing murder? Why, it would set Scotland Yard buzzing like a wasps' nest. But if the two sets did not coincide, what had McNab to gain from those fingerprints? Nothing that I could see. For, if no separate set of Kinloch's impressions existed, those taken from the ostensible Dick Hollins that day were useless: they could not prove that Dick Hollins and Alexander David Kinloch were one and the same person. And it mystified me more than ever to remember that McNab was sure the two were one even before he took the fingerprints.

But I was not yet convinced Hollins was a fraud. So, as the taxi pulled up in a traffic block at Marble Arch I said as much to McNab, bluntly too, to draw him out of his contented silence. He turned to me, laying a hand on my knee.

'You must learn to be a better observer, my son. It's almost as essential in your own profession as in mine. An observer is what few are. Most folk have sight but few have insight.' He paused before adding, as if quoting from someone: ' "They look on what I look on but they see not what I see." That is why they need such aids to apprehension as journalists and detectives.'

He spoke with seriousness, but his adroit double use of the word apprehension made me smile.

'You've been a first rate jackal to me this day,' he resumed. 'I was anxious the man should not hear my voice just yet, nor even know another person was there. But you kept all his wits riveted on yourself. And you showed him you believed he was what he affected to be.'

'Because I did believe it. His Cockney accent appeared perfect.'

'Oh, but the Cockney accent is easy – a mere matter of changing "a" into "y" and saying fyce for face – that sort of thing. But behind the Cockney accent is the Cockney idiom, a very different matter. And this man's idioms were all wrong.'

'Give me an example,' I said as the policeman's extended arm was lowered and we began to move again.

'Take this one, then. You remember his saying to you that he never forgets voices when they come into his ears along o' 'arf a crown? That "along o'" was wrong. He used it in the sense of "together with". But in the East End you will find "along o' " means "because of". A wife beater will tell the magistrate it was "along of her tongue" as an excuse. So this fellow I was certain was no true Cockney.

'And this matter of the idiom did not stand alone. There was, again, his rendering of that passage from his book. Yes, it was well done. As Cockney English you might think it perfect unless you were, like myself, very suspicious. But for all that he blundered badly.'

'Will you tell me where? I, too, was on the watch and detected nothing.'

'It was very obvious. He put in the r in reading the word "Lord".'

'But,' I objected, 'there *is* an r in the word "Lord".'

'True. But no Cockney sounds it.' McNab laughed. 'All you English now treat that letter r as if it were an intruder from Scotland. You try to cold-shoulder it out. You deny it? Very well, take this same word "Lord". You attend the Law Courts, don't you? Tell me, did you ever hear Counsel address the judge otherwise than "m'lud"? And you go to church too.'

'Not so often.'

'Often enough to know that the parson, like the generality of you, says "Laud" for " Lo-r-rd",' McNab snapped. And as I turned to protest he added with a laugh: 'Oh, I dare say you *think* you sound the r, but it is an illusion on your par-rt. But there was no illusion about the blind man's r, which you heard yourself, no doubt.'

'Yes, he put in about three in the one word,' I said mischievously.

'So you would think. But he did nothing of the sort. He put in one with just the right distinctness and precision to prove to me that he was not only no Cockney but also that he was no Englishman.'

'And the colour of the hair convinced you he was Kinloch?'

'The texture more than the colour; there's more variation in texture than in colour. I put that wisp found in the room at Ealing close to his head and found a perfect match both in colour and texture. But that wasn't all. While you had his hat in your hands it was possible for me to examine the man's head. You remember the photograph of Kinloch in uniform? It showed him wearing the glengarry bonnet which, more than any other headgear, allows one to see the wearer's forehead. This was very fortunate, for the forehead is the most changeless feature of the human face, more so even than the eyes, which of course I could not see. Then as I looked at his forehead I regarded the identity as established. In configuration, shape, in the way in which the hair followed the contour of the temples and arched up to the broad straight forehead I knew the truth – this was my man at last!'

There was a glow in his eyes as he finished, and a hint of colour in his usually pale face. His feeling of triumph was stronger than he usually permitted it to be; and I did not wonder, for he had met with many checks in this most baffling case.

As we neared the *Record* office where he was to drop me I asked about his next move.

'What are you going to do about him?'

'Kinloch?'

'Yes. He may refuse to tell you anything, or he may tell you a faked-up story.'

'I'm not going to ask him anything. I'll leave him unquestioned where he is, roosting on that stool. He knows his chances of making contact with those he wishes to meet better than we do. He isn't sitting there for the fun of the thing. So we'll let him sit, and see what comes of it. He will serve admirably as bait, the unconscious bait, for the bigger fish we have yet to land.'

'But you intend to have him watched?'

'Of course. That will be fixed up inside the next hour. Two gardeners will be hoeing and weeding the beds behind him, a painter will be at work on the gate close up on his right, and if you happen to pass that way before five tonight you will find a match-seller has stationed himself under the overhanging tree five yards to the left. Come, here you are,' he said, throwing open the door as the taxi drew up at the office.

Reluctantly I got out. There was so much more I wanted to learn.

But Matheson saw to it that I did not learn more that night. Matheson had lately become rather soured over the case. It had been of little value to the paper so far. 'The blind looking for the blind,' he muttered one day after questioning me about our progress. I could have told him enough to whet his keenness, but my lips were sealed, since the secrets were not mine but McNab's, at whose service Matheson himself had placed me. Indeed, towards the end of the case, I felt that to be between Matheson and McNab was like being between the devil and the deep sea. Matheson naturally was all for publicity while McNab's instincts inclined him to closeness. So it was pull devil, pull baker, with myself between the pair. And that night Matheson had the pull, for as soon as my news job was complete he gave me, before he himself left, enough other work to tie me up till after midnight. And all the time McNab, I knew, was out there, putting the last touches to the trap by which he meant to make his big capture.

But about nine o'clock, a few minutes after I had resigned myself to go on with work our most inexpert junior could have done equally well, I was called to the telephone. It was McNab. And the moment I heard his voice it was apparent that something fresh was in the wind.

'That you, Chance? Come round at once. Something has happened.'

'What?' I asked involuntarily, forgetting that he would not tell me over the telephone. But to my surprise he breathed the words:

'*She has seen him.*'

For the moment I did not realise what this meant.

'Do you mean Kin –'

'Yes. Come now. I'm expecting Howley every minute.'

Promptly I handed over my work to the inexpert junior. As I hurried round to the Adelphi I remembered that Howley was the name of the smart constable who had spoken to McNab over the telephone about the blind reader he had noticed in Enderby Gardens.

He had not come when I arrived, but McNab soon told me as much as he himself knew. He had, it appeared, just come in when Howley rang him up from the police station. Almost apologetically the officer said that as we had questioned him about the blind man in Enderby Gardens we might perhaps care to know that some others seemed also interested in him. At first McNab thought Inspector Snargrove had got on the right clue at last, or that his own watchers had been clumsy; but, when Howley informed him a lady seemed to be in it, the startling truth came out. There had been an incident, a very curious incident close to the blind man's pitch, which had called for the constable's intervention. Howley said he was approaching the Gardens from the west about 12.30 when he heard a cry, a woman's cry, and coming nearer, saw a lady leaning against the garden railings half supported by a man who appeared to have been accompanying her. A few people had gathered round the couple. Howley assisted the man to get her into a passing taxi, in which they drove off, the lady in a state of collapse.

'But where does the blind man come in?' I asked.

'I couldn't quite follow Howley there. That's chiefly why I asked him to come along. But notice the time the incident happened – 12.30, about two hours *before* we ourselves saw him and took his fingerprints. That's the curious feature. Of course it's possible it was merely a coincidence that the lady took a faint turn just there. And I gathered from Howley that no sort of communication passed between the blind man and the pair. Kinloch certainly would not see what was happening. Still, that is all the more reason why we must ascertain what led Howley to associate the lady's faint with the blind man. There's this other circumstance. At 8.35 Jenkins – he's the match-seller – rang me up to say he's just returned from shadowing the blind man to his lodgings in Hollis Street. Jenkins was inclined to be sore about it. I had led him to believe his job would be finished by five, whereas the man had stayed on his pitch till almost eight. That is another fact that makes it necessary for us to see Howley. For, if this extension of time from five to eight is exceptional, it is highly significant when taken in conjunction with the incident earlier in the day.'

'Looks as if he expected her to come back.'

'Certainly, if this extra long stay of his turns out to be exceptional. And it looks as if we had got at Kinloch in the nick of time. Another day and it might have been too late. We have got him all right though. He cannot escape. Day and night he will be under perpetual surveillance; and his blindness makes that an easy job.'

'You have set an all-night watch on his lodgings?'

'Better than that – something less conspicuous. My match-seller is in the same lodging house, probably in the next bed to his.'

Just when I was thinking how easy it all was and how impossible for a blind man to escape in such circumstances, or even to be aware he was under observation, there came a knock at the door, and Howley was ushered in.

The constable was a fresh-complexioned, clear-eyed fellow, of the usual well-set-up build, and though now in his off duty clothes, there was no mistaking what his duty was. Sitting bolt upright on the extreme edge of a chair he related the facts already given, and it was not till McNab began to question him that anything fresh was elicited.

'What made you suppose the lady had any interest in the blind man?' McNab asked.

'Well, chiefly it was the way she kept looking at him over the gentleman's shoulder while I was helping to get her into the taxi.'

'She seemed unwilling to go?'

'Yes. And yet she kept staring at the man as if he had been a ghost, as you might say. So I asked the gentleman if he had any complaint to lodge against the man.'

'What did he reply?'

'He did not reply – he just smiled.'

'Did you form any idea as to the relationship of the lady and gentleman? Did you think they were, for instance, husband and wife?'

Howley fidgeted momentarily.

'Well, sir, at the time questions like that didn't enter my mind; but I can say they were on intimate terms, for she used his Christian name.'

'Oh! What was it?' McNab inquired.

'She addressed him as Sandy. Several times she said quite low, "Oh, Sandy," like that; almost into his ear, as she looked along at the blind man as if she was frightened.'

Swiftly McNab exchanged a glance with me.

'Ah, I see.' There was disappointment in his tone. Then he added: 'And the blind man, do you think he overheard her?'

Howley was surprised.

'Oh, no, the name wasn't more than whispered. And, although my attention was given to the lady, I had my eye on the blind man just then, thinking he might have annoyed them as they passed him. The man had stopped reading and had turned his face our way. Though of course he could not see he was no doubt aware from the noise of feet on the pavement that something was happening close to him, for he seemed to be listening hard too.'

'A dramatic moment that, eh, Chance?' McNab nodded meaningly to me.

And if, as now seemed proved, he was right about the blind man being Kinloch in search of the lady, it certainly was a thrilling situation.

'Tell me, constable,' McNab said after a long pause, 'are you certain no communication passed between the blind man and the lady?'

The question obviously amazed Howley.

'Not after I arrived. What happened before I cannot say. The incident lasted no more than a couple of minutes or so before they went off in the taxi.'

'Did you hear what address the gentleman gave to the driver?'

'I did, sir. It was 3 Brook Street, Belgravia.'

McNab drew the writing pad towards him as he sat down at the table. Howley seemed to be developing increasing surprise and some uneasiness at the minuteness with which he was being questioned. But, from the almost nonchalant way in which McNab pulled the writing pad across, not even I could have guessed that he was writing down the first definite address obtained in connection with the Ealing murder.

'And the taxi's number?' he inquired.

But this Howley had not observed. In response to McNab's lifted eyebrows he explained that he had been too busy in getting the lady into the taxi and in keeping back the inquisitive onlookers to notice the number. This looked like one of our old checks till Howley, looking up from the contemplation of his boots, hesitated the suggestion that he could obtain the number since he knew from a recent case in which he had been concerned the driver belonging to a rank at the top of Campden Hill Road. McNab picked up his pencil again, and down went the particulars the officer supplied. While these were being taken I got hold of the London Directory and turned up Brook Street, Belgravia. It was, I discovered, a short residential street behind Grosvenor Place, and the occupier of number three was given as Christopher Agate, M.D. Accepting the hint I next opened McNab's copy of the Medical Directory and learnt that Agate, after studying in London, had graduated M.B. at Cambridge in 1903, joined the R.A.M.C., served in India, in 1909 contributing to the *B.M.J.* a series of articles on military hygiene.

But I pulled up in the act of transcribing all this information on hearing McNab say:

'And now, constable, I am sure you can supply a pretty accurate description of the gentleman and the lady?'

Howley could. There had been nothing to distract his attention from them. And he had got the particulars entered in his notebook. As his big hand went to his pocket, and fishing out the book he began to turn the pages, my pulse suddenly quickened. Now, at last, we were to have a glimpse of the hidden man, the actual criminal. Howley found the page and cleared his throat.

'Height about 5 feet 11 inches. Age between 35 and 40; pale complexion, dark, quick-moving eyes, and dark hair with close clipped moustache; features regular, small tight-lipped mouth; figure upright, looks like soldier in mufti; wearing smartly cut brown suit and soft hat to match.'

As Howley looked up from his book to see, I suppose, if this conveyed anything to us, I was sure McNab was silently visualising the man. On that there came back to my memory a thing McNab had said to Matheson in the office – that he had no doubt the murderer was a man in a high social position and that probably his portrait had more than once appeared in our columns. But if McNab made an identification from the officer's description it was more than I could do. The description failed to be sufficiently individual. It would have fitted hundreds, and if helpful at all it was so more from those it excluded than from anyone at whom it definitely pointed. McNab himself did not appear to find much help from the description to judge from the way he sat, hunched up in thought, frowning, elbows on knees, and with his long, thin fingers thrust into his much ruffled hair.

'And the woman?' he said at length.

Howley hesitated, rubbing his square chin as he eyed his notebook doubtfully.

'I had a good look at her of course,' he said, 'but I've made no entry. In her excited state it's difficult to say what she is usually like. Even her height, for example, sir – it's hard to judge a female's height when she is half-leaning against another person.'

McNab nodded.

'Just shut your eyes, and describe her as you see her.'

Howley at least contemplated the toes of his boots through lowered lids.

'Young,' he pronounced, 'tallish but of slender build, wearing a navy blue costume and small hat with light stockings.'

'And her looks?'

'She looked ill – like what I've already said, as if she had seen a ghost.'

'Yes, but normally would she be considered, well, fine looking?'

'Oh, she was certainly of prepossessing appearance.'

McNab smiled at this.

'That tells us little – prepossessing appearance. I've often wondered whether the police got that phrase from the reporters or the reporters got it from the police. Just tell me what her points were: eyes, nose, mouth, hair, voice, anything distinctive or peculiar.'

Howley did not take long over that.

'She had fine eyes. Yes, I remember that, as she stared – brown eyes, very big at that moment, anyhow; and the eyebrows dark. That is why I was surprised at the colour of her hair.'

'What surprised you?'

'Well, sir, in that close-fitting hat you couldn't see her hair. But in getting her into the taxi the hat was displaced, her hair showed, and it was fair hair which she wore long, in coils about her ears, with a square-cut fringe that came almost to her eyebrows.'

'Would you say then that these were her most distinctive characteristics?'

'The colour of her hair and her eyes, yes,' Howley replied with conviction.

'Good. That is all we need, I think.'

McNab rose and Howley heaved himself up, pocketing his notebook.

'I can take it, I suppose, that something lies behind this?' he asked doubtfully.

McNab preceded him to the door.

'Something very serious may lie behind it,' he replied, taking him by the arm. 'If it does, you can take it that your work will not go unmentioned nor unrewarded.'

When the door closed on P.C. Howley, McNab flung himself into the big wicker chair. He seemed tired. I passed him the note I made on Dr Agate.

'Ah, that will keep,' he said with a yawn of weariness. 'It may be useful, but I doubt if that taxi ever reached this address. The man who carried out the murder with such foresight was not likely to give away such a clue at such an awkward moment in the hearing of a policeman and almost in the presence of Kinloch. That, you'll allow, was hardly the moment for such a man to make a slip. Still' – he glided the paper into his pocket – 'I'll see the taxi man in the morning and verify that.'

'And those fingerprints – have you verified them yet?'

'I have. Those I took from Kinloch do not coincide with those found on the glass.' Lying back he put his hands lazily behind his head. 'Queer how the value of a thing changes with a change in a situation. Once I hoped the two sets of impressions would coincide. But when I had no need to be certain Hollins is Kinloch, my hope was that the two sets would not coincide. For if those at the Yard were not Kinloch's fingerprints they must be those of the murderer, and in themselves they will be enough to hang him. Yes, our work is nearly over. Anyway, there's nothing more you can do tonight, laddie.'

Seeing what he meant I got to my feet, picking up my hat.

'And – tomorrow?' I asked.

'Tomorrow,' he said, 'the teeth of the trap will close on him.'

The grim certainty in the quietly uttered word arrested me. That McNab regarded tomorrow as the end of his work on the Ealing murder was clear. And my thoughts flew back to the beginning. For the man on whom the trap would close tomorrow would go to his doom merely because this other man now lying with legs crossed in that chair had happened to observe the unusual manner in which the end of a walking stick had been worn away. It staggered me to think of it. Everything that had followed, and that which was to follow tomorrow, would have, as it were, *emerged* from the end of a blind man's stick!

So seeing this miracle in the art of observation, I had not the least shadow of doubt as to what would happen tomorrow. The woman, as McNab counted on, would undoubtedly come back to rescue Kinloch from the wretched plight in which she had unexpectedly found him. For obviously Howley's account supported McNab's inference that the woman had at least pity if not a warmer feeling for the blind man with whom she had lived. She would come back – alone, next time. All Howley had reported was the warrant for that. She would come. Kinloch had all along counted on her coming; and he had been right. And she would walk straight into the open trap. But another thought came as I turned to go, and I addressed the back of McNab's head.

'At what hour will the arrest be made?'

'That is not in my hands,' he replied. 'The lady will doubtless choose her own time for visiting Enderby Gardens.' He broke off with a laugh. 'Oh, I see what you mean. You want another "exclusive" for the Friday *Record*, and so you would prefer the arrest to be rather late at night.'

'If possible. Matheson has spent a lot on the case.'

'Well, I'm not likely to be in a position to swear an information before tomorrow evening, if that's any comfort to you. So at least the evening papers will get nothing. But after that the control will be in Snargrove's hands.'

'Snargrove?' I cried.

'Of course. I have no power to arrest the man. When I have sworn my information and led the inspector and his men to the door with the warrant in his pocket my work is finished.'

'And Snargrove steps into the limelight!'

'Yes. He takes that notoriety off me. A sore handicap for a detective it is to be well known. To be able to remain unknown is almost the one asset the private agent has over the official. But keep your mind easy about the other newspapers. No other paper will contain more than a mention of the arrest, if as much.' He waved me away. 'So go home and get to work on those columns for your Friday's issue. That will provide England with another sensation.'

And that is what I set about doing the moment I got home. It was somewhere about three in the morning when I dropped into bed.

But I had no mind to miss getting the full story of the actual arrest. Therefore I was on McNab's doorstep by 10.30 that morning. We went out to Enderby Gardens together. Alighting at the Campden Hill Road corner we walked along towards the square, the centre of which was occupied by the Gardens. McNab was quietly elated, but I fancy my own excitement was not equally well controlled. He pointed out how admirably the place adapted itself to our purpose – a quiet, smallish square with just one rather narrow road leading into it and another leading out into the road beyond.

'We may have to wait for hours, you know,' he said. 'But there's a seat inside the garden gate where we can sit and smoke at our ease without attracting attention. And,' he added with a chuckle, 'if we run out of matches there will be a match-seller at our elbow just outside the gate.'

'You seem very sure she will come.'

'Very sure. So, it would appear, was Kinloch when he chose his pitch. And who could doubt it after hearing Howley's account of the incident yesterday? Evidently she wanted to speak to Kinloch then when she saw him sitting there as a blind beggar. As evidently the man bustled her into the taxi to prevent that. Howley described him as pale. I bet the gentleman was – at that moment. Think of it! He found himself unexpectedly within ten feet of the man who could denounce him as the murderer, an excited woman on his hands, and a policeman at his elbow. Nerve? Yes, the fellow must have nerves of steel. Lucky for him that Kinloch, though a fraud as Dick Hollins, was no fraud as a blind man.'

'So he could not know either of them by sight,' I interjected.

'Quite true, but Kinloch counted on her speaking to him when she was startled to see him sitting there as a beggar. He had, no doubt, his own reasons for that belief, and what happened yesterday proves that his belief was well founded.' He looked at me quizzically as we walked on. 'You don't know much about the ways of women yet. When a woman has made up what she would call her mind to do a thing, do it she will. You might stop her once, you might stop her twice, but sooner or later when you have to think of something else, or are only looking the other way –'

The words ended in a sudden, queer gasp, and he pulled up short, catching at my arm. As I looked round he pointed with the other hand. We had by this time advanced sufficiently far along the road to open out a view of the gardens in the square. As usual the south pavement showed a fair number of pedestrians coming and going, but the north, next the gardens, was empty enough to let us see even at that distance that Kinloch was not there.

'I don't see Jenkins, either,' McNab said, 'nor Peters,' he added as he began running towards the gardens.

McNab reached the spot ahead of me. I had no idea he could sprint so fast. But a closer inspection of the spot yielded some information. Of Jenkins and his matches there was indeed no trace, nor of Roberts and Pilcher, the two who should have been weeding and hoeing inside the railings. And of Peters' presence there was just the evidence given by the green paint on a length of these same railings. We could see where he had left off – halfway down one of the bars, the upper being a brilliant fresh green, the lower colourless and rusty, with the half-filled pot at its foot. But all that we saw afterwards. What took the eye first was the blind man's three-legged stool standing there unoccupied, with the blind man's big book lying face downward on the pavement. McNab's four men had vanished, and the man they were watching.

After surveying the scene for a moment with narrowed eyes McNab stepped up to the railings and, touching the paint, regarded his fingertips.

'Still quite fluid,' he murmured. 'It can only just have happened.' Then, indicating how close the stool was to the point at which the painting had stopped, he said: 'Peters got his chance, anyhow.'

But I could see McNab was gravely perturbed.

XVIII

McNab said nothing for a long time. He stood gazing, hands clasped loosely behing his back, at the various articles and implements which had been abruptly abandoned by the blind man and the men set to watch him. One or two pedestrians, seeing him thus absorbed, cast half curious eyes on him as they passed, glancing about to see what attracted his attention. McNab did not seem to like what he saw. When at length he turned to me with a question there was a quiver, a nervous sort of quiver about the corners of his mouth.

'Well, Godfrey,' he said, 'what do you make of it?'

'Your bait's been taken,' I hazarded.

He nodded gravely.

'No nibbling at it this time. Swallowed, and carried away.'

'And presently your men will come back and tell us where it was taken to. All according to plan, isn't it?' I asked.

'I hope so,' he rejoined slowly. 'I hope so. Still, something my men didn't expect to happen has happened here. They were certainly taken by surprise.' His eyes travelled over the place again. 'Look at Peters' brush. It dropped handle downwards out of his hand into the pot. And he was wearing an apron. Did he follow them in that? It isn't anywhere about. The hoe, too, looks as if it had been dropped in the midst of a stroke; and Pilcher appears to have gone off still wearing his weeding gloves, though he has left his cap behind.' McNab indicated the cap, which I now perceived lying under a shrub on the dark mould inside the railings.

'Something took them unawares,' he said.

He gazed up and down the road. As usual, our side had little on it except nurses with perambulators and a few toddling children. And on the busier side, if any in that stream had witnessed anything startling, they had already passed on elsewhere.

For some fifteen minutes, which must have seemed as many hours to McNab, we paced up and down, waiting.

'Peters is a reliable young fellow,' he said once. 'Never has failed me. Jenkins is up to a thing or two as well,' he went on, stooping to lift the Braille book from the ground.

'Then,' I said, 'Peters and Jenkins between them will have followed Kinloch. It's only a matter of the distance from here to the house they've taken him to. Sooner or later one of your men will come back with the information.'

'That was the plan,' he replied as mechanically he smoothed out the crumpled leaves of the book. 'But the best laid schemes o' mice and men sometimes miscarry. And I begin to suspect this one has. It all looks as if the bait had been lifted clean out of the trap. And that means we have lost contact with Ponsonby Paget's assassin – lost contact just at the one point where contact could have been established.'

He shut the Braille book and laid it on the campstool.

And within the next few minutes the proof came which justified McNab's foreboding. It was the little man, Peters, who first turned up, looking both hot and sheepish. His crestfallen look was eloquent of failure, and the shake of the head which he gave as soon as he met McNab's eyes was not really necessary.

'So he's got clean away?' McNab said.

Peters nodded breathlessly.

'A blind man, from four of you? It should be interesting to hear how.'

Peters found his voice at last.

'He gave us the slip, sir, all right, but he isn't a blind man; no more a blind man than I am.'

'What!' McNab cried. 'What's that you say? Not blind? Are you gone crazy, Peters?'

'No more blind than myself, he wasn't,' the man repeated stubbornly.

I well remember how McNab stared. Stared at first in almost angry incredulity. And then a change shot over his face. The look of blank unbelief vanished from his eyes to be replaced by a swift light that revealed understanding.

'I see,' he said slowly and as if to himself. 'Yes, I see now. So that was why Dunn laughed.' He turned and nodded to Peters. 'But come and tell your story. There's a seat near the gate inside the gardens.'

And there presently we were sitting with Peters between us.

'It's not yet an hour,' the little man began with a sigh, 'since the thing happened. We had all settled down to our work, Jenkins with his matches, the others at their weeding and me with the brush. Between Jenkins and me the man on his little stool. Safe as houses it all seemed. Jenkins, of course, had the best chance of seeing what was up, for he had nothing to do, and his face turned on the road all the time, whereas I naturally had my back to the road. It was a cry from Jenkins that came first. I looked round and saw him being grabbed tight by a gentleman and him shouting out something which I didn't catch. But what I saw next was that blind man bolting out into the road, and him neatly dodging a cyclist too.' Peters paused momentarily. 'I own up to it, I was so taken aback at that sight that I didn't act near quick enough. In fact, sir, I was in a manner of speaking so struck all of a heap by discovering the man wasn't blind at all that I stood all agape and paralysed. He was so mighty spry too – quick as lightning. You'd never have guessed he was the same sort of down and out looking chap sitting so quiet on his stool. The result was he got pretty well into the car before any of us got a move on.'

'The lady had stopped her car on the other side?' McNab asked.

Peters looked up quickly.

'That's right, sir, on her near side coming from Campden Hill Road, that is. But she hadn't stopped her engine, though she had the door open and was in the act of rising to get out, I thought, when the man seemed to say something to her and jump in by the offside door. The lady seemed taken by surprise. She did nothing for a second or two. Then I dropped my brush and ran. I'd have got there, too, but for a taxi that nearly ran into me. It blocked me out just long enough for the car to get moving.'

'What was the car's number?' McNab asked.

Peters fairly wrung his hands in despair.

'Oh, sir, all that sort of thing had been taken thought of. The number was hidden by a rug hanging over the back; the front wasn't in sight, and all I saw as I made a grab and missed was the letter "K" when the rug swung up a little as the car accelerated.'

A groan came from McNab.

'No need to ask what happened next,' he said.

'Well, sir, by this time our other two men had scrambled somehow over the railings and Jenkins had got free from his gentleman.'

'So you all four ran down the road after the car, didn't you, with a crowd at your heels, eh? What good did you think that would do?'

Peters looked rather aggrieved and perplexed.

'Well, sir, we divided at the end of the road, Jenkins and I getting a taxi there. We went up towards Bayswater, leaving the other two to go down Kensington way, whenever they found another taxi. And, sir, there wasn't a crowd following us, not what you'd call a crowd; it's – it's too genteel a neighbourhood for that, sir,' Peters protested.

McNab replied with an impatient snort.

'Peters, you might just as well have gone on at your painting. Better, indeed, for then you might have helped Jenkins to collar his gentleman.'

'Collar the gentleman!' Peters exclaimed. 'But, sir, it was the gentleman that collared Jenkins. He had stopped for a box of his matches just as the car came along, giving him half a crown, and he held on to Jenkins till he got his change. Jenkins told me in the taxi, said the man thought he was doing a bolt with the half-crown.'

'Rubbish. That man was there to delay Jenkins, to divert the attention of the one man who had his eyes on the road, and to draw the eyes of you others towards Jenkins and himself. Jenkins was a fool. But not,' McNab declared, with flashing eyes and an outward lift of his clenched fist from which Peters quailed, 'a greater fool than I have been.'

His wrath and disgust, however, quickly simmered down. And when, after a few more questions, Peters was sent away, in his dour, tenacious fashion he set about making the best of what seemed a very bad job. That the upset to his plan had stunned McNab I did not need to be told. For a little he seemed like a man dazed by a blow, incapable of connected thought. He needed a minute or two to recollect himself. And without fuss or flurry he took those few moments' rest on that seat in the gardens, sitting there stolidly, unmindful of the children's shouts, and the subdued expostulations of the genteel nurses as they strolled past us.

At what point of time McNab again got a grip on the situation I could not tell. An unforgettable impression he made on my mind as he sat there. Every sense, every nerve and muscle, even his breathing, appeared to be stilled, so that thought might function unimpeded. In the end I saw him, as it were, come back to an awareness of a world outside his own mind, and I wondered what, if anything, he had salved from the wreck of his plans. Yet his first words to me seemed unconnected with – his defeat that day.

'This,' he said gravely, 'now becomes a race to prevent a second murder.'

The words startled me. Then I saw what he meant.

'You mean he will murder Kinloch?'

'Yes, he will eliminate Kinloch.'

This was so far away from the directions in which I had supposed his thoughts to be running while he sat there that I was taken aback. That Kinloch might be in danger had not occurred to me. He had been our quarry so long that it was somehow hardly possible all at once to apprehend he might be also another's quarry.

McNab took me by the arm.

'Hurry up. There's no time to lose.'

We turned our back finally on Enderby Gardens. Where we were hurrying to I had no notion. He had called it a race to stop a second murder. But whether he knew what direction the chase was to lead us, north, south, east, or west, was more than I could tell; and certainly it was more than Peters, or any of his men, had been able to tell him. The pace which McNab set as we hurried along the road, however, revealed a definite purpose. It proved to me he had a definite objective before him; but I spared him questions, saving my breath for the pace he set me.

A few minutes later and he doubled into Notting Hill Tube Station. We got clear of the lift as a train came hissing and rumbling out of the tunnel. It was not a 'rush' hour – with any except ourselves at least – and the carriage into which we tumbled proved to be nearly empty. The sprint through the corridor and down the steps had been hot. I flung myself into one of the cross seats facing McNab.

'In an ideal world,' I complained, as breath returned, 'Peters would have got that car's number, and except for the hanging the case would be over.'

'Maybe. But in an ideal world nobody would need hanging.'

This wasn't quite what I meant. What I meant was that if we had merely been two figures in a work of fiction we should have had an easier job. This I explained in repeating my remark.

'But Peters did get us something,' he objected. 'Peters saw the letter K on the registration plate. And that information, though not all I schemed and hoped to obtain, is good enough to go on with.'

'Sure it isn't false?'

'No, I'm not. For though the registration was draped by a rug over the back of the car, it may have been false all the same. Still, half an hour or so will decide whether the K is genuine.'

On that I learned where we were going. An odd place, it struck me, to go for the purpose of deciding whether the K on the car was genuine or not. For I learned we were heading towards the docks, to Trinity House in fact, the headquarters of the Channel pilots. How the Channel pilots could be connected with a motor's registration I could not imagine. But McNab, though ready enough to talk after that long meditation of his in the gardens, would not enlighten me on this particular point. I dare say my wide-open stare was responsible.

'It's just a hint picked up,' he said. 'I'm acting on the off chance there's something in it. If we draw a blank it's all up with Kinloch.'

Now it seemed to me that if he did not overrate Kinloch's danger at least he underrated Kinloch's ability to take care of himself.

'He's a wily bird, Kinloch,' I said. 'Look how he took you in about being blind.'

McNab smiled ruefully.

'He did. But it was a part he could play to the life, for he had been blind for years.'

The carriage was now filling up at every stop, and it became safe to talk only when the train was roaring through the tunnels. McNab bent towards me.

'If the hint I'm working on turns up trumps,' he said, 'a lot will depend on you. But don't be deceived about this man's danger. This Kinloch is nearer death now than he ever was in Flanders.' He tapped my knee and almost roared at me. 'Be clear on that point or you'll make a mess of the job I'm now forced to place in your hands.'

Then the train shot out into daylight and we were crossing Tower Hill towards Trinity House.

To the official in the hall McNab explained his visit. He wanted to see someone familiar with the Kent coast. The official scratched his chin, however, in doubt, when McNab said it was not shoals, tideways or lighthouses, but roads, bays and headlands, on which information was needed.

'Looks as if you'd come to the wrong shop, sir,' he remarked. Then he brightened. 'There's old George; he was in the coast-guards, in Kent I fancy 'twas. He'd be the very man if he's anywheres about.'

Something passed from McNab's hand to the other's palm, with the result that old George was quickly produced from somewhere in the basement. He was a ruddy-faced, blue-eyed old fellow, still with a wind-blown appearance for all his service in the serene quietness of Trinity House.

'You know the Kentish coast?' McNab began at once.

'Reckon I do, sir, every inch of it from Rochester to Rye.'

McNab beamed satisfaction.

'You think you could identify any part of it from a descrip-tion?'

'For sure, sir, provided you gave me enough to go on.'

'Ah, that's where I'm doubtful. This is rather difficult. Lis-ten.' McNab spoke slowly – softly and very slowly. 'There's a road down a steep, long hill, a road with a sharp, right-hand turn. At the foot of the hill there's a village. In a car you'd be through the place in a couple of minutes. Then you'd find yourself suddenly running close to the sea, so close that on a stormy day you might feel the spray on your face. After about a mile you turn away from the sea and don't hear it again.'

Old George, who had listened intently, rubbed his ear thoughtfully.

'That is hard and no mistake. There's a score of places from Whitstable to Margate, and nigh Broadstairs too, like that. And besides them –'

McNab put up a hand.

'You would feel both the spray and the sun on your left cheek,' he said.

The old coastguardsman's face brightened.

'Ah, that's better. Wipes out all the north coast, that do.'

He pondered for a moment and then looked up. 'Sounds like a bit o' Pegwell Bay after you leave Ramsgate, except that the hill ain't right. And it would be Walmer to a T if you were going east instead of west. Dover 'ud do for that steep hill, and the right-hand turn all right, only Dover's 'ardly a village, and they wouldn't thank you in Dover to hear it called such.'

'The sea is very noisy on the beach – a shingle beach,' McNab said half despairingly.

Old George shook his head.

'All the beach's shingle thereabouts, leastways till you get to Dymchurch, but in Dover it ain't what you'd call noisy on account of the breakwater.'

'Mingling with the noise of the surf,' McNab interjected, 'you might hear the notes of a bugle on your right, on higher ground.'

I fancy this was McNab's last desperate throw. But at the mention of the bugle the old coastguardsman suddenly looked up, slapping his thigh.

'Dang me if I ain't a proper fool,' he cried excitedly. 'Why, for twenty years I lived on the very spot! Lies between Folkestone and Hythe, it do. There's the long hill down afore you enter Sandgate. Then soon as you pass the coastguard cottages you open out the sea till you lose it again when you reach Seabrook police station. And all along you've Shorncliffe Camp on your right. Suits it to a T if you've joined the main road by coming down the steep lane from the Downs nigh to the top of Sandgate Hill. That's your spot, sir, though if there's any prize going for this here guessing competition I 'ardly deserve it.'

'The sea comes over sometimes there?' McNab asked.

'On a spring tide following a strong south wind it do. More than once the road's been washed away then.'

McNab seemed contented by the information, and George got a prize before we left which appeared to make him equally content.

Recrossing Tower Hill McNab's satisfaction increased as he took out his watch. It was then twenty to four.

'We're beating the clock, as your cricketers say. Looks as if we might be in time to save him yet,' he said. Then he added, 'You can catch the five o'clock from Cannon Street, after we've had something to eat.'

'Catch the five o'clock from Cannon Street!' I echoed in surprise. 'Where to? What for?'

But nothing would he tell me then. He was hungry, he said, even if I was not, and we must go straight to the Adelphi. He had things to say before I left which could not be said except in private, and at his place he could give me my instructions while we ate. I was certainly hungry enough, having had nothing since my unusually early breakfast, but at the moment the hunger of my curiosity was even sharper.

Of what food passed my lips once we were again in McNab's flat I have no memory. But for the quick, almost fierce way in which he spoke to me I have an unfading memory, for this was McNab in a moment of crisis, when success or failure hung balanced on a hair. Even while he was poring in silence over the large-scale road map of Kent I recognised that his whole capacity for action, mental and physical, was at its fullest stretch. Yet he began his instructions quietly enough.

'I have decided not to call in Snargrove and the Yard,' he said. 'Partly because there isn't time – this is a matter now of hours at the most – and partly because Howley's description of the guilty man is too indeterminate to act on quickly. Heaven knows how many men in brown suits with toothbrush moustaches would be detained all over the country within the next twenty-four hours. The man is like too many other men.'

'Yes,' I cut in, 'that's what I meant before. If this were fiction that man would have had a drooping eyelid, an acid mark on his forehead, a finger missing from his left hand, ears pierced for earrings or –'

But he stopped me.

'We have no time, either, for that sort of talk,' he said sharply. 'There isn't even time to write out your instructions. Listen attentively or you may not remember them.'

'If I can carry a political speech practically verbatim I'm not likely to forget this,' I declared.

'Right. Listen, then! As I've said, I am taking the risk of not calling in Scotland Yard for the reasons given and also – mark this – because we are acting at the moment less with a view to the murderer's arrest than to prevent a second murder. That, after all, is what the law intends, even when it hangs a man. Hanging the murderer does not restore his victim to life, but it doubtless has kept many others alive.'

'You are sure Kinloch really is in danger? He himself doesn't–'

He almost stamped his foot at me.

'Listen! What motive do you suppose led to the murder of Ponsonby Paget? You know Paget and his paper. What was the motive for the murder but the fear of exposure and disgrace? Paget knew something and threatened him. Paget misjudged his man and paid the penalty. Well, at this moment with arrest threatening him he has a much stronger motive for murder, for it is not his name only that is in danger, but his neck. Further, don't forget that Kinloch *can now see*. That fact was not known to the pair when they carried him off today. It was, indeed, only known to the doctor who laughed at me. They didn't know it, though. You remember Peters telling how the woman was in the act of getting out of the car, obviously with the intention of leading him to it? Well, once it is known he can now see he becomes for the first time really dangerous. Got that?'

I nodded understanding.

'You are convinced?'

Again I assented in the same fashion.

'Good. Now you know what we are up against we can get to business.'

He rose and began to pace about, hands deep in his pockets.

'Follow this carefully, Chance,' he said. 'It will take some time, but you can go on eating. I now want to show you that you are not being sent off on a wild-goose chase.' He paused a moment. 'You recall, perhaps, Dr Dunn's assertion that Kinloch heard the surf once, and once only, after leaving the house where they had sheltered since the murder? You will also remember that he said Kinloch at the same moment heard a bugle sounding. The coincidence of these two sounds – the surf and the bugle – tells us much. The surf could only spray the car during the high-water period of a spring tide. Now the Tide Table tells me that the spring tide of March 22nd at Folkestone was high at 10.5 a.m. and 10.57 p.m. Which was it – the solar or the lunar tide – that sprayed the car? The bugle answers that question for us. The bugle call came from the military barracks at Shorncliffe. But at no barracks is a bugle blown after 10.15 p.m., at which hour the "Lights out" is sounded. Therefore it was not the "Lights out" Kinloch heard while the spring tide sprayed their car. It is also certain it was not on a date before the 22nd, for though the tide would have come up earlier than 10.57 its high-water mark then would have been too low to bring it over the road in any wind. The conclusion is therefore that it was the morning spring tide that was coming over as they passed, and that the bugle heard was the 10 a.m. "Orders" call. And the inference I draw from the fact that this point was passed so early in the day is that they had not come very far. That inference, however, hardened into a conviction the moment I looked at this map.' McNab here spread the road map of Kent on the table before me. 'You have but to look at the mere *shape* of the county. See, it is like a spear head, with the place they passed at 10 a.m. well inside where it begins to taper to a point. Very well.' McNab slapped me on the back as I bent over the map. 'Unless they came into this eastern extremity merely to go out of it again, that unknown house in which they sheltered securely from about the 15th of January to the 22nd of March lies somewhere within this small spear point of country.' As I stared at the map he added, 'That's where we shall run them to earth. But there's no time to tell you about that now.'

'And what am I to do?' I inquired.

'Go to Folkestone, hire a car – a four-seater open tourer – and try to locate that village alleged to be shut in by gates at each end. Don't believe in it myself. But we can't afford to miss the chance of its being a real place, so cover all the ground possible before dark. Explore, examine, question. In a crisis don't hesitate to call in the police. You know all the facts better than anyone, and you could identify Kinloch at sight. As soon as it is dark be at the Westenhanger crossroads to wait for me with anything you have gleaned.' He indicated Westenhanger on the map. 'See, there on the London road, where the road to the right leads to the Lympne Aerodrome, and that on the left is the old Roman road over the downs to Canterbury. That is your job while I do mine here – see Snargrove perhaps, but at all events get hold of Dr Dunn at Ealing.' Then he added, 'Look, you have just fifteen minutes to catch your train.'

When I rose, pocketing the road map, McNab spoke in another tone as he opened a drawer in his bureau.

'One thing more I'd better warn you about. After the way affairs were mishandled this morning this case is not likely to end with the quiet arrest I like. More probably it will be a nasty, messy, violent business. So you'd better carry this.' He stood up with an ugly-looking automatic pistol in his hand.

'As bad as that?' I whispered.

'Desperate,' he nodded, handing over the weapon.

Then I bolted down the stairs for the five o'clock Folkestone express.

XIX

Long before dusk came on that glorious day, long before I was due to meet McNab at the Westenhanger crossroads, I had done the job on which he sent me. Dunn had not been drawing on his imagination about that village. McNab was wrong there. It was a real place. It had an actual existence. Unlike any other village it might be, but it is there today for anyone to go and see; and by eight o'clock that night I not only knew its name but was lying among the gorse of the wide common watching the house for which we searched.

What had happened was this. On arriving at Folkestone I went to a garage close to the Central Station and explained to the proprietor, a Mr. Large, that I wanted a good car and a driver who knew the countryside. Whether or no Mr. Large from the further particulars I gave him thought me mad, I cannot say. But as if to keep a close eye on his property he declared that as none of his drivers knew the country better than he did he would drive me himself. His doubts about my mental condition must have been strengthened by what followed in the next hour. For all the time I kept him running up and down over and across and along that ridge of Downs lying behind Folkestone and extending towards Canterbury. It must have seemed aimless to him.

'But isn't there anywhere you wish to go?' he asked at last, after I had put many questions about this or that lonely house as we whizzed past.

Well, by this time it seemed aimless even to me – just a filling in of hours till McNab came. Then I remembered the village. Not that I believed in it any more than McNab did. And I mentioned it to Mr. Large more to give a rational look to our excursion than in any hope that he would know of such a place. But the moment its peculiarities were mentioned I saw him cock up his ear.

'Common about half a mile wide ... gates at each end,' he muttered reflectively. Then on went the brakes and he laughed. 'Why, we're going right away from it,' he said.

I was utterly astonished.

'You don't mean it's a real place you *know*?' I cried.

'Sounds like Stelling Minnis,' he said, beginning to jockey the cab round. 'Anyway, you'll see for yourself in half an hour.'

And just on eight o'clock, after sliding down into the Elham Valley and climbing the far ridge of the Downs, we ultimately reached the lonely and lovely place by way of a narrow, tortuous lane from the long, straight Roman road called the Stane Street. As soon as we cleared the gate I knew this must be the place. A queer thrill sent my pulses leaping. Before us the wide common stretched, sprinkled with gorse and young green bracken, on either side the old houses widely separated, but all standing on the two extreme edges like soldiers, toeing a line. Straight down the middle ran the road, and evidently to reach any of the houses one had to leave the road and run over the turf among the gorse for quite a quarter of a mile. But I hadn't come there to appreciate Nature's beauty. So after the first catch of the breath when that common opened before my eyes I stopped the car. On our left near the gate there was an inn, a white house with the neat red signboard bearing the words 'The Rose and Crown'.

'Wait here,' I said to Mr. Large, 'I've some inquiries to make.'

Towards the inn I advanced very slowly. I had to get a grip of myself. For it staggered me to perceive that here at last was the end of our search, the end of all concealment. Here the people concerned must be known. Two men stood at the bar as I entered. Beyond the usual country salute no word passed till I had tried what the Rose and Crown's' ale could do for a dry, a very dry, throat.

'Nice place this,' I said to the elder man, an old fellow with a fringe of grey beard round his neck.

"Tain't that bad in summer,' he replied grudgingly.

'You seldom see a stranger except in summer?' I went on.

'That's so, and not a many then, neither.'

Here the landlord, leaning his folded arms on the counter, joined in with:

'It's a God-forsaken spot, sir. Many's the day I don't draw three quarts.'

'But some people like lonely places. Even in winter I've known a man seek for a spot like this, even when he'd got money and the whole world to choose from,' I added.

'That be like what her ladyship does,' the young man said, rolling some tobacco in his palms.

'That's right, Bob Ames,' the old fellow nodded. 'It don't surprise us to see her little car a-rolling through the gorse at no season of th' year. But she ain't been at the Minnis not lately.'

'She were here last January, Jacob Wytch.'

'Ay, so she were, all alone too, a matter o' six weeks. But then a Hardress ain't no stranger like what the gentleman was a-speaking of.'

I set down my glass on hearing that, and if I spilt none of its contents it was because the glass was half empty.

After that a few deft questions yielded all I sought. The lady it appeared, belonged to a family called Hardress, formerly resident in the neighbourhood. She had married during the war Sir Stephen Wye, a soldier. But he wasn't a soldier now, I gathered. He was going into Parliament. It all came out bit by bit. Yes, they lived in London, but Lady Wye had a little house on the Common, for she liked to live there better than in London, she did. No, she wasn't there now, but I could see the little house for myself if I didn't believe them.

Fifteen minutes later I was lying among the gorse and bracken with the house under observation. At first I watched the little white house with the dull red tiles and the wooden garage at one end to see if I could detect any sign of life within. McNab seemed confident, not only that they would again seek refuge there, but would only approach the house in darkness. And after watching for some time I concluded he was right. No sign of life could I discern. No smoke rose from its chimneys. I should, of course, have liked to go right up and make a close inspection. That, however, I could not do without seeming over-curious if

I happened to be seen. And anyway I soon became convinced that no one had yet arrived at the house. So I stayed where I was, well concealed among the bracken and gorse bushes.

And then as I lay on that spring turf waiting, to put it plainly, for a murderer to come, a trifling incident happened that touched my imagination queerly at the moment. For presently there came slowly along the grassy pathway between the bushes a sheep and her lamb. Both seemed tired and neither saw me. I think they were making at the end of a long day for the nook in which they passed the night. Then stepping between me and the sun now dipping into the far side of the common, their fleeces became outlined in silver, like a halo, surrounding their darkened bodies. An incongruous picture that was to establish itself in my mind as it did among the terrible memories of the night then closing in!

Soon after that, as the dusk of that golden evening deepened, I began to think of my appointment to meet McNab at the Westenhanger crossroads. There was now just enough light to let me see the various positions on the map, and as far as I could make it out, I was not less than eight miles from the crossroads. Mr. Large I had sent to the 'Rose and Crown' to await my return, letting him suppose I was looking up a friend somewhere on the common. But with darkness coming on I had to make a quick decision between keeping my appointment with McNab and staying on to watch that house. Wisely or not I decided for the latter. What weighed with me was the conviction that, if McNab were right, the four walls of that house now empty would presently surround the murderer. It would be good to know he was there! And whether he came alone or accompanied by his wife or the misguided man, Kinloch, no entry could be made without my knowledge. Then I saw what to do. I must send Large to meet McNab and bring him back to Stelling Minnis. Creeping away on hands and knees for a hundred yards or so I rose and made for the inn. Large soon understood what I wanted, and as I saw his red tail light vanishing into the gloom my thought was that it was just as well not to have the lights of a big car glaring over the common.

By the time I got back to my nook among the bushes night had set in. I had forgotten how dark it can be in the country, how dark and still. A hush seemed over everything. Once, far away, a dog barked, and the sound came thin yet clear in the distance. Later I began to feel cold, for the turf was now damp with the dew that had followed the day of bright sunshine. Yet I had to be wary, for on that turf at that hour anyone might pass unheard and unseen.

Half an hour passed and nothing happened. Then came the thought that I could now safely take a closer look at the cottage and its surroundings. Indeed I felt compelled to move up nearer since the house was no longer visible. What I wanted above all was to see if there was any approach to the house from behind, through the fields beyond the trees. This was my first intention, and after that to get myself established at some point from which, since so little could be seen, I would be able to hear the slightest sound even to the cautious opening of a door or a footfall on the step.

But as I crept round the gable of that cottage it gave me a queer feeling to recall how, much in the same way, I had stolen round behind the house in Ealing on that fateful night. Then I had come on the murdered man. Could it be, I asked myself, that I was now to find myself face to face with the murderer? Well, I went round the house as carefully as if that was about to happen, for I crept on step by step with my hand on the butt of the automatic McNab had given me. Of course I met no one,.and an inspection of the enclosure behind the house convinced me that no car could approach from that direction. To surmount the loose stone wall under the trees would be easy, but on that still night I knew no car could come within a mile without giving ample warning of its approach. So I moved over with a freer mind to have a look at the back of the house.

What I discovered there did not at first startle me at all. It was apparently such a little thing: a pane of glass broken in one of the windows. Some mischievous boy? So I said to myself till I observed that it happened to be the pane next the catch. That made me stand and listen, holding my breath. But the house seemed all dark and dead. The mischievous boy, I told myself again. Such things do happen to the windows of empty houses. Then I remembered the garage on the far side. There I might be able to get a hint as to whether the house was really as tenantless as it looked. Thither I went next, feeling along the rough-cast walls till I rounded the corner and arrived at the doors. A little manipulation showed me that, though shut, the garage door was unlocked. For a moment I stood speculating on the amount of noise likely to be made if I tried to open that door. Little used as it must have been, the hinges were sure to be very dry. Still, after finding the door unlocked like that, I simply had to find out whether there was a car inside. I risked the noise. It sounded almost like thunder in my apprehensive ears, and I opened it only just enough to let me squeeze inside. Then I stretched out my hands as I took a couple of steps forward.

It was there all right. And when I had felt my way along the side of the car and found the radiator still warm I did not doubt that the house was less empty than it looked. But after that garage discovery I made my first blunder. If only I had been content with what I had achieved! For after that discovery all I need have done was to go back to my old position in the bushes and wait there till I saw the flashing of McNab's headlights when he drove along the road over the open common. But no! I must needs try to better my best. Not content to leave well alone, I must needs try to paint the lily. And so I ran into trouble at once. For on going round to the back of the house once more to have another look at the window I saw something that looked no more than a deep shadow moving towards me from the direction of the loose stone wall. Had the man's eyes been turned my way he must have seen me, for I must have been more visible against the white background of the house than he himself was against the gloom of those trees. I dropped to the ground and lay still. He passed within a few feet of me. Then there came a double knock on the kitchen door. I began cursing my foolishness, knowing that if a light showed from the door I must be seen where I lay against the wall of the house. Eventually the door creaked open. Unluckily I had fallen with my head towards the door and had no chance of seeing anything. But I heard probably all the better.

'Well?'

This came from the man who opened the door, and it was almost a snarl.

'It's all fixed up. The boat leaves on the ebb about eleven.'

'Where is she?'

'She will meet you on the quay and go on board with you.'

This time I recognised the voice. The accent was different, but in tone and pitch it was Kinloch's voice.

The other sniggered.

'I meant the boat this time,' he said. 'Eleven o'clock.'

'Yes; it gives me just time for what I'm going to say to you,' Kinloch snapped.

'Step in then. Sorry I'm in the dark. But of course you are familiar with every corner of the house.' The sneering voice was cut off by the closing of the door.

Lying still I thought over what I had heard. The hostility existing between the two men I didn't bother about. What troubled me was that Kinloch and the woman had obviously made arrangements for the man's escape. And she was to meet him somewhere – the place had only just escaped mention – and go away with him. How? Not in a mail boat, since they were independent of the tide. Nor in a small boat either, for the same reason. Some tramp it must be, now berthed in some inner harbour in any of the south-eastern ports. Which? There were half a dozen within thirty miles. For a moment I wondered how much Kinloch had to say to the other man. If there was just time to say it that man might be away almost at once, before McNab turned up. The possibility got me to my feet at once. At all hazards I had either to find out more about the port of departure or somehow to prevent him from getting there.

The door stood ever so slightly ajar. It appeared to open into a passage, for I heard voices some way off as I pushed it carefully open. Those raised voices made things easier, for they both guided me on and covered any slight sound I might make in feeling my way along the passage. By this time, however, the two men seemed to have thrown all caution to the winds, so far as sound went, anyhow. More like a couple of angry dogs they were, and the thought came to me that this probably was their first meeting, their first, anyhow, at which the woman was not present. I was glad, though, the woman was absent. Beyond question she would have heard me. As soon as I got within earshot of their words the first I heard was my old friend's name. Kinloch's voice had ceased. He had had his say.

'By God, this is just too much,' the other cried. 'Too much from an associate of Ponsonby Paget's. I tell you I had no more scruple about removing him than in killing a rat. It made England a sweeter and safer place.'

'For your sort.'

'Look here, you'd have gone the same way if she hadn't come into that room and heard you whining.'

'Whining! Did you say whining?'

'I did. The old blackmailer dead and his accomplice whining for his life. That, I think was the situation.'

An odd sound came in the silence that followed – a kind of choking sound. Then Kinloch said quietly:

'You are a fool to presume at this moment on what I was that night. Your wife has told you I was in that room only by accident.'

'My wife has told me many things. What she has not told me is how you contrived to – alienate her affections.'

'You blackguard! You'd better go now if you want to go at all.'

Both men had jumped to their feet. It sounded as if they were about to fly at each other's throats. But there was no certainty that our man was not about to clear out. There was that in Kinloch's tone which might well have made him decide to take the hissed-out advice. So I backed away down the passage. Somehow or other I had to prevent his escape. Somehow or other I had to hold him up till McNab arrived. And the safest way I could think of was to put the car out of action. Throwing caution to the winds the instant I got outside I ran for the garage. Knife in hand I squeezed through the door, my notion being to slit the tyres. But as soon as I got my hands on the tyre I knew this was impossible, for I found it to be of solid rubber. I ought to have remembered what McNab had told me about this peculiar type of car.

What else could be done? Little enough I knew about motoring, but there must be a dozen other ways of putting the mechanism out of action. And the necessity for being quick about it hindered coherent thinking. Then as I stood trying to think I heard from the direction of the house a door bang, like a shot, and I began to feel feverishly about in the dark for something heavy with which to strike the car, to damage the mechanism, smash the switchboard or the steering wheel. Before my hands found anything, however, and almost at once, there came the patter of feet outside. In a second someone was tugging the garage doors wide open. Despair swept over me like a flood. Was the man once more to escape? I seized hold of the car as if to stop it leaving the garage. Then a swift inspiration came. Putting a foot on the running board I vaulted on to the back seat and slid down to the floor of the car, off a fur rug lying on the seat. There I stayed, crouching low.

Of course the moment the engine started I saw what I could have done. Though ignorant about motors, I had some electrical knowledge and knew how quickly and silently I could have put the battery on the footboard out of action. But it was too late to retrieve that stupidity, and I tried to comfort myself with the thought that run where he liked he could not run away from me.

There was but one moment when I feared discovery, and that came when he got down to shut the garage doors after we had moved out. Fortunately, though, he had not switched on the headlights, and so there was no back radiance from the wall of the house by which he might well have seen me lurking in the gloom. When I heard him busy with the doors I drew the fur rug over me. Then I felt fairly safe, for the space between the seats on that type of car is narrow, and the floor behind being much lower than in the front I found myself well down below the seat level.

We went across the common without lights, running on the turf with surprising silence and smoothness. But once through the winding lane and out on the long, straight Roman road he switched on the lights and increased the pace. That the lights were on I was made aware by a narrow beam which came through a small spy-hole in the back just above the seat, a contrivance peculiar to the car, to let the driver see that the rear-light was showing.

Thrusting a hand from beneath my rug I used this spot of light to look at my wrist watch. On seeing the time was 10.33 I made two inferences: first that something must have happened to McNab, and secondly that the unknown port for which we were bound could not be very distant. What was I to do? The responsibility McNab's absence threw upon me was grave, and I didn't like it. Meanwhile we were travelling fast along the straight, empty road, and before long I felt the descent from the ridge begin. Down and down we went at a headlong pace. I took a peep over the side when the numerous twists and corners of the road must have kept the man's whole attention.

Out in the open country again, past solitary, darkened houses, I judged him to be making for Folkestone. By and by I saw from the regular, recurrent flashes that we were passing lampposts, and the pace steadied down. The problem I struggled with was

how to get the man into the hands of the Folkestone police before he knew what was happening to him. And I was desperately
anxious to see the job done as neatly and nicely as McNab could
desire, without mess or fuss.

He was heading for the harbour. But could I depend on a
policeman being there? I did not know. Then a trick occurred
to me. Taking out a long lead pencil I thrust it through the
spyhole already described, and smashed the tiny bulb which
illuminated the transparent registration plate: the car had now
no rear-light. Hopefully I crouched down again, hidden by my
fur rug, and wondering whether I could rely on the vigilance
of the Folkestone police. We had not gone far among the streets
before I had my answer. There came a peremptory shout to stop,
followed by the sound of running feet. A half-smothered oath
sounded above my head, but the speed increased. Farther on
there came another shout, and then a shrill police whistle. If this
was meant as a signal to some comrade farther on it failed to
effect its purpose, for the car was swung violently down a side
street. Then indeed I saw the mistake I had made. The man was
frantic with fear. Not knowing why the police tried to stop him
he had jumped to the conclusion they were after him for the
murder. My opinion is that under the shock of this the man's
mind became unhinged. We flew through the streets at a pace
which brought shouts and calls from right and left, and from
people other than the police.

After we rounded the right angle bend, before the steepest
section of the ascent begins, and he could see no lights of a
pursuing car down below on his right, it is possible he thought
the outcries were raised solely on account of excessive speed.
Indeed most, almost certainly, were so caused. And I have a
notion that he had persuaded himself into the belief that all
were so caused before we reached the summit of that mighty
ascent. McNab once said in my hearing that no pessimist is ever
a murderer. But we had not gone more than a mile or so along

the top, past the Valiant Sailor Inn, before coming to the thing that broke him finally.

I knew something was up ahead of us. He swore and slowed down suddenly. Yet it was something he was not sure about. I inferred that from the fact that the car still travelled forward, though at a crawl. Obviously he was creeping up for a closer look. So knowing his attention to be thus fixed I rose on my knees to have a look myself. Right ahead a long stretch of the near side of the road seemed to be 'up' for repairs. In front of the night watchman's booth an open brazier burned freely, and I could see the red lamp in the centre of the road and a string of others extending behind, marking the space on the offside left available for traffic. It bothered me to guess what there was to rouse suspicion there. It all seemed open and above-board. I could see the lonely old watchman quite distinctly, poking the brazier into a blaze. Perhaps it was instinct, perhaps it was his recently rattled nerves, perhaps he didn't like being guided into that long narrow strip of road on the off side, but at last he made up his mind and set his foot down on the accelerator. We jumped forward for the opening.

And the next moment I saw that the instinct that had made my man hesitate had been, however blind, a sure one. For from the watchman's booth a helmeted figure stepped into the road with uplifted hand while others not in uniform seemed to spring from nowhere in front of us, and as if to clinch the thing I saw at the far end of the string of lamps the brilliant headlights of a car which moved into and completely blocked the narrowed road. He must have seen the game was up. But perhaps he still thought he had a chance by swerving on to the turf and rounding the car at the far end. We have been unable to agree on the point. But swerve he did, and that violently to the right. It was the cry from the men in the road that warned me – that and the gathering speed of the car on the grassy slope. I was aware that the sea lay on the right, but how far below I did not guess till I recalled the long ascent we had made. But that remembrance, flashing into my mind, sent me first to the seat and then with one mad leap over the side. Over and over I rolled and then slid head first after the car, gripping at tufts of bent grass and trying to dig in my toes. It seemed an eternity, but it could have been but a mere fraction of time, for as I came to rest I could see the lights of the downward plunging car. At once it seemed to leave the earth and drop into space. Then something white loomed up below and the car struck a projecting spur of the cliff and, passing on with one headlight out, left behind it a cloud of white dust.

The final plunge into the abyss followed, and this was traceable only by the single remaining headlight, which went down like a falling star. Far below the one little disc of light shone for a second on the tops of a clump of pine trees. A far away faint crashing and rending of branches came up to me and the light went out. A moment's strange silence followed. Then the startled seagulls on the ledges below, launching themselves into the air, rose past me, with noisy flapping wings and wild raucous outcries that seemed to rend the night. Then the tussock of bent grass to which I had been clinging gave way in my hand, and after a frantic clutch or two I slid forward and fell into space.

*

When I opened my eyes again I was in a room flooded with sunlight. A nurse moved softly about the room. I watched her drowsily for a moment or two. Something told her I was awake, for she turned towards me watchfully. Then she smiled, and her smile seemed to increase the sunlight in the room.

'What hospital is this?' I asked.

She moved noiselessly over.

'Hush,' she said. 'You must not talk.'

'What happened?' I demanded.

'You fell over the cliff while bird-nesting.' She held up a forefinger. 'But no more questions till Dr Cadbury has seen you.'

She slipped from the room, and I must have fallen asleep again, for the next I remember is hearing two men's voices talking in subdued tones.

'... and you got hurt yourself they told me when I went to view the body,' the deep voice that had probably awakened me was saying.

'A sprained ankle only,' the other voice murmured. 'We did not know he was in the car or how he got into it. But when we were hunting among the wreckage after the body had been removed, someone noticed him lying halfway down the cliff. He'd been there all night. I slipped in getting to him. A mere nothing, but I rest the foot in sitting beside him till he comes round.'

'What do the doctors say about him?'

'Concussion, dislocation of the right shoulder and exposure. But he was conscious yesterday for a few moments, Nurse Jones tells me.'

'Well, the inquest ought to have been adjourned till he came round, and Kinloch, too, if he does.'

'But, Snargrove, there was no evidence he was in the car. And I wasn't there myself when it went over. Look here, this is what happened,' McNab went on after a pause. 'I was to have met Chance at the Westenhanger crossroads at dusk. But I was late through a breakdown beyond Ashford. When I got to the place I found the driver of Chance's car waiting with a message. I was to come on to where Chance had been left. I did not go, because a few questions to the man convinced me that Chance had scored a success and had not himself kept the appointment because he had located our man, So I went on to the police station at Seabrook, where I provided information while the car was filling up at a garage opposite. The station soon had the wires humming, the smart detective constable there taking the precaution of telephoning the harbours to cut off every possible avenue of escape. That is how he learned of the Dutch tramp *Van Helder,* due to leave Dover on the ebb at 11p.m.

And it was he who fixed up the roads, including the one on the Dover-Folkestone road where repairs were going on.

'Then I got Large to take me to Stelling Minnis. So far I knew only the name of the place Chance had lighted on, but not the name of the man, though I had given the police the description of him we had got from Howley. At Stelling Minnis there was, however, no sign of Chance. But a few questions to Large sent me to the inn, and from the landlord, whom I pumped as to the questions Chance had put there earlier that evening, I got all that was necessary for me to know. The landlord, I believe, thought we were police searching for Chance, whom we suspected of planning to burgle Sir Stephen Wye's cottage. So it was from the landlord's lips I first heard the name of the Ealing murderer. We found his house in a few minutes, and, as you know, we found, too, that he had gone, this time leaving Kinloch behind.'

'Wye was our man right enough,' Snargrove agreed. 'I took his fingerprints this morning. But the name did not come as a surprise when you telephoned it to the Yard.'

'What?' McNab cried. 'You suspected him?'

'Had him on my list of possibles. You will understand that, in addition to the private letters and papers, I went through the *Eye Opener* pretty thoroughly. Well, among other items that took my eye there was this item: "The rumour that Sir Stephen Wye will be nominated for the Byewich division in Suffolk is without foundation. We have the best authority for asserting that Sir Stephen will not stand." That appeared in the issue dated Saturday, 13 January.'

'And Ponsonby Paget was murdered on the 15th. Wye, of course, went to see Paget about it, and there learned that Paget had acquired certain information about him which if published would wreck his political ambitions.'

'Beyond doubt,' Snargrove agreed. 'But you will understand that Wye's name was only one among a number of other possibles – some far more promising. So when we inquired into his doings that night we found he had an alibi that seemed beyond doubt. You are interested in alibis? This is a good one. Notice, Wye's house, Whitelands, is five miles, roughly, from Ealing. We began with an investigation of his movements on the Monday, the day of the murder: Lady Wye had been away in the country for a week, but was to have returned that night. Wye had a chill, and went to bed about eight. Somewhere about ten he rang, with a request for some hot whisky, at the same time asking if Lady Wye had arrived. The butler answered in the negative, saying that the fog would account for the delay. To this Sir Stephen agreed, and, with the order that he should not be disturbed, bade the man good night and switched off the light.'

McNab laughed softly.

'And then he got out of bed again, eh? And left the house by the window. After that he loitered in the road to stop Lady Wye before she reached the house. He would know her car by the very distinctive note of its two-stroke engine – in time to stop her before she passed in the fog. He then got her to drive him to Ealing for his interview with Ponsonby Paget. Next morning the butler enters to pull up the blinds, and finds his master asleep, eh? Then the master is informed that Lady Wye has not, after all, returned.'

'Exactly the butler's testimony; the thing was an absolute success,' Snargrove agreed.

'Oh, a relative success, please,' McNab pleaded. 'Have you forgotten an inquest has just been held on the man?'

'That's more of your logic, I suppose. Still, I'll admit it's served you well in this case. But for your inferences from that walking stick there would have been no inquest on the body of Stephen Wye this morning. But the verdict – think of it: accidental death, with an expression of sympathy for Lady Wye, and a censure of the road surveyor. I'm going to have a word or two with Lady Wye presently, but not of sympathy.'

'You can't proceed against a wife for not turning informer against her husband. And, after all, she did not necessarily know why he wanted her to drive him over to Ponsonby Paget's – not anyhow till after the crime had been done.'

'True; but I did not mean that. As accessory we lay our hands on this man Kinloch if, and when, he recovers.'

'My dear Snargrove,' McNab's voice protested, 'how can you prove him an accessory? You might as well try to prove myself, or poor Godfrey there, accessories. All the evidence we have goes to prove that Kinloch was as keen as you or me to discover who the murderer was. And so far from assisting him to escape it looks beyond doubt as if he had been shot by Wye just before he bolted for Dover. A greater crime that than the removal of a blackmailer! And I'll warrant Lady Wye, at least, would agree with me. I'd like to have seen the man hanged. Still, a six-foot drop on the gallows would hardly be as terrifying as that two-hundred-feet drop over the cliff, and hanging, after all, would not make the man any more dead than he is.'

McNab's unconsciously raised voice brought Nurse Jones into the room.

'I'm sorry,' she said, 'but if you have more to say would you mind coming into the next room. Talking may disturb the patient.'

'Sorry. I am just going,' Snargrove said, rising like a lamb.

MacNab also got up.

'I'll try my ankle along the corridor. Doesn't do to let it get stiff,' he said, taking Snargrove's arm.

When they were out the nurse turned to me.

'Oh,' she said, 'so you have come round.'

'I may relapse if you run away again,' I warned her.

But this time she rang the bell instead.

'You look better, much better,' she said, looking at me fixedly from the foot of the bed. 'So what they say can't be true.'

'What do they, say?'

'That those two men are detectives.'

'But they are.'

The pretty, fair-haired nurse opened her eyes wide.

'What have you been up to? Not bird-nesting; they wouldn't be watching you for that, surely.'

She was so astonished that she did not see McNab in the doorway.

'One of them,' I said, 'is my best friend.'

'Oh, you mean the smaller one – the lame detective?'

A laugh that made her wheel round came from McNab.

'No, no, nurse,' he said, 'a lame *man*, if you like, but not, *not* a lame detective.'

And when Nurse Jones had fled from this logic to summon the matron and the doctor or both, I got in the question I had burned to put.

'Kinloch – is he dying, then?'

McNab looked at me solemnly.

'Kinloch is in Paradise, my son.'

He sat down on the chair beside my bed and took hold of my hand.

'You've just had the news?' I gasped.

'Saw him in it this morning. He, too, you understand, has what is called a ministering angel at his bedside. I took her there from Dover yesterday.'

Then as I stared he affected to have misunderstood me.

'Oh, I see what you meant – the bullet wound. Well, a week or two will see him cured of *that*. He's in no more danger of going to the real Paradise than you are yourself.'

THE END

Visit our website to explore the list of great Golden Age
books and sign up to our infrequent Newsletter
to be told of our latest titles first:
www.oleanderpress.com/golden-age-crime

OREON titles in this series

The Essex Murders
by Vernon Loder ~ 9781915475053

The Middle of Things
J.S. Fletcher – 9781915475060

The Boat Race Murder
R. E. Swartwout ~ 9781915475039

Murder at the College
Victor L. Whitechurch – 9781999900489

The Charing Cross Mystery
by J.S. Fletcher – 9781909349711

The Doctor of Pimlico
William Le Queux – 9781909349735

Who Killed Alfred Snowe?
by J. S. Fletcher – 9781915475015

The Yorkshire Moorland Mystery
by J. S. Fletcher – 9781999900472

Fatality in Fleet Street *
Christopher St John Sprigg – 9781909349759

* Free ePub & PDF on sign-up to the
OREON newsletter:

www.oleanderpress.com/golden-age-crime

Printed in Great Britain
by Amazon